NEVADA LOWBALL

ANTONIO NICASSIO

NSP
NEXT SHOT
PUBLISHING

ISBN: 979-8-9884768-0-1 (Hardcover)
ISBN: 979-8-9884768-1-8 (Paperback)
ISBN: 979-8-9884768-2-5 (Ebook)
ISBN: 979-8-9884768-3-2 (Audiobook)
Library of Congress Control Number: TXu 2-421-046

Any references to historical events, real people, or real places are used fictitiously. Names, characters, and places are products of the author's imagination.

First edition 2024.
Next Shot Publishing, Las Vegas, Nevada
TheNextShot.TV

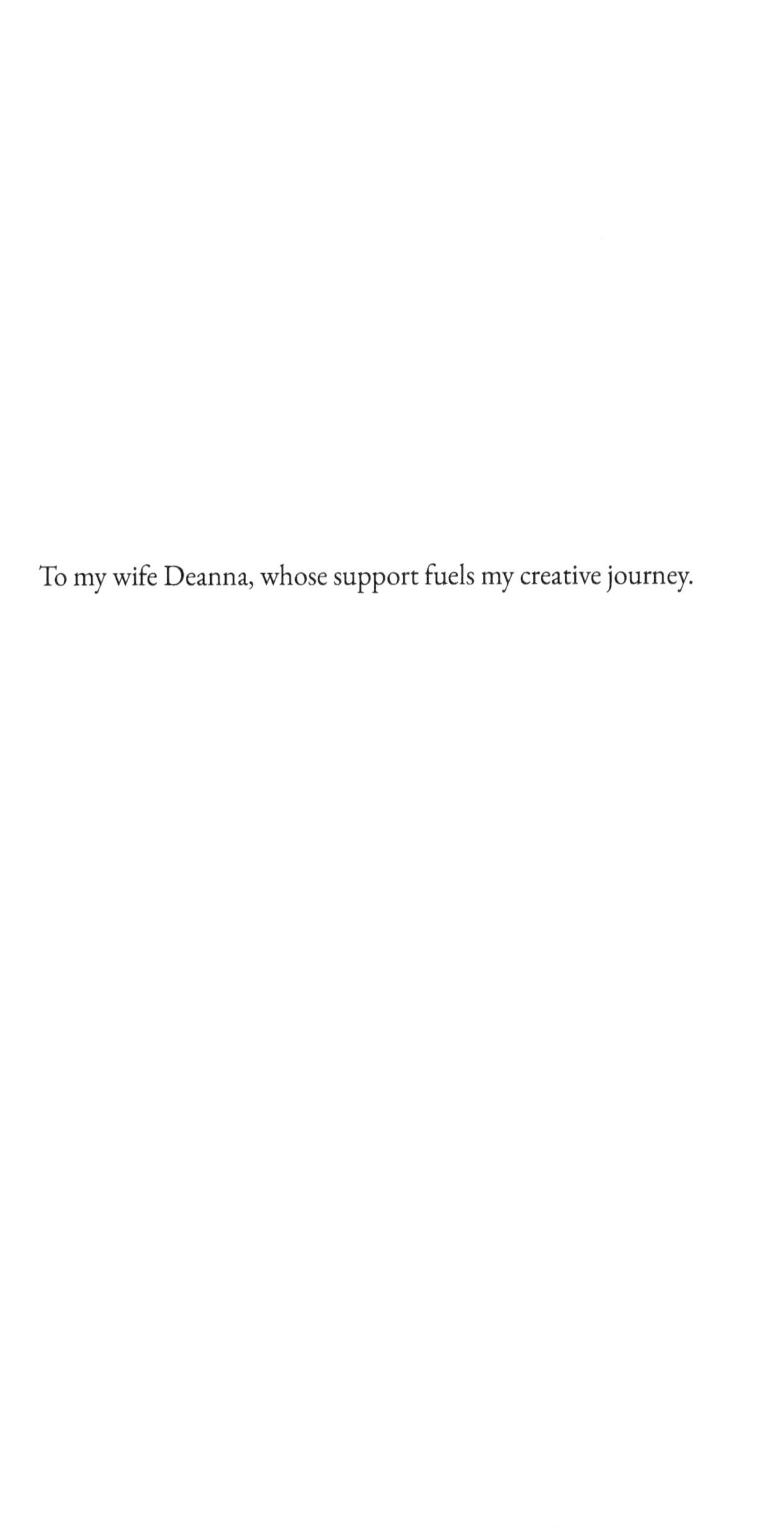

To my wife Deanna, whose support fuels my creative journey.

NEVADA
LOWBALL

"The commonest mistake in history is underestimating your opponent; happens all the time at the poker table."

General David Shoup

PROLOGUE

O N A ROOFTOP, UNDER an early-morning sun some-where in Mogadishu, Somalia, two young US soldiers over-watch local movement from their OP, or observation point.

The first soldier, a gangly young man with shaggy brown hair, Specialist Wesley Erickson, is positioned next to his black M16A2 rifle. A large man-pack radio chirps at him as he peers through high-powered binoculars. To his front lay a laminated topographical military map. Taped to the upper-right corner of the map is a wallet-size picture of a young brunette high school cheerleader. This is Wes's girlfriend. The young girl stares back at him, frozen in time, with a big, bright smile.

Lying next to Wes is his best friend, Caleb Fincher. Built like a college wrestler with short red hair, Caleb eyes a dilapidated building through a high-powered optical scope mounted to his M14 7.62 sniper rifle.

Their platoon sergeant, Sergeant First Class Sean Lynch, in-spects their work. A Boston native with broad shoulders and a square chin, Sean is your typical combat-arms senior non-commissioned officer, or NCO.

Checking Wes's work on the map, he notices the picture of Maggie. Displeased with seeing the photo out in the field, Sean asks Wes smugly, "Who's the broad, Erickson?"

"This is my girlfriend, Maggie."

"Let me guess. You're going to marry her when you get back?"

"That's the plan."

This time the older platoon sergeant chuckles out loud and says, "I hope she's not with Jody right now while you're out here eating Somali shit." A Jody is any guy back at home who ends up dating the girl of a soldier deployed overseas.

"I've got three ex-wives who told me they would wait for me too."

Wes smiles politely, more amused than insulted by his boss's comment.

Sean continues. "Look here, troop. You need to take that picture off your map and keep your head focused on the mission."

Wes nods in acknowledgment, stuffing the picture in his assault pack. A voice comes over Sean's radio. "Dealer Seven, Punisher Base."

"Go ahead, Punisher Base."

"The Hooligan element located eight blocks west of your position needs a reinforcement element. Displace and link up with Hooligan Seven."

"Dealer Seven copies all—out." Sean tells the young soldiers, "Secure your junk and let's get moving."

"Roger that, Sergeant," they respond in unison, grabbing their gear.

Sean leads the small element down the decrepit building. Cautiously, Sean exits the building first onto the main dirt road. Suddenly, sharp snapping sounds of gunfire zip over his head. He leaps back inside.

Sean yells over his shoulder, "Okay, gents, basic movement 101."

"Roger that, Sergeant."

Concrete and dust spit up around the doorway. Sean readies his position. Tactically exposing himself enough, he lays down a base of fire. Wes and Caleb burst out the rickety door. With rifles up, sending rounds down the street, they hustle to their next position.

Hitting the dirt behind cover, they both yell, "Set!"

Sean yells back, "Moving!" Wes and Caleb send rounds down the street. Sean runs to their position. All three scan the road.

Sean tells Wes, "We're going east on that next block. Get some smoke out to cover our movement."

Wes quickly pulls a white smoke grenade from his pack and tosses it down the street.

Within seconds the alleyway is filled with thick smoke. On Sean's signal, the US soldiers move quickly.

They get a hundred yards up the alley unopposed before being peppered with enemy fire again. The Somalis' AK-47 bullets echo loudly down the alley, skipping off the walls and over their heads. Several enemy bullets chew the dirt road in front of them. Wes yells, "Contact front!"

Caleb returns fire first. A Somali fighter reveals himself from a nearby building. Caleb shouts, "RPG ten o'clock."

A flash of light comes from the enemy's tube. The screaming sound of a small rocket engine races in their direction. All three dive for cover. The rocket-propelled grenade streaks across the alleyway, ricochets off a hard building, and smashes Wes square in the chest. The impact slams him to his back, knocking all the air out of his body. But there's no explosion. For a split moment of calm, Wes looks down at his chest. Frantically, he yells, "Sergeant, this fuckin' RPG is stuck in my armor!"

"Don't touch it—I'm coming to you."

Sean and Caleb run to Wes, shooting at the rooftops, covering their movement.

"Find us a route out of this alley," Sean says to Caleb.

Caleb pulls his map from Wes's assault pack. The picture of Maggie falls to the dirt floor. Caleb doesn't notice it.

Sean examines the embedded grenade in Wes's body armor. He grabs the RPG firmly. "Don't fuckin' move."

Carefully, he dislodges it. Once it's free, Sean looks closer at the unexploded munition.

He laughs at Wes for only a moment and says, "You are a lucky son of a bitch. That fuckin' Sammy didn't pull the cap before launching it." Wes is speechless. "That piece of plastic is the only thing that kept you from turning into chucky soup."

The safety cap Sean is referring to is usually removed before firing, but for some reason it is still on the tip of this grenade. The young Somali must have been in a rush to kill Americans.

Still concerned with the faulty explosive in his hand, Sean tosses the munition down the alley. Again, no explosion.

Sean stands up, but Wes pulls him down by the arm. "I owe you big time, Sergeant."

Sean gives Wes a toothy smile. "Yeah, you do." Looking away from Wes toward Caleb, he asks, "Did you find us a route?"

"Yes, Sergeant, I did."

"Then grab your buddy and let's get the fuck out of here."

Caleb helps Wes to his feet and the two run down the alley.

Covering their rear, Sean sees the picture of Maggie on the ground. Running to catch up with his soldiers, he intentionally steps on the photograph, with disdain.

CHAPTER 

Three Years Later - Pahrump, Nevada

THREE YEARS AFTER WES returned home from Somalia, he and Maggie got married and moved into a small, single-wide mobile home together. Wes, deciding not to reenlist, now is employed at the Golden Nugget Casino as a card dealer. He also works part-time with Maggie's father, Gary, doing cabinet installs, while Maggie has gotten to work on her theme-based catering business.

Coming home to spend time with his wife is something Wes always enjoys doing. Every day, he looks forward to being squeezed around his midsection by Maggie's short and petite frame. Her smooth and distinct facial features, complemented by her green eyes and dark hair, have more power over Wes than he would like to admit. And more than Maggie realizes.

Tonight is especially enjoyable. Maggie has decided to go above and beyond with dinner. Wes, wearing the casino's mandatory uniform that includes black slacks, a white tuxedo shirt, vest, and bow tie, scurries up the steps to his home. A nameplate embossed with his name dangles from the gold-colored vest. His shoulders relax as he enters the home.

Walking into the house, Wes pauses in the doorway, head moving side to side. *Italian, I love Italian.* The living room is decorated with a plethora of Italian-themed décor. Green, white, and red colors adorn the small living space as plastic grapevines hang from the room's curtain rods. In the middle of the living room, a small table covered by a red tablecloth waits. On top of the table, an old wine bottle converted into a candle sits prominently. A modest flame flickers, throwing warm ambient light against the walls. Opera music plays low in the background from a small portable radio. In the kitchen, cooking over the stove, Maggie works on a new dish she's auditioning for her small catering business.

Once a month, Maggie decorates the living room to match the type of meal she's preparing. It's an opportunity for her to try out new themes for her business. It's also a way to push back against the mundane day-to-day meals she usually has ready for Wes when he gets home from work.

Last month, the living room looked like a Chinatown neighborhood in San Francisco. Red and gold colors covered the room. Asian music accompanied paper lamps hung from the ceiling. Maggie prepared a sour chicken meal. She also wore a long silk robe with nothing underneath. An added treat for Wes.

Being the loving husband Wes is, he appreciates his wife's creative side. He also values her entrepreneurial spirit. Though sometimes Wes feels Maggie can be a bit quirky with the décor and music, he plays along. Especially if there's a little late-night activity in the bedroom following the elaborate meal.

Wes takes in the powerful aroma of Italian herbs. *The smell of oregano and baking bread is making me hungry.* He follows it into the kitchen and finds Maggie hard at work. She is wearing a thin white silk blouse and a black miniskirt, with her hair pulled up in a ballroom array.

"Dinner is almost ready. I laid out an outfit I'd like you to wear tonight," Maggie says.

"Well, hello to you too," he says, teasing. "What meal will I be sampling tonight?"

"Gorgonzola pasta."

"Wonderful," Wes says. *I loathe anything with bleu cheese in it.* But if eating something he doesn't like earns him a little *dessert,* Wes would eat a dog. *It would have to be cooked, of course.*

Wes follows his wife's instructions and hops in the shower. Though tired from the day, he scrubs up fast and gets out. Looking in the mirror, he styles his semiwet hair and slaps a little cologne on. On the bed, he finds a black shirt and gray slacks. Putting on the garments, he debates whether to tuck his shirt into his pants. He decides he will. *Give her something to unwrap.*

Back in the living room and quite hungry, Wes sits down at the table. He watches Maggie stroll across the small kitchen toward him. She sets a bottle of wine down, giving Wes a sly smile. *We're definitely getting busy tonight.* He pours wine into the glass. "Would you like a little?"

"Not tonight," Maggie says, a small grin on her face.

She's more excited tonight than usual. Normally when Maggie puts these dinners together, she exhibits a level of focus, double-checking all the fine details. But not tonight. She's flirting more with her eyes and smile.

Maggie makes two more trips back to the kitchen, bringing pasta, bread, and salad. When she finally sits down, the couple take turns dishing the meal onto their plates. Wes reaches for a piece of bread and notices Maggie eyeing him with a playful look. "What's going on with you tonight?"

She draws out her response. "Nooothing ..."

"Well, okay. You're kind of acting like a weirdo right now."

"I'm telling you, Wesley, nothing is going on," she says, still kidding with him.

Wes plays along. He scoops a small ball of pasta onto his fork and holds it like a catapult. "If you don't tell me what's going on in three seconds, you are going to be covered in gorgonzola."

She giggles. "You better not."

"You've got to the count of three," Wes says, jokingly. He warns her again before starting his countdown.

"One."

Maggie still giggling.

"Two."

More giggles.

"Three!"

As he playfully takes aim, his attack is repelled with an announcement.

"I'm pregnant."

Wes freezes. Feeling joyful, he slowly lowers his fork. He goes to his wife. Maggie, sitting upright like a princess in the royal court, smiles at him, glowing. Wes kneels on one knee and places his hand on her stomach. She covers his hand with hers. In a soft tone, he asks, "How far along?"

"Almost eight weeks," Maggie says, matching his tone.

Out of nowhere, a thick swell of emotion rises from Wes's chest and bursts through his eyes. He sets his head in Maggie's lap and basks in the moment. She caresses his head, running her fingers through his dark hair. The two sit like this for a long minute.

Enjoying their moment, Maggie breaks the silence. "Do you want a boy or a girl?"

Not moving his head from her lap, he says, "It doesn't matter to me as long as the baby is healthy." Another moment passes before Wes runs through each gender scenario to himself. *A boy would be cool. I'd make him tough. But a girl, oh shit.*

Having an epiphany, Wes pops his head up and looks straight into Maggie's eyes. "If it is a boy, I'd like to name him after your father."

The gesture is not wasted on Maggie. Her eyes become moist. "I think that's a great idea, Wesley."

"When should we tell everyone?" he asks.

"Can we wait until we find out if we're having a boy or girl?"

"Of course."

CHAPTER  2

E ARLY THE NEXT MORNING, on the outskirts of town, in a somewhat hilly desert area, the sound of gunfire echoes into the air. Dirt roads form a simple spiderweb pattern on the desert's surface. Many of them leading to makeshift shooting ranges littered with broken bottles, old televisions, and aluminum cans. Off one of those roads sits a blue-and-white 1989 Ford Bronco truck, and three men are positioned next to it. One man is lying flat on the ground with a large rifle in front of him. Another stands behind him at his feet. The third sits casually on the tailgate.

Posted joyfully three hundred yards out on top of a small dirt mound is a porcelain garden gnome wearing a red pointy hat with a goofy smile on its face.

Caleb buries the rifle's buttstock deep into his shoulder. He brings his eye close to the scope. His shoulder blades pump as he takes in the last bit of oxygen before squeezing the trigger.

A light hiss of air escapes Caleb's mouth, and his body goes completely still. Wes, positioned behind his feet, stops moving around too and stares at the gnome. Sean sits quietly on the tailgate of the truck behind the two young men. The world is frozen in time, for a moment.

A sharp crack exits the barrel of the rifle, and the gnome explodes in a shower of porcelain fragments. Dust and the residual gunshot ring out and echo throughout the empty expanse of the desert. No one moves, appreciating the minor explosion. The silence is broken when Caleb celebrates the impact. "That's what I'm talking about! I'm a motivated killer!"

Wes laughs, kicking Caleb in the legs. "Motivated killer? If I remember right, you didn't get to shoot a single Sammy from a sniper position when we were in Somalia."

Caleb rolls to his side and barks up at Wes, "Hey, dickwad. You know a sniper's secondary mission is reconnaissance."

Wes maintains a stoic stare at Caleb. Sean hops off the tailgate and joins the ribbing. "How many Sammies did you actually kill from any of your ops, Ginger Bits?" Sean asks sarcastically.

"Fuck you, clowns," Caleb says, face growing red. Sean and Wes bust out laughing. Caleb has always protected the reputation of his sniper skills. And when they are called into question, he can become intense. Wes enjoys shooting, but Caleb is a beast when it comes to firearms. His ability to calculate distance, windage, ballistics, and target type before placing a round within centimeters of his intended objective is second to none. Caleb has always been competitive that way. Even before he and Wes were US soldiers.

After graduating from high school, the two enlisted in the US Army together under the Buddy Program. This allowed them to go to basic training, infantry school, and their first assignment together. After training, they were assigned to the Tenth Mountain Division at Fort Drum, New York. This is where they met Sean, who became their platoon sergeant. Immediately, Sean recognized the young Nevadans' individual potential. With a deployment to Africa on the horizon, he sent the two young men to advanced training. Wes attended the forward observer course and Caleb, sniper school. Three months after they returned, they were with Sean in Somalia.

Still irritated by the ball busting, Caleb takes a kneeling position, ready to address this sensitive subject. The question wasn't whether Caleb shot anyone while deployed. Wes and Caleb both terminated targets while in Somalia. Mostly during firefights they had while patrolling the bazaar shopping areas. But every time Caleb was posted on a sniper overwatch position, the opportunity to take a combatant's life never presented itself.

He has since taken several targets while in a sniper role on other deployments. But Mogadishu was his first, and he trained hard to get ready.

Not being able to engage a living target as a bona fide sniper on his first deployment felt like not getting any action from your date on prom night. Especially after buying tickets, renting a tux, paying for dinner, and taking those ridiculous pictures. This is why Wes and Sean like busting his balls about it.

"And how many deployments did you do?" Caleb asks, challenging Wes's deployment record. "One?"

This is a fact. Wes deployed only once. And that's all Maggie would tolerate. She wanted him home full-time. He sometimes regrets getting out. But Wes's record isn't up for debate right now. He deflects the question and keeps pressing Caleb.

"How many, sniper?"

"Fuck you, Wes."

Wes and Sean continue laughing until Sean offers up another target to Caleb. "Do you think you can hit something a little farther out?"

Caleb gets back behind his rifle. "Call it, then."

Displacing any humor left in his body, Wes searches a target. Looking through a set of binos, he spots one. He brings his tone to a professional level. A remnant of when they all worked together. "Green frog, five hundred and fifty meters west of T-R-P-2."

Caleb makes a few adjustments to his scope and announces with a deadly calmness, "Identified."

Sean issues the order: "Fire when ready."

Caleb steadies himself. The beautiful silence encompasses the veterans once again. Then another loud crack, followed by raining green porcelain. Sean and Wes cheer mockingly by saying, "Motivated killer" in unison.

The three head back to the truck. The old platoon sergeant reaches into the cooler and throws everyone a beer. Sean starts in. "I know you guys think this security gig with the Professor is a little shady, but the money is ridiculous. You should let me get you in."

"I'm not trying to stand around watching a bunch of rich motherfuckers as they gamble and bang hookers," Caleb replies crassly as a beeping sound comes from his pants. Caleb grabs the black beeper and holds it up to Wes and Sean. "Besides, I've got my own security gig with the racetrack." The track he's referring to is a professional track on the outskirts of Pahrump. They designed it for private parties wanting to race their sports cars. It is also used to teach Hollywood actors how to drive fast for upcoming action films.

Wes chimes in, "Yeah, and I told Maggie that I hung up runnin' and gunnin'."

Annoyed with Wes's comment, Sean says, "I'll never understand why you'd rather be a limp-dick card dealer and play house mouse with Maggie. Especially with the skills you have. You both know the three of us make a great crew. Definitely better than any crew working for the Professor right now."

"Look, Sean. Honestly, I wouldn't be opposed to the idea, but without Wes, I'm out."

Sean looks at Wes with an expectant expression on his face.

"I'm a family man now, gentlemen. I promised Maggie."

Caleb throws his shoulders up in an *Oh well* gesture. With a plastic smile, Sean nods in acknowledgment.

CHAPTER 3

AFTER HIS TIME AT the range, Wes finds himself standing in front of an ambiguous tin building. A loud table saw screams from inside. The sound is broken up with periodic blasts of a nail gun. Maggie's father, Gary, also known as Mr. Bennett to the young men he has given employment to over the years, owns the place. Even before Maggie and Wes started dating, he had Wes in the shop with his son, James, and their friend Vinnie. Gary, who had the belief that all young men should learn to work with their hands, welcomed any neighborhood boy wanting to learn a trade. And that trade had been cabinetmaking.

Ever since meeting James, Wes has been at the shop, learning how to work like a man. The shop itself is the ultimate man cave. Power tools line the walls. As do different calendars of years past with half-naked women posing with those tools. The floor always has a light coat of sawdust that drifts with every stride taken. The scent of burnt wood lingers as saw blades meet every variety of lumber. Knotty pine, red oak, mahogany, hickory … all the wood Gary says has "good character."

What Wes likes most about this place are the stories Gary tells about being in Vietnam. And they usually get colorful after he has pulled a little too much from a bottle of whiskey he keeps in his bottom drawer. Sometimes the story is about an old buddy. Or some asshole lieutenant who had almost gotten them killed. Often, he talked about the good leaders he served under. And how those experiences translate into day-to-day life.

One story that has stayed with Wes is about Gary's platoon going into a northern village. According to Gary's recollection, his platoon leader ordered them to burn down all the huts in the immediate area. Gary and several other soldiers protested the order, knowing there were only women and children living in those huts.

Through a drunken slur, Gary said, "That motherfuckin' LT told us they were the enemy. And all I saw were poor people trying to survive. But we ended up doing it because we were following orders. Biggest fuckin' regret of my life."

This had been the first time Wes saw Gary tear up.

Wes saunters into the shop and spots James working over an ear-piercing table saw. Like a true craftsman, he runs a piece of lumber through the raging blade. Next to him, Vinnie works a chop saw, beads of sweat running down his bald head into his scruffy beard. Neither James nor Vinnie notices Wes at first. Wes gets James's attention by waving his hand at him. James catches the signal in his peripheral, acknowledging Wes with a nod. Wes puts his finger over his lips, shushing him. James knows exactly what Wes is thinking.

Carefully, Wes scoops up a handful of fine sawdust off the floor and pulls a lighter out of his pocket. With the sawdust and lighter in hand, he flicks the lighter on. James watches, a shit-eating grin on his face. Wes throws the sawdust through the flame. This ignites a fireball that engulfs Vinnie without warning. Frantically, Vinnie waves his arms like a baby bird trying to fly, panicked, trying to escape the momentary flame.

"What the fuck!" Vinnie says. James and Wes explode into a frenzy of laughter. "Damn it, Wes! Why you guys always gotta mess with me?"

James shuts down the table saw and says, "'Cause you make it too easy, little guy."

Vinnie puffs out his chest as he approaches James. "Fuck you! I'm sick of your shit!"

James glances at Wes, amused by Vinnie's temper. "Look here, Wes, we got a real-world tough guy."

James gives Vinnie a two-finger poke to his forehead, pushing him back. Ever since the three were kids, James has always given Vinnie the same poke. He does this when he wants to push Vinnie's buttons. James picked up the move from an old kung fu movie the three used to watch when they were kids.

Wes gets between the two of them, hugging Vinnie. Doing a horrible impression of a Cuban Scarface, Wes negotiates with Vinnie. "Come on, Vinnie, take it easy."

Vinnie remains proud, his bald head growing redder by the second. Regretting the prank, Wes tries to help Vinnie out of his standoff with James. He grabs him by the cheeks and apologizes.

"I'm sorry, Vinnie, I was just fucking around."

The commotion is halted by the sound of a gravelly voice yelling, "Hey!"

The three young men stop, turning their gaze toward the door. A grizzled old man with a brown curly Afro and a graying beard stands glaring back at them, angry and frustrated. "I told you boys not to burn Vinnie with the sawdust! I can smell that shit all the way outside!" Gary approaches the three. They all stand up straight, lowering their heads. "I'm sick of you boys messing around in here. You're going to burn my shop to the ground."

"All right, Pops," James says. "So, what kind of bullshit work do we have today?"

"If you don't like your job, quit," Gary says. "You boys need to fix the crown molding at the Russo house." Gary looks to Wes, lighting a cigarette and throwing the used match to the sawdust-covered floor. All the young men's mouths drop in shock. "You working today, Wes?"

"Yeah, if I can. I could use the extra cash this week."

Gary chuckles. "Got to keep our little princess happy, don't we?"

Wes tries to hide his smirk. James and Vinnie look at him like he's pathetic.

"I hate that guy," James says.

Gary takes a puff of his hand-rolled cigarette and exhales the smoke. "He's not that bad."

James continues. "He complains about everything. We've changed the color of the doors three times. If he's not so bad, why don't *you* go over there?"

"Don't you fucking tell me where I need to be!" Gary says with a loud boom, pointing a finger at James.

"Pop, I'm just saying—"

"Well, don't say! Just shut up and do what I tell you. And you better do it right this time!"

With this, Gary storms out of the shop with a little hobble in his stride, slamming the door behind him, shaking the tin walls. The three workers stand, defeated.

CHAPTER 4

J AMES, VINNIE, AND WES eventually get to Mr. Russo's house. Wes tries to push them along, but James and Vinnie are moving like frozen molasses. James sneers at Vinnie as he off-loads crown molding from the truck with Wes.

Wes rubs his clean-shaven face, trying to cheer James up. He strikes up a conversation on a subject everyone enjoys. And of course the subject is sex.

James and Vinnie always perk up when they get to brag about their latest conquest. Wes usually avoids getting into the dirty details of his and Maggie's sex life. Unless Wes is trying to get under James's skin. But today Wes is taking a more diplomatic role.

"Yo, Vinnie, whatever happened to that fine Mexican chick you were seeing?" This gets the desired effect from James.

"Yeah, Vinnie, the one with the mustache?" James asks.

Not fazed by the comment, Vinnie responds to James first. "The only woman with a mustache I ever fucked around with was your ex, and I haven't seen her in a while." James isn't amused. Vinnie continues. "Wes, the Mexican broad you're talking about... " He then takes a horrible salsa dance position and in a horrific Ricky Ricardo accent says, "ah, mucho gusto, Papi."

James and Wes exchange a confused look and start laughing hysterically.

"Do you even know what that means?" Wes asks.

"No, but it sounded good."

More laughter from the trio. The moment is cut short by an angry shout coming from the front of the Russo house. They look up and see Mr. Russo standing on his front porch in a maroon silk robe with his hairy chest protruding from the overtly extravagant garment. With his hands on his hips, Russo's fifty-five-year-old squat frame supports a round belly. "Does this motherfucker think he's John Gotti?" James asks out loud. No one responds.

Sweat is already rolling down Mr. Russo's receding hairline. His creepy molester mustache twitches with every syllable exiting his puffy old lips.

Wes and Vinnie stay outside as James follows Russo into his house. Russo leads him into an immaculate kitchen. Spanish tile floor, steel appliances, and large marble countertops welcome anyone entering. The cobblestone walls are framed with six-inch crown molding and hickory cabinets. All installed a week prior by the three-man crew.

James calculates the hours in labor for this job. *We have already spent twice the time it would usually take for a project like this. Hell, anyone else would be thrilled with the work we've done.* Unfortunately, Russo yells at James about their progress so far.

"Look at this crap!" Russo says, waving his hand at the cabinets. "This crown doesn't match up at all! The doors are all crooked—"

Interrupting Russo, James attempts to explain where they are in the process. "We still need to adjust the doors. And we brought new crown."

Russo continues yelling. "The doors don't match. You see? They're different." He stomps on the tile floor like a spoiled child, yelling, "Different, different, different!"

James scowls back at Russo. *Is this grown motherfucker throwing a temper tantrum right now?*

Reaching his boiling point, James fantasizes about grabbing Russo by the ears, forcing his head into an open cabinet, and smashing his skull with the door as blood flies through the air in slow motion. Also, in his fantasy, Wes and Vinnie cheer him on as screams for mercy echo off the decorative walls.

Come back to reality, James. When he finally returns from his fantasy world of carnage, Russo is still fretting about their work. Russo only slows down to stop to catch his breath. Huffing and puffing, his fat, round face is now bright red. *Maybe he'll die right here.*

CHAPTER 

JAMES, VINNIE, AND WES have been at the cabinet install for at least seven hours when Russo saunters into the kitchen.

"Hey, morons, pack up your stuff and be out of here in fifteen minutes. I have someone coming over, and I want you out of the way when he shows up." Looking at James, he asks, "Do you understand me, moron number one?"

With a thick, exaggerated, inbred southern accent, James says, "Right away, suh."

Russo's eyebrows and mustache jolt with disgust as he marches out of the kitchen.

"Quitting time, bitches!" Vinnie says.

James doesn't say a word. Absentmindedly, he picks up his tools and heads toward the truck. Wes and Vinnie follow. Outside, James is hurling his tools into the bed of the truck. He jumps into the driver's side and slams the door. Vinnie and Wes are a little more careful with their tools as they load them in the back.

The sound of a loud sports car approaches. Behind the steering wheel is Sean, driving a black Porsche that sits low to the ground. He pulls up to Russo's house. Tires screech when the vehicle comes to a stop.

Sean takes his time getting out of the sports car. Wearing a gray blazer, white button-down shirt, slacks, and dress shoes, he looks like a casino pit boss. His athletic physique and chiseled Irish chin complement the ensemble. Sean has a gold chain around his neck and a ring on his pinky finger.

He and Wes shake hands. "I didn't know you were working on Russo's house."

"Just a little longer," Wes replies.

Looking at Wes, dirty and covered in sawdust, Sean says, "I'm telling you, I got better work for you. It pays a shit-ton more, and you don't have to haul dirty equipment around."

Wes changes the subject, introducing Vinnie and James. Sean looks through the cab of the truck and nods at James. Starstruck, James nods back with a slight smile.

"I don't know what's wrong with Wes, but I'd be down to work for you," James says.

Amused, Sean cocks his head back and looks over the old dirty work truck. "Be *down*?" Sean asks, sarcasm in his voice. "What is it you do exactly?"

James straightens up in his seat. "I can do anything you need. Want me to collect? I got you. Make runs? I'm your guy—"

Sean interrupts him, offended now. "James, is it? I don't know what you've heard about me, but it's not that. I only manage a security company." James's shoulders lower. Sean proceeds. "Unless you have any sort of overseas military experience, you're not qualified. Besides, if I were the type of guy you implied I was, you wouldn't approach me the way you did." Sean looks at Wes sympathetically, shaking his head as he strolls toward Russo's house. Over his shoulder he says, "Time to get on a winning team, Wes."

Wes tries to break up the awkward moment by shoving Vinnie into the passenger side of the cab. He hops in next to him.

Vinnie whines for a minute and asks, "Why do I have to ski?" He pumps his hands up and down over Wes's and James's groin areas as if pleasuring both simultaneously.

"Because you have the softest hands," Wes replies.

James misses the joke, staring at Sean, who is shaking hands with Russo in his front yard. The three cabinetmakers pull out of the driveway.

On the road, James is driving more aggressively than usual. Out of the blue, he shouts at Wes, "How in the fuck do you know Sean Lynch?"

Caught off guard by the question, Wes answers, "He was my platoon sergeant in Somalia."

Not believing what he heard, James verifies the information. "Sean Lynch was with you overseas? What the fuck, man? He's offering you a job and you're telling him no. Don't you know who he works for?"

"I've heard things, but who knows?" Wes replies. "Besides, a lot of what I heard are only rumors. Either way, I don't want to get involved in his work."

"Wes, this motherfucker works for the Professor."

"So what if he does?"

"So what! If you don't want the job, can you talk to him about me?"

"He made his position pretty clear about you."

"Bullshit—he was testing me."

"If you say so."

The old work truck pulls up to the front of Wes's house. Wes invites James and Vinnie inside. "You wanna come say hello to your sister?"

"Nah, I have to catch up on some drinking," James says, irritated.

Wes gets out of the truck and moves up his long dirt driveway.

The truck peels out on the gravel road behind Wes. It fishtails, kicking up dirt all over him. He stands for a moment, stunned at the way James drove off.

Wes enters his small castle, clean and decorated well with secondhand home décor from the local Goodwill. From the back room, he hears Maggie going back and forth with someone on the phone.

"What do you mean they didn't accept the offer? Well, what's the next step?"

She comes out of the bedroom and points at Wes's feet, cueing him to take off his boots, which he does. He takes a moment to look at Maggie's long dark hair, which always melts his heart. He watches her petite frame pace in circles as her sweet, feminine, and confident voice brings her negotiations to a close.

"Okay, I'll tell him, thank you." She hangs up the phone and greets Wes with a kiss and hug. A light, sweet aroma from her hair sneaks into his nose, causing him to squeeze her tighter.

"Who was that?"

"The Realtor," she replies, a bit annoyed.

"And ..."

"And they didn't accept our offer. But ..."

"Ah, there's a 'but,'" Wes says, attempting charm.

Maggie changes her tone too. Being sweet and optimistic, she says, "But they countered."

Of course they countered, Wes thinks, sitting down, taking off his socks. The couple has been working a pending house deal for the past two weeks. "And?" Wes asks.

"It's a little more than what we wanted to pay."

"How much more?"

"They went up five thousand."

"Five thousand! I can buy you a brand-new pair of titties for that kind of money!"

Maggie playfully slaps him on the arm. "Wes, I thought you liked the girls the way they are?"

Let her know you still like them—now! He kisses her on the neck as he grabs one of her boobs. "I do, I do." He follows up with a more serious question. "Are you willing to pay that much for the place?"

Maggie coos at Wes as she kisses him on the lips, grabbing his inner thigh. "You know I love that place. Besides, can't you see us in that house?" She kisses him on the neck now as her hand moves a little more up his leg. "Having all our friends over for parties?"

"Yes, I can," Wes says, playing along. "I'd want to plant some grass too. We could also have James and Vinnie update the kitchen."

Maggie pulls away from Wes. "I am not letting those two touch my house."

"Slow down, turbo," he says, defending their honor. "You're not exactly qualified to put in a new kitchen. Besides, what's wrong with them? We all grew up together."

"I don't know about them anymore," Maggie says. "James is always getting into something sketchy, and Vinnie follows along like a dummy. Does he even have his own brain?"

"You should try to have more respect for your brother and his friend," Wes says, playfully chastising his wife.

Maggie cocks her head at her husband, displaying authentic indignation.

CHAPTER 6

A FTER DROPPING WES OFF, James and Vinnie head to the local R Bar. Vinnie hopes a little liquor and a decent-looking lady will settle James down before they head home. But the plan is falling short. James is still acting like a top-shelf asshole. Vinnie would take a little ball-busting at this point if it would put James in a better mood.

The two sawdust-covered men go inside. It's a fairly dark establishment. The only decent light is an overhead fluorescent fixture mounted above the pool table. Gathered around the table, locals challenge each other for a couple of dollars.

There are no beauty queens in this place. But the bartenders have heavy hands, and a few of the waitresses like to chat the young men up. Most nights, James and Vinnie can find a chick to go home with. But the way James is acting tonight, chances for some little late-night action don't look promising.

The two men find a place to sit near the pool table. A blinking red neon light from an old Coors beer sign on the wall flashes above the table. The entire bar is busy tonight. Local women in jean skirts and cowboy boots shake their goods to a mediocre band playing on a small stage. Neither James nor Vinnie dances; instead, they drink, fuck, and sometimes fight.

Kelsey, a waitress Vinnie knows, greets them. With her cleavage protruding out of a red button-up shirt, she totes a drink tray, sporting her typical smile. Vinnie considers Kelsey to be good-looking. Not "model hot" but more like "you won't hate yourself in the morning" cute. She's in her early thirties and shaped well for having one kid. Vinnie met the kid one morning after an all-night coke and sex binge with his mother.

"Hey, Vinnie. What can I get you guys tonight?" Kelsey asks.

"I'll have a whiskey."

"And you?" Kelsey asks James.

"Beer," James says, who is staring into space.

Kelsey prances off, trying to be cute. Vinnie leans over to James, trying to talk over the music. "Are you gonna be shitty all night?"

"Fuck you, man," James says. "Aren't you tired of being a clown?"

"What are you talking about?"

"Sean didn't give us a second look," James says.

"Fuck him."

"You don't get it, bro. What I'm saying is ... there has to be more out there for us."

"You want to do bigger jobs?" Vinnie asks, a bit confused.

"Not bigger jobs," says James, becoming serious. "I want *the* job. I'm tired of selling a few ounces of weed, stealing copper, and hanging cabinets for my old man. I want to hit something big."

"Your dad's cabinet shop isn't that bad," Vinnie says, not believing his own words.

"For fuck's sake, Vinnie! We've been trying to leave that dump forever."

"But it's safe and the cops aren't always on our back."

"Look. The shop is for my dad. He loves that shit, not me. There's an entire world of cash out there. We just need to sink our claws into it. Maybe then Sean will take notice and put us on the payroll."

Did this motherfucker forget Sean told us to go fuck ourselves?

Kelsey is now back at the table with their drinks. "Here you go, boys."

"Get the fuck away from us," James says in a harsh tone. "Can't you see we're talking?"

The entire establishment looks their direction. Including a giant goon at the pool table and a couple of bouncers standing behind the bar. Kelsey doesn't flinch but gives it right back to James.

"Don't yell at me because your dick is small."

Vinnie thinks, *Why do women always attack the size of our dicks when they get mad?* She continues at Vinnie now. "You better keep your boyfriend in line, or both of you will be out of here."

Vinnie raises his hands in surrender, and Kelsey storms off. The bar settles back into its routine. They both take a swig from their drinks.

"The thing with Sean, we can change that," says James. "All we need is one big job. After that, word gets out we can handle our shit. Then we have Wes put in a good word for us."

Vinnie reminds James, "Bro, he said if we ain't military, he's not interested."

"That's bullshit. He wants motherfuckers who can fight and have balls. And we're both."

"But Sean is shady, man," Vinnie continues. "Plus, Wes didn't want to work with him either. Why should we?"

James sneers at Vinnie. "Wes is so pussy-whipped on my sister he can't see straight. But you and me, we could be an asset to Sean. Besides, all Wes would have to do is talk to him a little for us."

They both sit for a moment in deep contemplation. Vinnie thinks, *Maybe James is right. Do a job, have Wes tell Sean about it, and then he might give us a second look.* "Let's say you're right. If we do this, what's our first move?"

James points to the goon over at the pool table and makes a booming announcement: "The first move is to slap the shit out of that bitch-made motherfucker over there."

The goon hears James's comment and straightens up, puffing his chest out. James slams his beer bottle down on the table, jumps to his feet, and heads toward the large man. *Fuck me, I'm not even drunk yet,* Vinnie thinks, following.

As James and Vinnie get closer to the pool table, the goon gets bigger and bigger. Vinnie notices his muscles, tattoos, and bald head. But what catches his eye is the leather biker vest he's wearing. It's covered with patches, including the infamous "1 percent" designation. Scanning the area, Vinnie spots four more biker types wearing matching vests. Vinnie is not too worried about their opponents being bikers. His concern are their numbers.

Now face-to-face with Goon Number One, James says, "You must think I'm pretty 'cause you keep eye-fucking me?"

"What?" Goon Number One asks through a gravelly, deep voice. Face tightening, eyes narrowing.

"Did I stu-stu-stutter, bitch?"

James flicks his cigarette. The cherry explodes like a firework on Goon Number One's face. He wildly swipes off the hot ash. His friends rush toward James.

"Motherfucker!" Goon Number One says. He punches James in the face, sending him into Vinnie. The impact almost knocks both of them over. James looks up at Vinnie with a smile. His lips are swollen and blood is gushing from his nose into his mouth.

"This is going to be fun," James says, sucking on his bloodied teeth. Having steadied his stance, he laughs hysterically.

Goon Number One gloats at his work. "I'm glad you think this is fun—"

James punches him in the throat. The massive biker drops to one knee. His four buddies charge James, their flanks exposed to Vinnie. Vinnie punches the closest one in the jaw. He stumbles back, dazed but not out. Immediately, Vinnie swings on another biker. Again, connecting fist to face.

James continues to beat on Goon Number One until one of the bouncers yanks him by the back of his collar, pulling him off the pummeled man and throwing him into the crowd. A blur of wild punches and yelling fills the bar.

Bodies and fists continue in Vinnie's direction, blinding him. Several blows scrape the top of his head. He feels his own strikes smash against hairy, fleshy meat several times. *Shit, I'm doing pretty good tonight.*

Still brawling, Vinnie is thrown backwards into the fire exit door, which sends him into the hot summer air. The backs of his heels trip over a concrete parking block. He lands hard on the gravel surface. Dizzy, he stares at the summer night sky. James slams to the ground next to him.

Vinnie sits up on his ass, ready for more punishment. But the fight is over. Three bouncers stand authoritatively over the two beaten friends, yelling for them to get off the property. Vinnie regains his focus when the bar door slams shut, and all is quiet. The silence is disturbed with James's heckling laugh.

"Hell yeah, that's what I'm talking about."

Vinnie, not as enthusiastic, stands up with James. "Let's get the fuck out of here."

CHAPTER 

IN HIS LIVING ROOM, sitting on leather couches, Russo and Sean exchange pleasantries before discussing business. Russo, a gaudy dresser himself, wearing a silk robe and slippers, looks Sean up and down, nodding in approval at his appearance. "You look sharp tonight, my friend. You got a hot date or somethin'?" Russo says in his thick New Jersey accent.

Sean displays a respectful smile. "Thank you, Mr. Russo."

"That's why I like you, Sean. You have the decorum of a true East Coaster," Russo says, slapping Sean on the shoulder.

Russo and Sean have found common ground since Sean has started working for the Professor. They both complain about not finding a proper cheesesteak sandwich and how there's something special about the smell, noise, and air of the East Coast.

Russo knows he shouldn't complain, though. The money is good, law enforcement almost doesn't exist unless you're drunk in a bar, and most of the residents care more about their gun rights and horses than they do about out-of-town commerce.

Even with their East Coast connection, Russo still looks at Sean as a working dog.

And anyone who knows dogs understands that hunger is necessary to keep them compliant.

So when Sean speaks with a formal tone, it gives Russo a sense of authority and importance. It shows Sean understands the food chain.

"Did you check out the new talent?" Russo asks, referring to several brothels Sean's been given to manage. Those brothels run from Pahrump up through US Route 95.

"Yes, I did. I also cross-leveled the girls again with the new ones eager to work."

"Sean! You Irish prick, you're always on top of things."

Cross-leveling is the process of placing girls, or "courtesans," as they like to call themselves, in different locations. Reassignments are based on looks and individual initiative. If they don't earn, they go to a more rural, slower location. Like Crystal, which is twenty minutes north of Pahrump. The process requires finesse and diplomacy. That's why Sean is in the position. He has a way with words that Russo lacks. But the role is mediocre in the grand scheme of the Professor's organization. And Russo always reminds Sean of this fact.

"God bless you, Sean. You know that shit gives me a headache."

"Yes, I know, sir."

A decanter filled with cheap scotch rests on a marble coffee table. Russo has good scotch hidden away. But never offers it to his subordinates. He considers his Irish dog unworthy of such decadence.

Russo pours two drinks, and the men settle back into their seats. Sean tells Russo about a new idea he has.

"Mr. Russo, I met this guy earlier in the week up at the Beatty house who drives cross-country. He also travels with this credit card lab setup inside his rig. All he does are his weekly runs and supplements his income with these fake credit—"

Raising his hand, Russo cuts him off. "Sean, you're busy enough. Plus, credit cards are tricky, and our boss doesn't like tricky." Like a well-trained dog, Sean heels. *Yes, still obedient.* Russo pats Sean on the back as he stands up. "Come on, let me show you what's next," Russo says.

Russo leads Sean to his master bedroom closet. He starts pushing clothes to the side revealing a magnificent safe. He flashes Sean a devious smile. Sean's face remains neutral. With a metallic squeal from the hinges, the door opens. Sean's eyes widen. His lips curl at the sides, as he holds back a smile.

"Our next endeavor," Russo says, a proud smile on his face.

CHAPTER 8

T HE NEXT MORNING, WES, James, and Vinnie are back
in the Russo house. Fortunately, for the three, Russo
left on an early-morning errand. Wes examines his two friends.
James's hands are red and swollen. A dark bruise spans over his
nose. Vinnie has a couple of lumps and fresh lacerations on his
forehead.

"Late night?" Wes asks.

"James was on his period," Vinnie says.

James deflects the comment. "I need a couple tubes of caulk
from the truck."

Wes and Vinnie sneak grins at each other.

Louder now, James talks to the walls. "Maybe those tubes of
caulk will grow legs and walk in here."

"Hey, James, you need some *caulk*?" Wes asks.

Vinnie snorts at the joke. "He always needs some *caulk*."

Wes and Vinnie chuckle.

James stops his work, intentionally dropping a screwdriver
on the tile floor. He shoots a sharp look at Wes. Wes throws a
toothy smile back at James.

"Since you're not *feeling well*, I'll go get your *caulk*," Wes says.

Once Wes is outside, Vinnie continues to plug away at the cabinet install like a good little worker bee. James takes this distraction to look around the house.

He strolls down the hallway, studying the tile floor. "He wants everyone to think it's Italian; I bet he got this shit at Ace Hardware," James says to himself.

At the master bedroom, James pokes his head inside. Against the wall is a large dark-wood bed with a diamond tuft headboard. Above the bed, a mirror is hung from the ceiling. *This fat, freaky motherfucker.* James fights the urge to throw up. *What kind of woman would roll around on Russo's fat belly? Fuckin' disgusting.*

Having to piss, James saunters into the master bathroom. More exotic marble and large mirrors. The entire space looks like it belongs in a casino. *What the fuck is this?* The toilet seat is in the down position. *What man leaves the toilet seat down? I bet this motherfucker sits when he pees.* Smirking, James throws the seat up against the tank and pisses straight down the middle of the bowl the way a man should.

"Dick control, Russo," he mutters through a low laugh.

After relieving himself, he notices a massive hunter-green safe in the closet. He yells, "Vinnie, get your ass in here!"

Vinnie yells back, "What now?"

"Get in here! I want you to see this."

Vinnie stomps down the hallway into the bedroom. "What's so—" His question is interrupted at the sight of the ceiling mirror. Confusion fills his face.

"Fuck the mirror. Look at this."

Vinnie looks at the safe. Not impressed, he says, "A safe ... great. So what?"

"What do you think he keeps in there?" James asks.

"Who knows? Kiddie porn if I had to guess."

"Be serious, numb nuts," James says. "Pop keeps ammo in his safe, but it's in the garage. A safe inside the house means something more valuable."

"Like what?" Vinnie asks.

"I don't know: money, jewelry, drugs—who knows? But something worth hiding in the closet."

Vinnie nods in agreement. "What are you thinking?"

"I'm thinking we found our opportunity to make a real move."

"Are you kidding me?" Vinnie asks. "Sean Lynch was here yesterday. Which means Russo most likely works with the Professor."

"Who cares?" James says.

"I don't know, man."

James knows he needs to insult Vinnie's manhood right now in order to manipulate him into helping. "Quit being a bitch, Vinnie! Fuck these old men and their bullshit suits and fancy cars. Whatever's in that safe can help us get our own crew going."

Vinnie rubs his head, brow furrowed. James has his attention.

"Look, bro, no one can say it was us if we don't get caught. We'll take what we get and launder it through some out-of-town sources. We give it a few months, use the earnings to make a name for ourselves. That way we get some attention from the Professor to show him we can run a crew."

"Hold on," Vinnie says. "Do you even know how to wash money?"

"It can't be that hard. Shit, all these businesses out here do it."

Vinnie nods. The two stand quietly, staring at the safe. James nudges him. In a desperate low tone, he says, "I can't do it without you, brother."

"Do what?" a voice asks.

Startled, James and Vinnie snap their heads toward the voice. Wes is standing at the doorway.

James recovers without missing a beat. "Go for round two with those biker bitches. You wanna come tonight?"

"Nah, I'll pass."

"Of course you will," James says sarcastically.

Rolling his eyes, Wes turns back down the hallway. James and Vinnie wait until the coast is clear. Vinnie finally speaks. "Fuck it, bro, I'm in."

James's recruitment strategy works again.

CHAPTER 9

EXCITED WITH THE PLAN to rip off Russo, James calls quitting time early. The three load their equipment back into the company truck. James is gleaming with a large, sinister smile. Vinnie has more of a concentrated look on his face. Wes's eyes are closed, his head leaning back against the cab.

Within thirty minutes of leaving Russo's house and dropping Wes off, James and Vinnie are in another bar. Because of the scuffle the night before, the two won't be able to return to the R Bar for about another week. It usually takes that long for the bar to reinstate their local membership.

Instead, they land in a darker and even more shady establishment. In this place, there's no pool table, no live band, no dancing girls, and no chatty waitress. There's only the bartender, Moby. The tats covering his arms and chest record the cumulative twenty-five years he has served in both state and federal prisons.

Named after the sperm whale in Herman Melville's novel *Moby Dick*, Moby is a large man made up of muscle and dense fat sitting on his six-foot-four frame. The former career criminal turned bartender has served time in some of the United States' toughest prisons, including stints in Folsom, San Quentin, and Pelican Bay in California. He also did time in Nevada and Arizona. Moby was also incarcerated in the Penitentiary of New Mexico in 1980. The same time twelve corrections guards were held and thirty-three inmates, mostly child molesters, were killed and burned. Word on the street was that Moby got his beefy hands on a couple of those kiddie touchers himself.

The bar itself matches the personality of its bartender. With a dark interior and tables spaced out enough for privacy, anyone involved in nefarious activities is most likely here. The general crowd of the bar is an older demographic, with the youngest being in their forties. Once in a while, you'll find a younger man having a drink with an older gentleman, but that's the rare occasion. This is why the entire place gives James and Vinnie a hard look when they enter. Tension is thick in the air.

Strolling in with exaggerated confidence, James nods at a table for Vinnie to go sit at. He takes his own seat at the bar waiting for Moby. When Moby approaches, James fights to keep his face tight and not stare at Moby's tattoos. Tall and domineering, with eyes reflecting all the carnage in his life, Moby asks, "What can I get you?"

"Two beers," James says, maintaining a confident tone.

Moby grabs two bottles of cheap brew. "That'll be ten dollars," he says, his voice deep and gravelly.

James throws a ten and a five on the bar. Moby nods in appreciation. James reciprocates the gesture as he heads over to Vinnie.

"Do you know who that is over there?" James asks.

"No, I don't."

"That's Moby," James says enthusiastically.

"Moby? Still don't know him."

Surprised by his response, James continues. "You remember that old dude Chuck who used to work for my dad?"

"The one with the fucked-up eye?"

"Yeah, that's his buddy Moby. I remember meeting him when I was a kid. He came by the shop to pick up Chuck. I remember him catching me staring at his tattoos. He scared the shit out of me."

Vinnie gives Moby a quick glance. "He scares me now."

"Chuck told me he robbed a few banks and got away with it. But ended up doing time for other shit. He also said he killed a couple of child molesters while locked up in Arizona. I have always been fascinated with the stories about this guy."

"Okay, so what?" Vinnie asks.

"I need to talk to him."

Vinnie's head drops in exhaustion. "Are you fucking crazy? Do you think you can walk up to a guy like that and ask him how he robbed a bank and got away with it?"

"Not like that, dummy. Plus, I wouldn't tell him who we're hitting or when. Just get a few pointers."

"James, I don't know. What if people talk after the job and he mentions us?"

James laughs out loud. "You think that hard motherfucker over there would talk to the cops? These old-school cons live by a code."

"And what's that code, James?"

"Don't talk to the cops," James says as a matter of fact. "How much cash do you have right now?"

"Maybe sixty bucks. Why?"

"Give it to me."

Vinnie does as he's told, pulling out three crumpled twenty-dollar bills. James pulls out two twenty-dollar bills of his own. He takes a quick second to iron out the bills on the edge of the table and glides back over to the bar. Vinnie puts his head down and continues nursing his beer.

James takes a spot near Moby. Looking at the television, Moby asks, "You want another beer?"

"Sure."

Moby gives James another bottle, barely making any eye contact with him. The two stare at the television, not saying a word. After another awkward moment, James asks. "They call you Moby, right?"

This gets the large bartender's attention. Moby pushes himself off the bar. Still towering, he takes a slight fighting stance. His demeanor, the look on his face, and the sound of his voice appear aggressive. "And who the fuck are you?" Moby asks, his voice booming through the bar. Several patrons lift their heads toward his voice.

James regrets his decision to mention his name but maintains a cool composure. "I'm James. I met you when I was a kid."

"And where the fuck was that?" Moby asks, not relenting.

"Over at my pop's shop. You picked up your buddy Chucky."

The bartender relaxes an inch. "Are you talking about Charles Barquin?"

"Yeah, the old man with the fucked-up eye."

Another inch of relaxation. "Where was this again?"

"At my dad's shop. He makes cabinets."

Moby's eyes jump back and forth, as he searches his mind. Finally, he pulls the memory. When he does, his posture relaxes its last notch. "Yeah, Chucky put in some cabinets for my mom."

"Well, I hope he did a good job."

Not impressed either way, Moby says, "They're still on the walls."

"That's good."

Moby starts wiping down the bar top. James continues. "So, how is Chuck these days?"

"Dead."

"Sorry to hear that."

"That's what happens when you stick needles in your arms."

"I didn't know he got down like that."

"He wasn't that way when he worked for your old man. Happened after his bike accident. Fucked his whole back up and got addicted to pills, which led to him shooting rigs."

"He was really cool with me back then," James says. Moby nods. Without skipping a beat, James continues. "I was hoping you could give me a little advice."

For the first time, Moby chuckles. "About what?"

In a lower voice, James says, "Doing rips."

Moby's face tightens, his eyes narrow on James. He postures again, standing up straight like a father getting ready to chastise his son. "What makes you think I know anything about that?" Moby asks with an accusing tone.

"Come on, Moby. Chuck used to tell me all your stories when I was a kid. I used to think how badass you were. I still do. I'm looking for any guidance you could offer."

Moby leans toward James. "Chuck always talked too much." He continues. "You want guidance? Here's a little: Don't do it. You're better off chasing those housewives at the R Bar than you are pulling off any real heist."

Surprised by the comments, James asserts himself with more force. "I'm tired of pulling shit jobs. I need to make a move, but I want to do it right."

Moby's next few words sound like rocks being pushed through a grinder. He growls at James, "You're tired of shit jobs? You're ready to step up to the big leagues? Bullshit! Let me ask you this. Are you ready to shit in front of another man for 1,100 days when you're locked down? Do you think you have what it takes to drive your thumb into another man's eye and pull his eyeball out while three of his buddies beat you with a pipe? Do you think you would enjoy fucking your own hand because they are no women around? Are you prepared to take another man's life when you thought he was the prey but becomes the predator? When he shows you his will to live is stronger than your will to steal?"

James sits quiet for a moment, contemplating Moby's words. With a serious look and tone to match, James says, "I already fuck my own hand."

This cracks the rough exterior of the infamous Moby. A small smile emerges from his face. He notices the twenty-dollar bills James is keeping under his hand. Nodding to the cash, Moby says, "Education isn't cheap."

James slides the cash over. "No, it's not."

Taking the tuition fees, Moby starts class in a lower tone. "What's the job?"

James takes the next couple of minutes to share his plans for the heist. Listening carefully, Moby asks insightful questions, causing James to make adjustments to his plan. Having laid out the whole job, Moby nods in approval. Receiving this endorsement from a man like Moby floods James's ego and fills him with brazen confidence.

The two men shake hands. James exits the bar with Vinnie following. With the two young hoodlums gone, Moby grabs the phone kept under the bar and punches a few numbers. "Yeah, that youngster just came by," Moby says into the phone. Now for the first time, a genuine smile appears on his face before he hangs up.

CHAPTER 10

T HAT NIGHT, AROUND ELEVEN, James and Vinnie sit in a stolen dark blue Toyota Corolla. They're parked a few houses down from Russo's home. James took great pains finding a spot well hidden with a good line of sight to Russo's place.

"Do you think we should be doing this tonight?" Vinnie asks.

"Absolutely!" James says. "We've got a solid plan, so why wait?"

They stare at the house for another minute and recognize Sean's black Porsche in the driveway. "Isn't that Sean's car?" Vinnie asks.

Before James can answer, the headlights to the Porsche light up and the vehicle zips out of the driveway. It heads their direction. Vinnie panics. "What are we going to do?"

James smoothly reclines the driver's seat, looking at Vinnie calmly. He holds his arm out against Vinnie's chest. Vinnie follows his direction, reclining his own seat. James says, "Relax, brother, relax. I've got everything laid out."

Vinnie's face twists in confusion. "What's gotten into you? You normally want to run in and out."

"It's a new approach," James says. His inspiration to work smarter and not harder coming from his conversation with Moby earlier in the evening. Besides covering the basics like hard entries and exit plans, Moby preached patience. And committing oneself to do what it takes to avoid getting caught. Even if it means shooting your mark in the face. "Yeah, I like this new approach," James says.

They hear the Porsche roar past the stolen Toyota. Both young men remain in their reclined positions. The thrill of hiding is reminiscent of their days playing hide-and-seek as kids.

"Are you ready to go?" James asks, a wild look of excitement in his eyes.

"Let's do it," Vinnie says.

Both men exit the vehicle. Crossing the street, they pull black ski masks over their faces.

James takes the lead, moving along a couple of parked cars, staying in the shadows. Vinnie is right behind him.

CHAPTER 11

L ATE IN THE EVENING, in the second bedroom of their mobile home, Wes and Maggie sit on the floor. Baby crib parts are scattered around them. Wes fumbles with a couple of pieces while Maggie thumbs through the assembly instructions. "Wesley, it says part 3A connects to 3B."

"Honey, please. I know you're trying to help, but I hang cabinets for a living. I can put a crib together."

Playfully indignant, Maggie stares at Wes struggling with part 3A.

"The pieces are color-coded too," Maggie says.

Not saying a word, Wes holds the two pieces up to Maggie. She takes them and, with ease, fastens them together. She looks at him with an *Aren't you proud of me?* look. Wes's pride is injured for a second before he smiles. He pulls his wife into his arms and they embrace.

"Are you scared?" Wes asks.

"Of what?"

"I don't know. Maybe the pain."

"Not yet. When the time comes, I probably will be. How about you? Are you scared?" Maggie asks.

"A little," Wes replies softly.

"About what?"

"Screwing the kid up."

Maggie puts her hand on his face. "You'll be a great dad. If we have a boy, you can be rough and tumble with him. And if it's a girl, she'll have you wrapped around her finger."

"Like you, right?" Wes asks.

"Exactly."

Wes stares at the ceiling, lost in thought. *I hope I can provide for my family. Especially with Maggie wanting a new home.*

He rolls over, facing Maggie. "You know, Sean offered me and Caleb a job again."

A tired look forms on Maggie's face. "Security work?"

"Yeah. But it pays a lot more than the army ever did."

"With more pay comes more danger, right?"

"I don't know, Maggie. Maybe. But with the baby coming and a new house, a better-paying job would be nice."

"But I thought you wanted to give up that kind of work. And you said Sean is sometimes involved in questionable situations."

"Yeah, that's true."

"I think you're much safer and much happier dealing cards. And you know my dad will want you to run the shop when he retires next year."

"But what about the house, sweetheart?"

Maggie kisses Wes. "We'll figure it out. Plus, I like having you home at night."

Wes smiles. "I like being home too."

Having to be at the shop early tomorrow to finish the Russo project, Wes stands up to go to bed. He helps his wife up.

Wes locks the doors and turns off all the lights.

Once in bed, he snuggles up next to Maggie and is at peace.

CHAPTER 12

Inside the desert castle, Russo stands over a Technics SL-1200 turntable. The song 'My Way' by Old Blue Eyes himself plays as he places the needle gently on the vinyl record. Russo selects a 1926 Padrón cigar from his tabletop humidor. He ganders at the vast selection of liquors. He decides on a thirty-year-old Zafra rum. A true top-shelf libation he keeps for himself, not made for the peasants who work for him.

Strutting to the couch with his evening vices, he stops midstride in front of a mirror. He admires his appearance. Standing proudly in his silk robe, holding the cigar and drink. *You still got it, Freddy.*

Snipping the cap off his cigar, he hears a loud knock at the door. "What the hell?" Irritated, he takes a quick sip of the rum and checks the front door.

Peering through the peephole, Russo only sees the darkness, except for a sliver of ambient moonlight breaking up the black night. He flips a light switch to the front porch. Nothing comes on.

"Fucking light ... who the fuck is it?" he says through the thick front door.

No answer. Russo snatches a snub-nosed .357 revolver from a small desk near the entrance. Tightly gripping the revolver, he unlocks the dead bolt. He takes a moment and cracks the door open. The night desert air is the only thing he can hear.

Carefully, Russo dips his head outside, looking left and right. He starts to close the door. With a loud, kicking thud, the door flies open. It crashes into Russo's face, smashing his nose and forehead. The impact drives him to the floor. His revolver flies out of his hand and across the tiled surface. Blood trickles down his face. Stunned by the blow and the pain, Russo grabs his face with one hand, looking for his revolver.

Spotting it, he crawls toward the firearm. His silk robe slides off his fat frame, tripping up his movement. His hands get lost in the wide sleeves of the plush garment.

While Russo fights with his robe, two men dressed in all black, wearing matching ski masks, barge into the house. The taller, thinner assailant kicks Russo in the back of his ass. Russo slides on his stomach across the floor past the revolver. He scrambles, getting one foot planted before his attackers are on top of him. Again, they knock him flat. He rolls over quickly and sits up. A black handgun, also a revolver, is in his face.

The short, rounder assailant picks Russo's gun up. He studies it like a museum curator for a second before tightening his grip around the new hardware.

"Good evening, you fat fuck." Thug Number One says.

Riddled with physical pain and feelings of disrespect, Russo is more pissed than scared right now. "Who are you two ass clowns?" he says, sneering.

Thug Number One pistol whips Russo. The gun's handle crashes into his temple. Russo lets out a painful grunt, falling flat on his back. Russo grabs the top of his face. He feels an open gash above his left eye. Blood leaks from the wound. And a goose-egg lump is forming on his forehead.

Thug Number Two mocks him. "Ass clowns?" he says, pulling Russo up by his thinning hair. He struggles to his feet. His scalp burns in pain. The two intruders face the hallway, now holding Russo by his beefy neck.

Guiding their target as if he were a wild horse, the two intruders lead Russo down the hallway toward his bedroom. Russo attempts to resist their pushing of his body. He tries to dig his slick house slippers into the smooth tiled floor but fails. Russo is practically slid down the long hallway, into the master bedroom.

Inside the room now, they throw him on the floor. "Open the fucking safe!" one thug yells.

"Do you assholes even know who I am or who I work for?"

His question is met with a kick to the midsection. A deep gasp, and all of Russo's air rushes out of him.

"Does it look like we care?"

Russo contemplates who his attackers might be. He considers Sean but dismisses the thought. *He doesn't have a crew. Then who?* Another hard slap to the ear. The blow throws his equilibrium out of whack. He becomes nauseated.

Russo, more afraid of the Professor than these two, lets out a small laugh.

"What's so funny?" Thug One asks.

Russo measures his words with a half teaspoon of sarcasm. "I seem to have forgotten the combination."

The metallic sound of the revolver cocking back brings the room to silence.

In a low serious voice, the taller thug says, "Let's see if I can help you remember it." With a bright flash, a loud, ear-piercing sound shatters the room. Sharp pain surges in Russo's foot and up his leg.

Screaming, Russo rolls back onto his ass and yanks his foot toward him. The tip of his silk slipper is blown to shreds. Burnt frayed material is clinging to his heel. The ringing in his ears makes it hard for Russo to check the damage done. After a moment, he regains his focus. Russo's big toe is completely gone. The only thing left is ripped flesh, some exposed toe bone, and a lot of blood. Wailing in agony and shock, he yells something nobody in the room can understand.

"Do you remember now?" the masked intruder asks, maintaining his serious tone.

With a shaky hand, Russo reaches up to the safe. He turns the dial to the left slowly. Then to the right one full turn. Before the final turn, Russo looks back over his shoulder. Through their masks, he can see both of their eyes filled with crazy anticipation. Like two dogs waiting for their master to give them the command to eat. Slowly, he turns the dial to the left for the final time. He pulls down on the sturdy handle. A grinding metallic sound unlatches from deep inside the safe.

"If I open this door, your lives are going to change forever," Russo says. For the first time, Russo sees hesitation in both thugs. They turn and stare at each other for a long moment.

The tall one turns back toward Russo. Pumping his gun at him, he says, "Open the safe!"

Russo pulls the heavy door open. It creaks with a low squealing sound. The assailants' postures loosen, their eyes growing bigger through their black masks. They take in the inventory of the safe.

"Holy shit," one of them says in a whisper.

"How much cash is that?"

"I don't know."

"Is that coke?"

"I'm not sure."

Inside the safe are ten straps of fresh hundred-dollar bills, totaling a hundred thousand dollars. Next to the cash are five bricks of tightly wrapped cocaine. Each brick weighing one kilogram. Each worth twenty-five thousand dollars. There are also some elegant timepieces and other valuables. One being a black-and-white DuPont lighter. A gift from the Professor to Russo for being a consistent earner. This is something the Professor has always given to those who have proven themselves worthy and loyal.

Russo, holding his bloody foot, scootches away from the safe. He watches the two young fools stuffing the money and dope into a black bag. They get the bulk of it, short of the watches and other valuables. In their haste, they lose one brick. The last package falls to the floor and breaks open. White powder flies out in a plume of dust, covering the floor and shorter intruder. He slaps the residue off his black pant legs.

"Shit! What the fuck, man?"

Russo chuckles through his pain.

"Let's go, we have enough," the tall one says.

They both run out of the bedroom and back down the hallway.

Russo yells, "You're dead! Do you hear me, you pieces of shit?" For added effect, he laughs hysterically, embracing his pain.

James and Vinnie can't get out of the house fast enough. Vinnie in the front, he hears James stop behind him as they round the corner of the house. "What the shit, man! Let's get the fuck outta here!" Vinnie says.

"We can't ..." James says but doesn't finish his sentence.

"We can't what? Let's go, man."

"We can't leave him alive."

"What?" Vinnie says, not believing what he's hearing right now. "What the fuck are you talking about! You said we weren't killing anyone! It's bad enough you shot him in the foot."

"We leave him alive, and we're dead."

"Bullshit. He didn't see our faces."

"Don't be a fool," James says, turning back toward the front of the house.

Vinnie can't believe his eyes. "I'm out," he says, getting into the stolen getaway car.

CHAPTER 13

IN THE HOUSE, RUSSO crawls around on the bedroom floor, trying to stop the bleeding from his foot with his robe. Blood continues to run out of his face, making his self-aid difficult.

Through heavy panting, Russo hears footsteps coming down the hallway. He gives up on his foot and drags himself across the floor. Leaning against his bed, he scoops up some of the loose coke. He snorts the powder quickly, preparing for more punishment. Someone enters the bedroom. With blood and sweat in his eyes, Russo struggles making out who's in front of him. He tries to wipe the blood off his face. He squints from the burning in his eyes. It takes a minute before he regains his focus. When he does, it takes another minute to process who is standing before him. He yells at the top of his lungs, "You motherfucker! You're dead, you mutt fuck!"

No words are exchanged as a black pistol is raised to Russo. He continues yelling, "You're not going to get away with this! You're all gonna—" Four rapid gunshots cut off Russo's last words. Blood spatters on the bed, walls, and floor. Russo's body stiffens from the impacts. Two bullets rip through his face and two more through his chest. Slowly, his body goes limp and slides to the floor. Blood pools around his lifeless body onto the Italian tile.

CHAPTER  14

ARLY THE NEXT MORNING, the sun shines in Wes's and Maggie's faces through the windshield of their Honda Accord. Like most days when Wes is going to work with his father-in-law, Maggie drops him off. She sometimes stays to visit with her dad for a bit.

Once inside the shop, Wes notices James and Vinnie haven't shown up yet. "They're late."

"Are you surprised?" Maggie asks.

Wes starts making excuses for his two friends when he is interrupted by Gary shuffling in from his office. "Your screwup brother is AWOL again."

"I see that, Daddy."

"Don't sweat it, Gary. There're only a few pieces of molding left. I can have it done by noon."

"I appreciate that, son," Gary says, handing the truck keys to Wes.

Maggie walks with Wes to the truck. Wes kisses her on the lips. He asks, "Are you sure you don't want to tell him now?"

"No," Maggie says insistently.

"Okay, sweetheart. I'll follow your lead."

The two kiss one more time and Wes drives off.

At about 8:00 a.m., Wes pulls up to the Russo house. When he gets to the front, he sees the door is open. He also notices a boot like scuff mark on its surface. Wes eases his way into the house. "Mr. Russo, it's Wes, with Gary's Cabinets." No answer.

Wes examines the kitchen. None of the stacked materials from yesterday have moved.

"Mr. Russo," Wes calls out, working his way to the living room.

In the middle of the floor, one cigar lies next to a shattered porcelain ashtray. There is also a broken glass with brown liquid still clinging to the curved shards. A leather hammock appears out of place, not in its usual position, pushed neatly against the couch. Wes is about to go outside when he sees drops of blood on the floor. Upon further examination, the drops continue down the hallway. Adrenaline fills Wes's chest.

Warily, he follows the trail of blood. Before reaching the master bedroom, he observes a white powdery substance covering the hallway floor; it appears to have been spilled and tracked out from the room by some heavy boots. Wes's body is now screaming at him to run away, but he ignores the feeling. He's been trained well to subdue his body's flight instinct.

He peers into the room and his eyes widen, his breath catching in his throat.

Lying on the floor, in a puddle of coagulated blood and white powder, is Mr. Russo. His lifeless eyes stare at Wes. The pain of his execution still recorded on his face. Wes observes two bullet holes under Russo's left eye and he's missing a significant portion of his foot.

Panicked at what he has discovered but steadying himself, Wes scans the room and immediately sees an open safe—empty. It takes milliseconds for Wes to remember James and Vinnie back here yesterday talking about something they didn't want him knowing. His body gets hot. His mind scrambles to make sense of the scene. *I gotta call Sean.*

Wes rushes to the kitchen phone and makes a call.

"This is Sean."

"It's Wes." His shaking voice betrays his panic.

"What's wrong?"

"You need to get over to Russo's house—now."

"What happened?"

"He's fucking dead, Sean."

"What do you mean?" Sean asks calmly.

"Russo is fucking dead." There's silence on the phone. "Are you there?" Wes asks in a panic.

"Yes, I'm thinking."

"I'm going to call the police."

Sean says, "Don't do that, Wes!"

"What?"

"Leave everything the way you found it. I'll take care of the rest."

"What are you going to do, Sean?"

"I told you, I'll take care of it."

Something in Sean's voice awakens a sense of protection and trust under his old platoon sergeant's care. He hasn't experienced this emotion since Mogadishu. Many times, under extreme circumstances, Sean got his and Caleb's asses out of some tight situations. And this one is no different.

"Just go home. I'll be in touch."

"Okay," Wes says, and hangs up the phone.

CHAPTER 

M AGGIE TYPICALLY ENJOYS EARLY-MORNING chats with her dad. Occasionally, their conversations get a little heated, depending on the topic. Despite this, they embrace their time together. Their ritual started years ago. Ever since Maggie wandered into her father's shop, finding him loading his own ammunition. He would have her help by measuring gunpowder or cleaning brass. Eventually, she ended up on the range with him. Nowadays, it's coffee and philosophical banter in his modest office at the cabinet shop.

Maggie can see her father is upset. The lines in his old face deepen every time James disappoints him. And this irritates Maggie. It always has.

"Have you thought about telling him to find another job?" Maggie asks.

Gary chuckles. "What would he do if not this?"

"Who knows? At least he wouldn't be stressing you out."

"You're too hard on him, sweetheart. He's not built like you."

Now Maggie chuckles. "You mean he doesn't appreciate what you do for him?"

Gary stares at his daughter, flicking his eyes up in thought. The hint of a smile stretches the lines in his face. With a subtle amount of pride in his voice, Gary says, "James is an excellent carpenter. Hell, if he actually tried, he'd be better than me."

"The only thing he's good at, Daddy, is being selfish."

Their conversation is cut short when they hear someone barge into the shop, the slamming door rattling the entire tin building. Gary gets up to investigate. Maggie follows.

Wes strides quickly toward Gary. A panicked look screams off the young man's face. "What's wrong, son? You forget something?"

"I need to talk to you right now. Alone."

Both Wes's words and his tone worry Maggie. "What's going on, Wes?"

"I need to talk to your dad for a minute."

"I'm going to end up finding out. You might as well say it now," Maggie says.

Wes shoots Gary a pleading look. Gary shrugs in response. "You might as well."

Wes rolls his eyes and shakes his head in frustration. He takes a breath. "Russo is dead."

Neither Gary nor Maggie moves. They stand still, mouths slightly agape, waiting for more details. Finally, Gary asks, "How do you know this?"

"Because I saw him. In his bedroom."

Still not appearing worried, Gary asks, "Okay. Did you call 9-1-1?"

"No!" Wes says. "Somebody killed him!"

This gets a reaction out of Gary and Maggie. "How do you know that, Wesley?" Maggie asks.

"Because I saw him in a pool of blood with his face shot off. It looked like an execution."

Maggie's hand jumps to her face, covering her mouth. Gary's stance tightens. "Then you need to call the police," Gary says.

"I can't." Wes says, desperation in his voice.

Gary's eyes narrow in on Wes. In a low tone, he asks, "Why?"

"Can we please talk by ourselves, Gary?"

Impatient with Wes, Maggie says, "That's not going to happen! Now tell us."

Wes runs his hands through his hair. "I think James had something to do with it."

Gary's head jolts back but only a little. His face drops.

"What!" Maggie asks.

Gary holds his hand up to his daughter in a gesture to calm her. "Let him finish."

Wes continues. "Yesterday I saw James and Vinnie in Russo's bedroom, staring at something in the closet. I didn't know what they were looking at. But I did overhear Vinnie saying he was willing to do something. Today, when I went over, Russo's door was open. His living room trashed. There was blood down the hallway. And that's when I found him."

Maggie paces in circles, almost on the verge of tears. "Oh my Lord, oh my Lord."

Gary remains stoic.

Wes continues. "Plus, there was an open safe in Russo's closet, emptied. And some sort of white powder all over the floor."

"White powder?" Maggie asks, confused.

"I don't know, some kind of drug, I think."

The three stand there for a moment, looking at each other. Processing the information. Gary breaks the silence. "And why didn't you call the police?"

"I called a friend of mine who works with Russo. He told me not to."

"Why?" Gary asks, not happy with Wes's decision.

"If this involves James and Vinnie, the cops are going to be on top of them. Letting Sean report it … buys them a little time."

"Sean, your old platoon sergeant?"

"Yes, Gary."

"He's good people, Daddy," Maggie says.

"And this Sean said he's going to call the police?"

"He said he'll handle it. Which I know he will."

Gary shakes his head. Wes continues. "This will buy us all a little time to figure this out. If we need a lawyer, we'll get one. If they weren't involved, even better."

"Okay," Gary says, not completely satisfied.

"I'll take Maggie home and we'll wait to hear something." Wes says. Gary concedes to the plan with a slow nod.

CHAPTER 16

W ES IS THE FIRST to ease through their front door. He told Maggie to slide into the driver's seat and wait in the car until he cleared the house. *Why is he being so paranoid? He would probably just say he's being hypervigilant.*

Wes quickly maneuvers through each room of his small mobile home. No one inside. Nothing out of place. He waves Maggie in.

Dropping her purse on the countertop, Maggie plops down on the couch. Her body goes limp. She lays her head back and closes her eyes. She can hear Wes rummaging through wooden drawers in the bedroom. Maggie knows what he's doing. And the thought exhausts her. She tries to relax.

"Maggie."

She doesn't respond, faking she's asleep.

"Sweetheart."

Not wanting to prolong the inevitable, she sits up. Wes is standing in front of her holding a black Glock 19 pistol by the barrel with the grip toward Maggie. He also has two magazines stuffed with nine-millimeter ammunition. He wags the grip at her, beckoning her to take it.

"I'm not in the mood, Wes."

"Take it."

She appeases him, grabbing the pistol. She holds it, with no signs of skill. But she ensures that the barrel is pointed at the floor and her finger is off the trigger.

"Let me see it," Wes says.

"Really?"

"Yeah."

She doesn't fight it anymore.

Her grip on the pistol moves to its proper position. Her index finger straddles the slide. The barrel tilts up toward the ceiling. With precision and experience, she performs the movements simultaneously.

Her thumb reaches around to the magazine release, dropping the mag into her hand with ease. She pulls the slide back, locking it to the rear. A round flies into the air, landing in the palm of her hand. Wes hands her a fresh magazine topped off with ammo. She slams the mag into the pistol and releases the slide, sending a bullet into the chamber.

"Happy?"

"Very much so," Wes says, kissing her on the forehead. "I'll be back later."

"Where are you going?"

"I'm going to get Caleb to help me find your brother and Vinnie. And hopefully find out what really happened."

Worried, Maggie asks, "Is that a good idea?"

"I'd rather find him first, before the cops do. Or worse, Russo's people."

"Who are Russo's people?"

Wes ignores the question. "Listen, please. If your brother shows up, don't let him in the house." Maggie rolls her eyes in disbelief. He continues. "I'm telling you, don't let him inside. Have him hang out in the back shed. I'll check in every hour or so. Keep the phone next to you."

Maggie nods, acknowledging the plan. He kisses her one more time and leaves.

CHAPTER 17

THREE HOURS AFTER RECEIVING the call from Wes, Sean is called out to Las Vegas to have a meeting with the Professor. Rather than meeting his boss at his office or at a restaurant, he brings Sean out to a golf course. Specifically, one of the Professor's favorite courses.

The golf course itself is one of Vegas's oldest golfing establishments. Nestled in the middle of an affluent neighborhood, the gated community is located in the middle of low-income housing, separated by a tall gate and minimum-wage security guards. Large custom homes surround the golf course. Most of them built in the '70s. Several "made guys" from the East Coast who came to Las Vegas to stake their claim live in the houses.

The course itself is a traditional-style eighteen-hole championship golf course. Designed in 1961, the course offers golfers a challenging experience. The par-71 course has many large trees, sand bunkers, and a couple of water hazards used to safeguard the lush fairways and immaculate greens.

Driving a golf cart in a light blue dress shirt, dark slacks, and leather shoes feels stifling to Sean in the early-afternoon heat. He stands out like a sore thumb passing other men on the course dressed in their typical golf attire.

Sean spots a teenage boy standing over a white ball. In his hands he holds a putter, taking practice swipes at the ball. Standing next to the boy is an older gentleman in his sixties, dressed in a light gray polo shirt and black pants. With a cigar hanging from his mouth, the older man, with slightly receding salt-and-pepper combed-back hair, observes the boy's performance. The older man's stance is relaxed but confident. He's not overly muscular but has the appearance of one who keeps himself in shape through regular exercise and a proper diet. On his clean-shaven face, a few deep lines are drawn under calm hazel eyes and his forehead. Behind grandfather and grandson, two additional men with athletic builds and short haircuts stand nearby.

The boy putts the ball in front of him. It glides along a curve on the short-cut grass and gently falls into a hole about thirty feet away. The clunking sound of the ball garners subdued celebratory reactions from the men standing behind him. *Impressive.* Not being a golfer himself, Sean appreciates the distance the kid moved the ball into the hole.

As Sean brings the golf cart closer to the group, he can hear the older man talking to the boy. Through a mild, indistinguishable accent, the older man says to the young golfer, "Nice recovery, son."

Sean stops the cart at a distance out of respect for the moment the two are having. He takes a moment himself and ponders, *I wonder how I would have turned out if my dad had taken me golfing.*

The older man looks over at Sean but continues with his grandson, pulling the cigar out of his mouth.

"Hey, Nicky, go ahead and move up to the next hole. I'll catch up with you in a minute." The older man nods at his associates standing nearby.

The muscle men wearing shirts too small for them nod back, getting into their own golf cart, delivering Nicky to the next fairway. The older man puts his cigar back in his mouth and waves Sean over.

Sean pulls up next to the older man. They shake hands. But the older man has a look of disappointment on his face.

"Sean," the man says, sounding a little morose.

"Professor."

"Tell me what you know."

Sean's posture tightens. "I have an idea who may have been involved."

The Professor takes a deep breath as he puts the cigar back in his mouth. He relights it with his beloved DuPont lighter. Sean must have waited too long for the Professor to light his cigar, causing the Professor to bark at him. This is something Sean is not accustomed to.

"And ....!"

"I met these two roughnecks a couple of days ago; they were working at Mr. Russo's place."

"And what were they doing there?" the Professor asks.

"Replacing his cabinets is what he told me."

"So, what about these so-called roughnecks?"

"They asked me for a job. They offered to do whatever I needed."

"And you told them what, Sean?"

"I told them I wasn't interested in hiring them."

"And you think they did this?"

"I think they are a good first look. I know they are both two-bit criminals at best. Like to fight in bars when they're not running low-level hustles. Plus, they're the only two I know who have been in Mr. Russo's house alone, as of lately."

The Professor takes a deep pull from his cigar and nods in contemplation. "Let me guess, trying to make a name for themselves."

"That would be my guess," Sean says.

"Well, they have my attention now."

"Do you want me to deal with them?"

"No. I've already made a call. They should be getting into Vegas late this afternoon. And knowing Lee, he'll be in Pahrump by tonight. What I need you to do is get Freddy's operation up and running again. Go ahead and move into his place. The sheriff should be at the house already. He assures me it will be cleared by the end of today."

"Sir, if I may, let me clip these two kids for you. I can handle it with no problems. And then I'll get things back up and running."

With a lighter tone, the Professor says, "You know, Sean, I appreciate your desire and abilities to take another man's life, especially on behalf of my business. But you're not in the army anymore. You need to go talk to somebody. Doesn't the VA have counselors? Besides, you've said you wanted to step up beyond managing hookers—well, here you go. Make it happen."

Feeling the Professor is being condescending with him, Sean readjusts his attitude and says, "Yes, sir."

"Now, if you don't mind," the Professor says, pushing past Sean, taking his golf cart, and driving off.

Sean curses under his breath, "Cocksucker."

CHAPTER 18

Eight hours after the Professor's meeting with Sean, a tan Crown Victoria with dark-tinted windows moves along I-40 West. Coming from Albuquerque, New Mexico, the vehicle's new destination is Las Vegas, Nevada. Behind the steering wheel sits an exquisite woman in her early forties. Dark mirrored sunglasses sit on her beautifully defined face. Her long auburn hair is pulled back in a ponytail. The woman navigates the desert highway with ease, humming to herself as she does.

Approaching Nevada I-172 toward the Hoover Dam, the woman reaches over to the passenger seat and rubs the leg of her husband, Lee, who is sleeping peacefully.

His eyes open. He turns his head toward his wife and smiles.

Amber, with an almost unnoticeable country twang in her voice, asks him in a sweet tone, "Did you sleep well?"

Lee, a handsome fellow with broad shoulders, salt-and-pepper hair, and a strong jawline, smiles back at her. A little more twang in his voice. "Course I did. With your hummin' and the way this car floats on the road, I slept like a baby."

Lee pulls his seat up from the resting position and looks out the tinted window. Recognizing the area, he says, "I love Hoover Dam. It's a symbol of human ingenuity and the American spirit."

Being playfully bored, his wife acknowledges his appreciation for the dam. "Yes, Lee, I know how much you like this place."

Lee cocks his head toward his wife and playfully corrects her. "Amber, I don't *like* Hoover Dam. I *love* it."

The Crown Vic pulls into a makeshift parking area. The flat, smooth dirt area overlooks the dam. The couple climb out of the vehicle and stretch their legs and backs, appreciating the massive structure below them. Lee, a history buff and a former lawyer, shares a short dissertation on the history of Hoover Dam. "This magnificent structure was built from 1931 to 1936."

They both stroll to the rear of the Crown Vic. "It was a government initiative to get hardworking Americans back to work during the Depression and was the tallest dam in the world."

Amber pops the trunk, and the lid opens. It reveals a bulky mass of rolled-up carpet wrapped in three coils of silver duct tape.

Lifting the bulk of carpet out of the trunk, Lee continues, a little strain escaping his voice. "They named this place after President Herbert Hoover. It has since provided power for Nevada, Arizona, and California."

With the carpet bundle over his shoulder now, Lee points to some of the designs embossed on the massive concrete walls. "Allen True was the artist commissioned to design the art you see on the wall's surface and on the floor of the dam. Many people did not like the Navajo and Pueblo Indian imagery he used, but Mr. True got it done."

"I bet a lot of people died building the dam," Amber says.

"There have been one hundred twelve deaths either directly or indirectly related to Hoover Dam," Lee says. He throws the heap of carpet over the edge down toward the bottom of the dam.

The bundle smashes into the concrete side walls as it falls. The impact causes a pair of human feet to pop out of one side of the bundle. "Make that one hundred thirteen," Lee says with a hearty laugh. Amber finds this amusing too. They both watch the bundle fall farther and farther until breaking the liquid surface below. They hear only a faint sound of breaking water.

The individual in the carpet roll had been a methamphetamine cook. Lee had been sent to shut him and his operation down. The cook, before ending up at the bottom of Hoover Dam, had left his previous employer to start his own meth manufacturing business. The cook's ex-employer didn't appreciate his ambitious spirit, so he hired Lee and Amber to come out to Albuquerque to deal with the rogue cook.

While in New Mexico, Lee received word the Professor required his services and that he should get to Nevada as soon as possible. Lee's initial plans were to bury the cook somewhere in the New Mexico desert, but he decided against it. He instead saved himself the trouble of digging a hole.

And that's what Lee and Amber are. A husband-and-wife hit team who relish doing this type of work. Both are skilled in the art of negotiation, interrogation, and extermination. Lee and Amber are two peas in a pod. They are excellent at what they do. And that's why the Professor wants to hire them.

CHAPTER 19

F OUR HOURS AFTER THE Professor met with Sean, Lee and Amber pull into a high-end townhome complex. They park in front of the main office, where new applicants get processed. Inside, high-end leather couches line each wall. Upscale coffee tables accompany the couches. Several televisions are mounted on the walls, displaying different programs. There is also an unmanned bar with both liquor and espresso machines available to anyone wanting to indulge.

Lee scans the office and notices a beautiful woman in her twenties with long, curly blond hair sitting at a desk behind a transparent glass wall. She is wearing formal business attire. The two lock eyes, prompting the young woman to greet the couple.

"How can I help you folks?" the assistant asks in an exaggeratedly cheerful tone.

"We're here to see your boss, missy," Lee says.

"I have several bosses, sir. Who specifically are you referring to?"

Becoming a bit annoyed at the assistant's good looks and the sound of her voice, Amber speaks up. "The Professor, young lady. That's who we're here to see."

The assistant's eyes widen. Her reply is curt. "Yes, ma'am. I will tell him you're here."

"Thank you," Lee says with a warm smile.

A few moments later, two thick-muscled goons in suits come into the lobby from a side door. They announce, "The Professor will see you now." Lee chuckles to himself, amused by the formalities.

Lee regards the Professor just as he does any other employer. But Lee likes to consider himself as more of an independent contractor than an employee. He prides himself on being a self-made man. Not a bottom-feeder like many of the Professor's personnel, whom Lee regards as surface-level tough guys who lack genuine grit. He appreciates the type of intestinal fortitude that propels a man to blaze his own trail wherever it might take him. The only thing Lee depends on is his beloved Amber. She is the fire in his soul. Plus, she has cut down more men than a 1970s karate movie star. She is the apple of his eye and as beautiful as a fly on a pig's ear.

When doing business, the Professor enjoys the ceremonial aspects of negotiating terms. It allows him to express his gratitude and appreciation for tradition's sakes. As opposed to Lee, who doesn't care so much for the dog and pony show. Amber, though, being a refined lady, thrives in these formalized social settings.

Another aspect of the Professor's operation Lee doesn't appreciate is his personal security team. He despises the oversize meatheads who can barely throw a good punch if they have to.

Yet here they are ushering Lee and Amber around like a couple of celebrities.

The couple are led into an office area and offered a seat in front of a massive wooden desk with an empty, executive leather chair behind it. They sit for a moment holding hands, exchanging bedroom eyes.

Lee sizes up all the men in the room. A few of the Professor's men look like they take their job seriously. Lee first looks at how rough each of the security guards' hands are. He also evaluates their firearms. Lee can tell, based on the wear and tear of their weapon systems, which ones train and which ones treat their firearms like fashion accessories.

One upside to these meetings for Lee is that he and the Professor usually have a smoke and a drink when they discuss business. Both men enjoy fine cigars and top-shelf liquor. The Professor has even gifted Lee with one of his famous DuPont lighters after Lee took care of a cartel problem he had in Arizona a few years back.

The Professor enters the office. The Oklahoma couple stand up. Lee lets the Professor reach his hand out first. *I and the wife are guests. We don't grovel.* The two shake like men with firm grips.

"Lee."

"Professor."

The Professor gives Amber a polite hug. In her true ladylike nature, Amber kisses the Professor on the cheek. Followed by her gorgeous smile that melts the hearts of all men. Everyone takes their seats. Lee sits quietly, waiting for the Professor to speak. *We're not desperate. Tell us what you need, Professor.* It also shows the couple can walk away if mistreated. But Lee knows the Professor pays well, so he keeps the dick measuring to a minimum.

"Lee, you know I never have problems, only challenges."

"Yes, sir."

"My current challenge requires a mature touch. Something more ... generational."

Here we go, Lee thinks. He hates when these contractors talk in fancy riddles. Even when arguing cases in one of Oklahoma's seven district courts, Lee had never thought of himself as sophisticated. He has always held the philosophy that normal people like normal talk. And that's how he used to get his clients cleared from their charges.

"Professor, I'm not sure what you mean. Can you dumb it down a bit?" Lee asks.

The Professor chuckles to himself. "There are a couple of youngsters that have overstepped their abilities and now require the direct mentorship of mature adults. I believe you and your lovely bride are more than qualified to provide that guidance."

Heat grows in Lee's chest, but he doesn't show it. He knows exactly what the Professor is saying. But Lee is not Italian, Irish, Russian, or part of any other groups that talk in sneaky, metaphorical Mafia codes. He's country, straight-up American built, Ford tough. And when you want someone dead, you say it. But Lee plays along in the spirit of customer service. He learned this with his first job, delivering newspapers as a young boy.

"I see," Lee says. "Developing young men has always been a passion for me and Amber. We feel it's our God-given obligation to parent those young bucks who have strayed from their rearing."

The Professor smiles back at the couple. "Great to hear, Lee. Whatever you get back from them, half is yours, plus your normal fees."

Lee nods in acknowledgment.

The Professor continues. "I'd like to wrap this up by the end of the week. So, if you can do that, there's another hundred K for you."

Lee and Amber now look at each other with raised eyebrows. "We'll take that action, fine, sir," Amber says playfully.

The Professor smiles again, handing Lee a black box. Lee removes the lid. Genuine appreciation fills the hitman's heart. He tilts the box toward Amber and says, "Our fine Professor understands a man's appetite."

Inside the box is a rare bottle of bourbon and ten beautiful Padrón cigars seated snugly next to the bottle. Lee tells the Professor, "Thank you, sir." The Professor puts a hand up, trying to appear humble. But Lee doesn't think it is sincere. Instead, he considers it to be more of a "throw the dog a bone" gesture. But this doesn't bother Lee. He knows he's a working dog. And he enjoys being one. *Man, I love my work.*

CHAPTER 20

IT'S BEEN ALMOST TEN hours since Wes contacted Sean about the Russo murder. And still no word. He and Caleb have been by James and Vinnie's single-wide mobile home twice. They also checked in with all their common friends but had no luck. After striking out on their search, Wes decides there might be something at Russo's house that could help.

Caleb pulls his truck up into the driveway. He and Wes find the front door locked up tight.

"Someone's been here. When I left earlier, I didn't shut the door," Wes says.

Caleb nods in acknowledgment.

Wes creeps down the side of the house. With cupped hands over his eyes, looking through the windows, Caleb follows. Head on a swivel, waiting for something bad to jump out.

Getting to the back door, Wes tries the doorknob and finds it locked. He pulls out a pocketknife and jams it between the door latch and the frame. He wiggles the blade up and down, left and right. The door doesn't open.

Caleb pokes Wes on the shoulder. "Holy shit, man, give me the knife." Reluctantly, Wes hands it over. Caleb stuffs the blade back in the door, and with a few subtle twists of his wrist, the door pushes open. Wes stands still, embarrassed by his lack of burglary skills.

Once inside Russo's home, the two friends creep through the living room. Wes's mouth goes agape as they enter the space. The entire room has been put back in its pristine condition. "There was broken glass and liquor all over the floor." Wes points down the hallway. "And blood spread all the way down."

"I don't see shit now," Caleb says.

Wes rushes down the hallway. No blood. No white powder with boot prints. Everything is clean. *Did I imagine the whole thing?* He peers into the master bedroom. Russo's body is gone. Even the bed has been stripped of its blood-covered linens, leaving the mattress bare.

He looks for the safe and finds it closed. Still inside the closet. But Russo's clothes are gone.

"Look, Wes, I believe you. But the way this place has been cleaned up so fast scares me. This looks like some real-world Mafia shit."

"I don't know. Maybe Sean ended up calling the police, and they cleaned everything up."

"Not a chance," Caleb says, cutting off Wes. "They might have swept up the dope and picked up the body. But sterilizing the place within a day? No fucking way. The place would be covered in yellow tape."

Wes nods in agreement. "Let's get out of here. I think we're in over our heads."

Wes and Caleb hurry out of the bedroom, down the hallway, and toward the back door. Before Wes can reach it, a smashing blow falls on the back of his head. He crumbles to the floor, face-first. Confused and afraid, he rolls to his side and looks up.

Caleb is standing behind some man about his own size, with his arm wrapped around his neck. The unknown man thrashes around, trying to buck Caleb off his back. Caleb holds on, squeezing tighter and tighter. It only takes seconds before the man drops to one knee. Then the other. His arms follow, falling to his side.

Caleb lets the man go, who is now resting on both knees. The unconscious man folds over at his waist, catching his fall with his face too.

Wes scrambles up to his feet. Still woozy from the strike to his head.

Caleb is now stretching the man out, pulling one arm out and turning his head to the side. A small grin on his face.

"Did you kill him!" Wes asks.

"Ha. Nah, man. Just put him to sleep for a few." Caleb takes a moment to appreciate his work. "We need to get going. He's going to wake up in another minute or so."

The two sprint out of the house.

CHAPTER 21

T HIRTY MINUTES AFTER ESCAPING the Russo home, Wes and Caleb pull up to find a black Porsche parked in Wes's driveway.

"Ah shit," Wes says.

"I know," Caleb agrees.

"That fucking guy you choked out must have called him."

"I know."

The two young men climb out of Caleb's truck as if nothing happened.

"What's up, Sergeant?" Caleb asks.

Sean looks at Wes. "Oh, I don't know. Somebody who works for my employer found two people in the Russo house about a half hour ago and got choked out"—Sean turns to look at Caleb—"by someone with red hair."

Wes and Caleb try to hold their stares, but their old platoon sergeant glares through them.

Wes says. "I got anxious waiting for you. So I asked Caleb to help me find—" Wes says, before stopping himself.

"Find who?" Sean asks. Wes shakes his head, knowing he has fucked up. Sean continues. "Were you looking for your loudmouth brother-in-law and his dummy sidekick?"

In a low voice, Wes says, "Yeah."

Like a disappointed father, Sean watches Wes.

"How did you know we were looking for them?" Caleb asks.

"Because his shithead brother-in-law asked me for a job."

"Of course he did." Caleb says. "And you said no."

"Without a second thought. Plus, they know those two have been in the house installing cabinets when Russo wasn't home. It's not rocket science."

Hearing this, Wes feels his breathing speed up. "I was in the house too."

Sean puts a hand on Wes's shoulder. "I spoke with the Professor this morning in Vegas. That's why I didn't get back to you right away. He doesn't know about you. And I'd like to keep it that way." Sean looks at both of his former soldiers. "That's why you need to keep your nose down and stay the fuck away from the Russo house."

Wes and Caleb say, "Roger, Sergeant" in unison.

Sean continues to stare at both young men for another moment. Finally, a smile cracks on his face. To Caleb, Sean asks, "So, did that motherfucker give you much of a fight?"

"Not at all. I took his back when he smacked Wes."

Wes says, "When he fell, he hit his face hard."

"Fuck him," Sean says. "I know the guy, and I don't like him much."

Caleb smiles. But Wes's face continues to contort with worry. "So, what's going to happen to James and Vinnie?"

"Depends. If my boss gets his shit back, maybe a good beat-down." Sean's voice becomes sinister. "If not, Maggie might be an only child."

His statement changes the tone of the group.

Sean grabs Wes by the face and pulls his head down, looking at the cut on the back of his head. "You good?" Sean asks.

"I'm good."

Sean's demeanor changes. He leans against his car. "Since you two are back to running and gunning, how about us three doing it together?"

Before Wes can answer, the front door to his house opens. Maggie pops her head outside. She greets Sean with a question. Her tone is pleasant enough, but her voice is tired. "Is that your car, Sean?"

"Yes, ma'am. Do you like it?"

"Well, of course I do. What woman doesn't like a fast luxury car?"

"You're right. Wes could buy you one, but he doesn't want to work for me."

Maggie tries to deflect the comment, attempting humor. "He said you never let him sleep when he did." Sean chuckles insincerely. Maggie continues. "You ready to come in, Wesley?"

Embarrassed, Wesley says, "Yeah." He addresses the group. "Duty calls."

Both Sean and Caleb roll their eyes and smirk. But instead of driving off, Sean focuses on Wes and Maggie until the couple go inside their home and close the door.

CHAPTER 22

IT'S BEEN ALMOST TWENTY-FOUR hours since James and Vinnie ripped off Russo. The two haven't seen each other since. James left the haul with Vinnie when he went back to finish off Russo. Instead of waiting for James in a stolen car to commit murder, while sitting on four bricks of cocaine and a hundred thousand in cash, Vinnie fled.

I didn't sign up to kill anyone, Vinnie thought, dumping the stolen vehicle in a desert area used by locals to abandon all sorts of debris. The dump site is located only a few blocks from his grandmother's house. With a duffel bag full of dope and cash on his back, Vinnie hiked the rest, taking back roads and staying away from the few streetlights scattered through the rural neighborhood.

Now, home almost a full day with no word from James, Vinnie became a ball of emotions. When Wes and Caleb came by and knocked his door he sat, deathly silent. Worried his two friends were there to deliver some sort of bad news. *Had James gotten caught by the police? Did he confess what they did?* To level off his roller coaster of emotions, Vinnie smoked through almost an ounce of marijuana. This therapeutic choice allowed him to feast on beer and cold pizza. And helped him to sleep through his anxiety.

At almost the twenty-four-hour mark since the heist, Vinnie hears a car pull up in the driveway and then drive off. He sits up straight and takes a quick swig of beer. He hears footsteps on the rickety wooden stairs and then the door opens.

James strolls through, relatively calm. He gives Vinnie a quick glance. He then grabs a beer for himself and plops down on the couch across from Vinnie. Not saying a word, Vinnie stares across at James.

They both sit quietly until Vinnie breaks the silence. "Where the fuck have you been?"

"Lying low. Any cops or anyone else come by?"

"No cops. Just Wes and Caleb."

"Did you talk to them?"

"No. They knocked a few times and left."

"Good," James says, relaxing more.

"What the fuck did you do last night after I left?"

"I had to find a ride since you took off like a bitch," James says, irritation in his voice.

Vinnie asks, "Did you kill Russo? It's on Channel 41 that he's dead."

James doesn't respond at first. Instead, he stares at Vinnie with a blank face. Vinnie takes this nonincriminating gesture as confirmation.

Vinnie shakes his head in disbelief and mumbles something incoherent to himself.

"Where's the stash?" James asks.

Vinnie gets up without a response and heads to his bedroom. A few moments later, he comes out with the black duffel bag and throws it onto the coffee table.

James smiles, unzipping it. He empties the bag of its contents. Two bricks and five bundles of cash fall out. He looks up at Vinnie, eyes narrowed. "Where the fuck is the rest of it? There were four bricks and close to a hundred K when we left."

Standing his ground, Vinnie says, "That's your cut."

"What do you mean, my cut?"

"Bro, as soon as you decided to start killing people, I figured we might have to run. So I took my half. Your half is right there."

"Where's your half?" James asks.

"Safe," Vinnie replies coldly.

James continues staring at Vinnie, not saying a word. He finally leans back, nodding. "You're right. You earned it." Grabbing his beer, he holds it up to Vinnie, wanting to toast their success. "To the baddest job we ever did," James says with an ear-to-ear smile.

Almost instantly, a feeling of peace washes over Vinnie. He grabs his own beer and holds it up. "Fuck yeah, brother." The bottles clank in celebration, and the two get drunk.

CHAPTER 23

ACROSS TOWN LEE AND Amber arrive in Pahrump, pulling up to a dark, rough-looking bar. The Oklahoma couple are here based on information they'd requested from the Professor. Lee's approach to hunting is simple. To find a thief, one must go where thieves hang out. And through the Professor's relationship with the local sheriff, this hole-in-the-wall dive bar is their starting point.

Lee and Amber enter the establishment and smile. Amber squeezes Lee's hand with excitement. Lee says to her in a low tone, "Let's try to behave ourselves now."

"I know, sweetheart," Amber says as the two stroll over to the bar. Patrons sitting at random tables eyeball the two.

"You're already turning heads, honey," Lee says. She smiles, throwing a little more hip into her stride. Amber loves this kind of attention. And Lee loves displaying his eye candy.

The bartender, a tough-looking man with a long gray beard and sleeve tattoos, stands up as the couple approaches. "What do you have on draft?" Lee asks.

"Coors and Coors Light," the bartender says in a gravelly monotone voice.

A condescending chuckle escapes Lee. "That makes sense. A shitty beer served at a shitty place," Lee says, intentionally speaking louder than usual. "We'll have two glasses of your exquisite piss water, fine sir."

The bartender's brow furrows. "Do you have a fuckin' problem?"

"I apologize for my husband, sir. We've been on the road all day, and he gets a little grumpy when he's tired," Amber says, smiling brightly. Holding up two fingers, she continues. "We'll take two glasses of whatever beer you have." The bartender gives Amber a look, fills two glass mugs, and roughly sets them in front of the couple. "Thank you," Amber says sweetly.

The large bartender turns to walk away. Lee calls to him, "I was hoping you could help me. I'm looking for another tough guy, much like yourself, but younger."

The bartender turns around and rushes toward Lee. Lee doesn't flinch a muscle but only displays his toothy smile. Now leaning over the bar, the large man is nose-to-nose with the Oklahoma hit man. "Look, fucker, I don't know what your problem is, but I suggest you drink your beer and shut the fuck up."

Another rough-looking man approaches Lee from the rear. Lee's posture doesn't change.

"Do you want me to take care of this, Moby?"

Lee laughs while looking at the bartender straight into his eyes. "Is your name Moby? Like *Moby Dick*? I bet you a hundred dollars you've never even read the book. Hell, I bet you two hundred dollars you can't even read."

Immediately, the man standing behind Lee grabs him by the shoulder and swings him around. Using the momentum, Lee smashes the man square in the jaw with the local piss water. Beer and broken glass fly in the air. The man drops straight to the floor like a bag of concrete.

Moby grabs Lee by the back of the collar and tries pulling him over the bar. But before Moby can get a good tug, Amber grabs him by his long beard. Wrapping the long hairpiece once around her hand, she pulls the giant to the bar, pinning him. Moby howls in pain, letting go of Lee and grabbing his beard. As he struggles to loosen from Amber's grip, his eyes flash with pain and anger. He raises his fist to her.

Lee catches Moby's fist with one hand and stuffs a chrome revolver under his chin with the other. Lee drives the business end of the gun into thick meaty flesh. "Whoa, big boy. You wouldn't hit a lady, now, would you?"

Moby lowers his fist. Amber takes a second coil of the beard around her hand. The once towering man sinks farther down to the bar surface. "Looks like you hooked yourself a big fish, sweetheart," Lee says, laughing. He continues. "You get it, Moby, 'big fish'?"

Lee lowers himself to Moby's pain-infused face. He glances at the prison tattoos covering the man's forearms. "Aren't you dotted up nicely?" Lee asks, using prison slang Moby would understand. Fighting the pain from his beard and the pressure on his back by being held in the bent-over position, Moby doesn't reply. Lee continues, more serious now. "I'm looking for a couple of youngsters. The ones who killed that Russo character a few days back."

Through gritted teeth, Moby says, "I don't talk to cops."

Lee laughs. "Now, what on God's green earth makes you think we're cops? No, Moby, we're not cops. We're concerned citizens who would like to talk to the young men who ripped off my employer."

It takes only a moment before Moby connects Russo, the Professor, and the Oklahoma couple. "You work for the—" Moby starts to say before Lee interrupts him.

"Yes, Moby, I do. But only on a contractual basis. Unfortunately for you, we're on the clock."

Moby shakes his head. "Look, man, I met the kid a few nights back."

"And ...," Lee asks.

"He wanted some advice on how to rip a safe."

"From you? That's rich." He looks at Amber. "Going to someone for advice on how not to get caught by someone who, in fact, has been."

Amber shakes her head in disappointment. "These kids today."

Lee puts his attention back on Moby. "How do I find him?"

Moby struggles through the pain. "All I know is ... he works for his old man who owns a cabinet shop. It's on ... the corner of Mesquite and Leslie Road."

Lee nods in appreciation, standing up straight. Amber loosens her grip on his beard but doesn't let go. "Well, thank you very much, Mr. Moby," Lee says. "Amber, sweetheart, I think we can table this until tomorrow morning during regular business hours."

"I believe so, my love." She continues to loosen her grip on the beard, but stops. She asks Moby a question. "Do you know where we can get some local souvenirs? We usually like to get something from where we've been."

Confused by the question and still in pain, Moby says, "No, lady, I don't."

Her lips pucker, disappointment registering on Amber's face. She says, "Too bad."

Like a snake adjusting its coils around its prey, Amber retightens her grip on Moby's beard. Violently, she yanks a large handful of hair, leaving a bloody patch of flesh on the tip of his chin. Moby screams in pain as he collapses onto the bar.

Through a surprised chuckle, Lee says, "Holy shit, woman, I would have bought you a shot glass at one of the gas stations."

Laughing and swinging the bloody, flesh-infused goatee over her shoulder like a high-end purse, Amber says. "You still can."

CHAPTER 24

T HE NEXT MORNING, MAGGIE leaves her home for her father's shop. Not wanting to wake Wes up or endure another one of his tactical tests, she leaves quietly. Usually, Maggie likes a little music to start her morning. But not today. Thoughts of her brother, James, and all the trouble he has brought to their family kept her up most the night. And to a degree, Maggie feels her father has enabled this deviant behavior in her brother. Now with Wes involved, especially after finding this body and getting smashed in the head last night, Gary needs some tough love. And Maggie is the one to give it.

At her father's shop with two cups of coffee in hand, she finds him in his office, riffling through paperwork strewn across his desk. *My poor father is getting old.* The strong, vibrant man who once sat through hours of dance classes watching his little girl twirl around in costumes is now old, gray, and tired. Much of his fatigue was brought on by the passing of her mother. But much more of it has been caused by all the trouble James has needed saving from. *Hopefully, I can talk some sense into my hardheaded father.*

She sits down across from him. He looks up at her with a tired smile. Taking the cup of coffee, he reaches into his desk and adds a little whiskey to the brew. Maggie wags her head. "You look exhausted, sweetheart," Gary says.

"I couldn't sleep last night."

"Yeah, me too."

"This whole thing with James has me worried."

"Your brother has been a pain in my ass for an awful long time. I don't see him letting up anytime soon."

"That's what I wanted to talk to you about, Daddy."

"You know I love you, sweetheart, but I don't need parenting advice from my child."

"I'm not trying to give you parenting advice. I'm telling you things are changing. And you might not want to waste the rest of your years saving James."

"Stop it!" Gary says.

Maggie flinches. It's been years since her father has lost his patience with her. She sits, trying to calm herself. But the more she tries, the more her anger rises in her chest. She blurts out, "Why me and not him?" Gary flashes his daughter a confused look. She continues. "You have always made me toe the line. But when it comes to James, there's always an excuse."

Gary cocks his head back, looking confused. "What are you talking about?"

With watery eyes, Maggie asks, "Why did you make me kill that dog?"

This causes Gary to lean back in his old office chair, pain in his face. He reflects on the incident.

When she was a child, Gary used to take Maggie shooting. She used to enjoy it. But her attitude toward it changed one late afternoon. While they were heading home after target practice, there was a dog lying in the road. Gary tried driving past, but a young Maggie yelped at him. "Daddy, please stop! We have to help him." Gary pulled his truck over and the two of them got out. Apparently, a car had hit the dog. It was also apparent the poor animal was beyond help and slowly dying.

"Come on, Maggie, let's go."

But Maggie would not leave the dog's side. "We have to do something."

Gary stood silent, with Maggie staring at him with tear-filled eyes. "Go grab your rifle," he said.

Maggie did as she was told and returned with a small, bolt-action .22-caliber rifle designed for children. He handed her a bullet. "Put one in." Maggie did as she was told. Gary took a deep breath. Calmly, he said, "Shoot the dog, Maggie."

Maggie reared back. Fear pushing against the inside of her chest. "What! Why?"

Gary crouched down to her. He asked, "Do you want to help the dog?" Maggie nodded. "Then you have to put it down."

"Why?"

"He's suffering and no doctor can fix him. We can drive away and let him die slow. Or you can do the right thing and stop his suffering. But it's up to you."

Maggie stared at the dog for a long minute. Slowly, she raised the rifle. She took aim and squeezed the trigger.

The dog was silenced by the bullet's impact.

Gary took the rifle from his daughter. Tenderly, he placed his hand on her shoulder. "You did the right thing, Maggie."

Back in Gary's office, Maggie is almost shouting. "You made me!"

In a stoic tone, Gary corrects his daughter. "No, Maggie, you chose. Truth over blindness. Because you're a good person and didn't want that dog to suffer." Gary shakes his head in disappointment. He continues. "Your brother, James ... I can't say the same. But he's my son, and I will always stand by him."

Maggie is now at a loss for words. Gary gets up from his seat and goes into the main shop area. Maggie sits for a moment, gathering her emotions. When they're back under control, she follows her father.

With a tape measure in hand, Gary is scratching a pencil on a piece of wood. She says to him, "I'm pregnant, Daddy."

The scratching pauses. He turns toward her. A light mist covering his eyes. He nods with a smile. "Do you know what you're having?"

"Not yet. But if it's a boy, Wesley wants to name it after you."

"What do you think?"

"I think it's a great idea."

And that's all it took. One teardrop runs down Gary's face. He doesn't let it reach his scruffy beard before wiping it off.

The two hug, and emotions settle. "I gotta go," Maggie says.

"Please be safe. And call me if you hear from your brother."

"I will. You do the same."

Maggie exits the building. Once in the parking lot, she crosses paths with a handsome middle-aged couple standing next to a tan Crown Victoria. The man, with a cigar in his mouth, asks, "Young lady, could you tell me where I can find Gary?"

Maggie points to the front door. "He's inside. Just go right in."

"You have such a beautiful glow to you," the man's wife says, lightly running her fingertips through Maggie's hair.

Maggie stiffens, unsure how to react to the older woman's compliment and unexpected touch. Awkwardly turning away, she says, "Thank you," and drives off.

CHAPTER 25

H AVING CROSSED PATHS WITH Maggie in the parking lot, Lee and Amber stare at the metal building. Lee looks upon the modest structure with a sense of appreciation for the entrepreneurial spirit. "It's small businesses that keep our great nation moving along," Lee says to Amber. "And now I get to see the inside workings of a cabinet shop." At first glance, building cabinets isn't sexy, but Lee appreciates the amount of hard work and artistic talent that goes into it. He also understands a well-designed kitchen with plenty of cabinet space can be a major selling point when buying a home. Plus, Lee has always had an interest in woodworking. Or the tools at least. He struggles to contain his excitement going inside.

As they enter the metal building, the smell of fresh sawdust fills the air. It's a refreshing smell, especially being out in this dry desert heat. The loud sound of a saw cutting through a piece of lumber rings off the metallic walls. They mosey into the main work area of the shop. A round man with a graying afro stands over a fine piece of American machinery. The man raises and drops a rotating saw onto a piece of wood. As the couple gets closer to the hardworking craftsman, the noise becomes almost ear-piercing.

Amber yells over the noise to the man working the saw, "Excuse me, sir. Excuse me." To no effect; the man keeps working. Impatient, Amber taps the man on the shoulder. He doesn't flinch or startle. Rather he turns his head around toward her.

This man must fear nothing, Lee thinks.

Amber pulls out her most deadly weapon, her southern smile. "Hi, sweetheart. Are you Gary?"

The gruff older man submits to Amber's charm. He turns off the saw and wipes his hands on his dirty overalls. He takes in Amber's beauty for a moment before noticing Lee. He replies, "Yes, I'm Gary. Can I help you folks?"

Lee takes notice of Gary's old-fashioned customer service—a thing lost on today's youth. Lee already likes this guy. "Well, yes, sir, you can," Lee says, imitating his tone. "We're looking for a cabinetmaker here by the name of James. Is he around?"

Gary's tone becomes cautious. "James is my son. Is there something I can help you with?"

"You're his father? That's interesting."

"How so?" Gary asks.

"Well, sir, you seem to be an honest American who finds value in a hard day's work. Your son, on the other hand, well ... he's a sneaky mutt who would rather steal than earn."

Gary stiffens up. He extends his arm toward Lee, pointing his finger to his face. "Don't come to my shop telling—"

A large square piece of wood crashes down on Gary's outstretched forearm. Gary screams in pain. He recoils his arm to his stomach. His opposite hand following. Amber recocks the lumber for another strike. In an experienced batting stance, she swings the piece of lumber lower. The board strikes Gary's knee from the side. It snaps inward from the joint. Gary's heavy frame collapses at the point of impact. He falls to the floor.

Lee cringes at the way Gary's leg is lying next to him like a broken toy. Amber celebrates with the chunk of wood raised over her head. She chants, "Oklahoma Sooners, class of '74, whoo!" The softball team had been the first to be added to the University of Oklahoma's sports program. A proud point in Amber's life before meeting Lee.

Looking down at the damage, Lee playfully chastises Amber. "Sweetheart, why did you hit Gary so hard? You damn near knocked his leg off."

Amber rebuffs the criticism. "I thought I was back on the field, honey."

Their tiff is interrupted. "You fucking bitch!" Gary says through agonizing pain.

The vulgarity expressed toward Amber sends a surge of anger through Lee. This happens periodically when the couple is on a job. And though it's understandable, Lee finds it difficult to let any insult toward his wife pass. Even if his wife just tore a kneecap from Gary's leg.

Lee snatches Gary by his jawline and pulls him up onto his good leg. He spots a large metal vise mounted on the workbench. With Amber's assistance, they put Gary's hand from his broken forearm into the vise and pinch it closed. The jaws tighten. The vise is snug enough to hold Gary's hand for a second, but it needs to be tighter, so he doesn't pull it out. Nodding at Amber to help, Lee asks, "Do you mind, sweetheart?" He looks away from Gary's hand.

Amber strolls over to the vise like a game show model. Her beautiful smile shining. She grabs the long metal handle and jumps up. When she lands back on the floor, she puts all her weight into turning the vise's handle. Her enthusiasm emulates a contestant on *The Price Is Right*, spinning the giant wheel with the numbers.

The jaws grab tighter on to Gary's hand like a bear trap. He screams as the sound of crushing bone is heard, drawing Lee's eyes to the vise.

Amber must have destroyed every bone and muscle in Gary's hand, leaving the outside edge of his palm blown like a popped tire, exposing a mixture of muscle, tendon, and blood. Lee chuckles at Gary's five fingers left in the vise swelling up like balloons. It reminds Lee of the old *Tom and Jerry* cartoons when Tom would swing a hammer at Jerry and miss, only to hit his own paw, making it swell the same way.

"Gosh darn, woman, his hand is thinner than my mama's chicken-fried steak," Lee says, laughing.

She looks back at Lee with her quirky little smile.

With Gary's knee readjusted, and his hand stuck in the vise, the Oklahoma couple takes a breather. Lee watches Gary attempt to support himself on his one good leg while being hunched over the workbench. Compassion fills Lee's heart for this blue-collared American.

Placing a stool under Gary's rear end, Lee relieves the pressure Gary's feeling in his old, worn-out frame. He gives Lee a look of gratitude underneath the groaning and sweat building up on his face.

I really like this guy, Lee thinks. He leans in toward Gary to emphasize his point. "Do you want your son to suffer the same fate as you? Or should I lay him down quickly? The choice is yours."

Gary struggles to speak through the pain. "I ..."

"You what, Gary?"

"I have a bottle of whiskey on the desk in my office. Can I get a sip?"

"Only if I can have a drink with you, Gary," Lee says, smiling. A painful smirk surfaces on Gary's face. Signaling to Amber to go fetch the whiskey, Lee takes in the entire shop.

With all the tools, wood, and sawdust on the floor, Lee is looking at a man's man. Even in this moment of Gary's depravity, Lee admires the old cabinetmaker.

Amber returns with the bottle and a couple of pieces of mail in her hand. Lee uncorks the whiskey and hands it to Gary. With his good hand, he throws back a full swing. He offers it back to Lee like the fine host he is. Lee takes a swig himself. It's not the best whiskey in the world, but Lee savors this moment with Gary.

Taking a breath, Gary says. "You know, I always knew my boy would be the death of me." He chuckles to himself now. "Ever since his mother died, he's gone down a dark path." He pauses before he asks Lee, "You got kids?"

"No, Gary, I don't—well, not that I know of."

Amber flashes Lee a snide look up from the mail she's been digging through. He winks back.

Gary chuckles, causing him to choke and cough. Lee hands him the bottle for another pull. Gary takes two deep gulps and says, "Look, I know my son is a piece of shit. I know he isn't even worth protecting at this point. But you know what? He always worked hard for me and respected me."

Lee is moved by the honest dissertation Gary is presenting to him.

Gary continues. "I love him … he's my son. And that's why it gives me great pleasure to say to you: go fuck yourself."

Holy shit, this is a true man. Even to his last breath, Gary's love for his son can't be broken. There's no greater thing than a man willing to die for what he believes in. "You know what, Gary? I have taken the lives of many men with much pleasure in doin' so. But you, my friend, are a rare breed. Killing a man of your caliber is something I won't enjoy."

Lee casually pulls his revolver from his shoulder holster and holds it to Gary's head. "But I will do it if you don't tell us where your son is ... right now." Lee leans in close. "I won't ask again."

"I got 'em," Amber says, interrupting the moment, holding up a piece of mail containing information they need.

A pain wells up in the pit of Lee's gut. Solemnly, he turns his attention back to Gary. He stands up straight out of respect for the older man. "Sir, it's been an honor."

Amber gently kisses Gary's forehead and steps back to get one more good look at the broken old man.

Gary glances down at the whiskey bottle and asks, "One more for the road?"

Lee nods and hands the whiskey bottle to him. Gary grabs the bottle and lifts it to his mouth. No fear escaping his tired face. While the bottle is up to his lips, Lee sends a round through the bottle and under Gary's right eye socket. Gary's head snaps back. The bottle shatters. Broken glass and whiskey splash to the floor. His body goes limp, sliding out of the chair like over-stretched clay.

Lee and Amber watch the remaining life of Gary trickle to the floor. The last bit of air in Gary's lungs expels audibly one last time.

Amber hands Lee a white envelope she found on Gary's desk. He reads a name and address on it. Complimenting Amber, Lee says, "Sometimes, I think you have the brains and I have the beauty." She smirks back at him, putting her arm around Lee's waist and kissing him.

CHAPTER 26

T HE NIGHT BEFORE WAS one for the books. After James and Vinnie figured out their shit with the Russo rip, they decided a little debauchery had been in order. Calling over a couple of young ladies with the promise of top-grade cocaine, beer, and Humboldt bud, the two-man crew celebrated the successful completion of their first heist.

Waking up the next morning, Vinnie notices the girl he hooked up with is no longer in his bed. *Oh well, what are you going to do?*

Pulling himself out of bed, Vinnie shuffles down the hallway and peers into James's room. He and his girl are gone too. The living room is littered with food wrappers and beer cans.

Finding a little weed left over from the night before, Vinnie packs the green substance into a short glass pipe and lights the top of the bowl. He deeply draws the smoke into his lungs and holds it in his body until the sensation of a cough forms in his chest. He quickly exhales. A thick cough through his nose and mouth follows.

Vinnie does this routine a couple more times. After, he curls up into the fetal position on the old leather couch. He wraps himself in one of those Mexican blankets found at a truck stop. He flips on the TV and lowers the volume. Adjusting an old pillow under his head, he watches a rerun episode of *The A-Team*. He loved this show as a kid. Within minutes, Vinnie's eyes get heavy. Somewhere between being awake and asleep, Vinnie can hear B. A. Baracus, saying, "I ain't getting on no plane, Hannibal," before the words change into melted noise. *If this is what a coma feels like, then sign me up.*

A few minutes into his THC-induced nap, Vinnie feels a light flick on his ear. Subconsciously, he swats at a fly that isn't there and resettles his head back on the pillow. He breathes deep, enjoying the comfortable squeeze of the well-worn leather couch and blanket. Another moment passes before his sleep is disrupted again. This time it's not from an imaginary fly. Instead, he feels two hard pokes on his forehead. Vinnie's eyes open. When they do, they struggle to focus on the dark, cylinder-shaped tip of a shotgun being held to his face.

Still half-asleep, Vinnie can only see the metallic surface inside the barrel. Hearing the universal sound of a shotgun racking a round into the chamber finally jolts Vinnie awake. He scans the immediate area. He finds a redheaded woman standing over him with a rifle shouldered. Still on the up-swing of his marijuana high, Vinnie tries to make sense of who this woman is, why she is in his home, and the reason there's a shotgun in his face.

A male voice draws Vinnie's attention. But he doesn't recognize him.

"Hello, Vincent. Where's your pal James?"

Still confused, Vinnie attempts to sit up, but the woman punches him in the face with the butt of her shotgun. Then everything goes black.

CHAPTER 27

MINUTES AFTER BEING KNOCKED out, Vinnie regains consciousness. A familiar female voice calls out to him. "Vincent, wake up." Stretched out on the backseat of somebody's vehicle, Vinnie lies still, petrified.

The vehicle pulls onto a gravel road and comes to a sliding halt. Car doors open and powerful hands hook Vinnie under his armpits and hoist him up. Quickly, he is yanked out of the vehicle, headfirst.

With his body airborne, Vinnie squeals. Having his hands fastened in front of him, he is unable to break his fall. His body slams flat on the ground. The impact knocks the air out of his lungs. Sharp rocks jab deep into the muscles in his back, increasing his pain. Pulling his bound hands to his face, Vinnie discovers they're fastened together with thick zip ties.

"Stand up now, son," the man from his mobile home commands. Vinnie lies there for a moment, trying to catch his breath. The redheaded woman kicks him on the back of his legs. The man says, "Get up now, Vincent." Vinnie struggles to his feet.

When upright, Vinnie looks around, trying to figure out where he is. He can see Pahrump out in the distance. Shuffling in a small circle, he finds a well built man in his fifties with salt and pepper hair standing in front of him with a welcoming smile. Next to him is an attractive woman in her forties wearing a devious grin. Vinnie remembers her and the shotgun she put in his face.

"Nice to finally meet you, Vincent." The man says, hospitality in his voice. "My name is Lee. And this beautiful woman next to me is my bride, Amber."

With a shaky voice Vinnie asks, "What the fuck is going on? Why did you bring me out here?"

Lee takes control of the conversation. "Do you hear this little rebellious turd demanding answers to his questions, sweetheart? Somebody with a little less experience might think he actually has balls."

Amber strolls over to Vinnie. She looks him up and down, not saying a word. She snatches him by the crotch. Vincent rolls up on his toes, trying to relieve the pressure of her grip. Keeping him under control, Amber takes in a deep smell of Vincent's aroma around his neck area. Looking over her shoulder, she says to Lee, "He doesn't have balls, honey. He's afraid. He's terrified." Amber lets his crotch go. Vinnie falls back onto his heels.

The three stare at each other. Not saying a word. The silence cracks Vinnie quickly.

He staggers toward the couple. Vinnie says. "Sir, I don't know why you brought me out here, but whatever reason it is, I know I can explain."

Lee laughs out loud. "Okay, Vincent, if you're willing to explain, can you tell me what happened at Russo's place?" Having presented his question to Vinnie, Lee now is looking for signs of deceit. Before answering, Vinnie reveals his intent to be dishonest by subconsciously wiping his mouth with his flex-cuffed hands. The Oklahoma couple have learned from years of questioning folks that touching one's face is a form of self-soothing when not being forthright. A lot of Lee's clients used to do the same thing. Even when they knew they had attorney-client privilege.

Vinnie answers Lee's question the way he expected. "Russo?" Vinnie asks.

Lee has seen this tactic over and over through the years from folks trying to buy more time. Lee picks up on the delay and waits for Vinnie to deliver the lie. Which he does on cue. "I don't know a Russo."

With a cupped right hand, Lee immediately slaps Vinnie in his ear. The strike inflicts a large amount of crushing and disorientating pain. A technique learned from his own father, who used to smack Lee and his mother around when he'd get a little too drunk.

The pain causes Vinnie to fall to the ground, clutching his ear. Eventually, he gets himself up on his hands and feet like a football lineman. With a burst of energy and a desperate shout, he rushes Lee. Again, Lee is several steps ahead of him. He laughs at Vinnie, catching his feeble tackle by wrapping both of his arms around Vinnie's head and neck. Lee counts out loud as he looks at Amber, letting her know to be ready. This isn't the couple's first rodeo. "One, two, three." On the third count, Lee rolls Vincent over onto his back with ease. "I've tossed bigger hogs than you, son." Amber reemphasizes her husband's point by stomping Vinnie on the face with the heel of her boot. He curls into a ball, reacting to the pain.

"Sit up, Vincent. Quit being so soft. I thought you were a local tough guy," Lee says. With watery eyes, the young man rolls back over onto his ass and leans against the Crown Vic's tire.

Lee considers several interrogation choices. With option one, he can ask Vinnie the same question again in a kind, southern tone. Option two would be the same as option one, but include cutting one of Vinnie's ears off. And of course there's option three: Lee can kill him.

Squatting down to Vinnie's level, the Oklahoma gentleman waits for Vinnie to speak again before making his ultimate choice. The two are now eye-to-eye. After a long pause Vincent speaks again, but this time much more carefully. "You wanna know about James, right?" Lee nods. "And about Russo's house?"

"Yes, Vincent, I do." *Now here comes fifty percent of the truth.*

"James told me he wanted me to help him rob Russo, and I said no. So he ended up doing it himself. I promise, sir, I don't know where he is right now. But I can find him."

Lee thinks, *It's like I'm bilingual and can interpret the bullshit coming out of his mouth.* He reasons that James probably did ask for Vinnie's participation. But Vinnie telling his buddy no, this is false. From the moment Vinnie first spoke, Lee could tell he's a people pleaser.

Lee also concludes Vinnie is too stupid to tell a lie that's more than one-dimensional. Thus, his last statement about not knowing where James is right now, this is true and false. True, he doesn't know where James is at the moment. But false that he will help Lee.

Lee pats Vincent on the shoulder. "Don't you feel better now?" The confused look does not leave Vinnie's face. Lee continues, pulling out a pocketknife. Snapping it open for theatrical effect, he points it at Vinnie's eye. "So, here's what we're going to do. I'm going to take something from you and let you go." Lee waves the blade toward Vinnie's eyeball. A deep moan rises from Vinnie's belly and through his throat. "And when James is found, I'll give it back to you," Lee says.

With full-blown crocodile tears, Vinnie pleads with Lee, attempting to grab his wrist without trying to overpower Lee. Rather, he appeals to Lee's good nature. "Please, sir, don't take my eye out."

"Take your eye out!" Lee says, pulling the knife back. "What kind of animal do you think I am, Vincent?"

Vinnie relaxes a little. "Thank you, sir, thank you so much."

"Of course," Lee says. And with one fell swoop of his blade, he cuts off the ear he slapped earlier. Blood gushes onto Vinnie's shirt.

Screams of pain and shock shoot out of Vinnie. "What the fuck, man!"

Lee laughs at Vinnie's lack of insight. "That ear was damaged, Vincent. But like I said, when we find James, you'll get it back." Lee raises three fingers. "Scout's honor."

Lee puts the mangled ear in his own front shirt pocket. Again, for dramatic effect.

Amber helps Vinnie to his feet. "We're about five miles outside of town," Lee says. "That means you'll be able to walk back in about two hours. After that, you'll find James and we'll find you. Do you hear what I'm saying?"

Amber flashes Lee a glare and chastises him. "'Hear what I'm saying.' That's awfully cruel, honey."

Lee corrects himself. "My apologies, Vincent. That was terribly insensitive. Do you *understand* what I'm saying?"

Vinnie nods, staggering backward apprehensively, toward town. When he gets a good distance away, he runs for his life down the dirt road.

CHAPTER 28

LYING IN BED COMFORTABLY, Wes is holding Maggie from behind as they both sleep peacefully. His hand protectively covering her belly. *Bang, bang, bang!* The loud knocking sound on their front door startles the young couple awake. Wes jerks up in the bed, frantic. Maggie lets out her own light gasp. Not knowing what's going on, Wes hurries to the door.

The banging continues. Wes can hear someone who sounds like James yelling his name. "Wes, open the fuckin' door!"

Still hazy, Wes opens the door. James is standing there with anger on his face, holding Vinnie up by his shoulders. Both friends are covered in blood. "What the hell are you two doing here?" Wes asks, upset and shocked by the way they came to his home.

Maggie races into the living room behind Wes. She stops dead in her tracks at the scene. "Oh my God, James," she asks, "what did you do!"

He snaps back at her, "What do you mean? I didn't do shit."

Wes examines Vinnie closer. He sees the mangled meat where Vinnie's ear used to be. "What happened to your ear, Vinnie?"

Vinnie responds with only a moan.

Vinnie's skin is pale, and it appears he's in shock. Wes helps James lift Vinnie's limp body into the house and onto the couch. Wes tells Maggie, "Go get some towels!"

Maggie doesn't move. She stands frozen in disbelief. Her eyes water. "Get some towels!" James says to his sister. This snaps Maggie out of her trance. She rushes down the hallway. Within seconds, she's back with a handful of towels.

Of course they're pink, Wes thinks. He takes the towels from Maggie, folds them up tight, and presses them hard against Vinnie's wound.

James tells Wes what happened. "They cut his fucking ear off."

Before Wes can respond, Maggie starts in on James again. "Cut his ear off. Who?"

James loses his temper with his sister. "Can you please shut the fuck up, Maggie?"

Even in the middle of this commotion, James's comment strikes a nerve in Wes. "Watch your fucking mouth, James."

James corrects himself with a shake of his head. Wes understands sibling rivalry, but *anyone* telling his wife to shut her fucking mouth is a no-go. Not wanting to expose Maggie to any more drama, Wes says, "Sweetheart, please go to the back room." She ignores him. Realizing Maggie won't cooperate, Wes turns his attention back to James. "Who did this, bro?"

James says, "Russo's people."

Hearing this confirms Wes's fear. James and Vinnie are somehow involved with the Russo heist. And probably the murder.

Wes can feel his face twist with worry. His voice shaky. "James, please tell me you didn't ..."

"No, motherfucker, we didn't kill Russo!"

Hearing the words *James* and *murder* in the same sentence triggers Maggie again. She starts pacing in a circle. Tears welling. "You killed somebody, James?"

"No! We didn't kill anyone!"

Maggie starts in on Wes. "I told you these two are no good."

Wes's patience grows thin with Maggie. But with control, he measures his next words. "Maggie, I need you to go back into the bedroom right now." Again, she doesn't move. And that's all it takes. "Now!" His bark cuts through her rebellious streak. Maggie concedes to his request.

Wes says to James, "We need to get him to the hospital, or he might bleed out." James nods in acknowledgment. Wes yells to Maggie, "I'm taking him to the hospital." She responds with a slammed bedroom door. Wes gives Vinnie a little smack on the cheek, trying to get his attention. "Hey, buddy, we're going to the hospital."

Vinnie comes to a little. He points at the Italian décor still hung up on the wall from Maggie's dinner a few nights before. He says, "I didn't know you were Italian." His two friends stare blankly at the question.

CHAPTER 29

The undercarriage of Wes's Honda Accord bounces off the asphalt as they race to the emergency room. Wes and James pull Vinnie rapidly out by the arms. The three young men burst through the front doors. Sitting behind the desk, a frumpy-looking nurse who appears to be in her late fifties casually looks up at the trio. Her eyes widen as she notices Vinnie, pale and covered in a mixture of blood and dirt. Before anything is said, Wes snaps his head towards someone walking across the waiting room. Wes turns to James, "Can you handle this for a moment?" James doesn't have a chance to answer before Wes marches off.

James watches Wes approach a man in a white lab coat. The individual looks middle-aged and somewhat overweight. His face is unshaven and he has dark circles under his eyes. The two shake hands and speak for a moment. The man in the lab coat shakes his head. Wes puts his arm around his shoulder and whispers to him. As he does, the man nods in agreement.

As James looks at Vinnie's goose-egg lump, his broken nose, and severed ear, paranoia engulfs James's expression.

He notices a security guard standing nearby who is giving him a stern look. James whispers in Vinnie's good ear, "If the cops show up, don't say shit. They don't have anything on us. No prints, faces, witnesses, nothing." Vinnie nods, understanding.

"What's your friend's name?" the nurse asks James.

"Vinnie ... his name is Vinnie." The nurse gives James a side look and hands him a clipboard with several sheets of paper attached to it. James takes the clipboard and helps Vinnie to a nearby chair. Once Vinnie is seated, Wes takes a seat next to James.

In a low tone, Wes tells James. "We're good."

"What do you mean we're good?"

"I asked that guy to help Vinnie—quietly."

"And he said yes?" James asks, surprised.

Wes chuckles. "Not at first."

"What do you mean?"

A sly smile flashes on Wes's face. "He's a degenerate gambler and has a thirty-day suspension at the casino for acting like an asshole at one of the poker tables. I told him I could get his suspension lifted."

"And it worked?"

"Not exactly. I also reminded him how his wife would feel if she found out he pays one of the cocktail waitresses to blow him in his Mercedes after a late night of losing."

"Look at you, Wes, doing gangster shit." James now impressed by Wes's savagery.

"No! It's more like trying to keep you two out of trouble."

A few minutes pass and the gambling doctor introduces himself to the trio. "I'm Nicholas Rosewell. I'm a physician's assistant here at the hospital. Since our friend here"—he points at

Vinnie, who is still out of it—"doesn't appear to require surgery, I'll patch him up myself."

"And you ain't calling the cops?" James asks, paranoia in his voice.

PA Rosewell's eyes open wide, and a panicked look on his face. He looks at Wes, who looks at James with an irritated look. "Are you stupid? Just do us all a favor and quit talking." Wes says.

James meekly acknowledges Wes's comment. The PA's face smooths out. He tells James, "I understand your friend requires some privacy as he recovers from the"—he makes finger quotes in the air—"'dog bite.'" James smirks. The PA continues. "With that said, I'm not mandated to report dog bites to the police when the victim is an adult. That's up to the victim to do if they so choose." The PA's eyes widen uncomfortably as he looks straight at James. "Do you understand what I'm saying, sir?"

"Yeah, I get it," James says with a slight nod.

The PA ushers Vinnie into a back room. Wes and James stay in the front.

An hour later, the PA comes back and tells the two friends that Vinnie is ready for visitors.

In the private room, Vinnie is still groggy but semiconscious now. The area where his ear used to be is wrapped in white gauze, tied off around his entire head. The cut on his forehead is stitched up, still swollen and bruised. Wes and James stand on each side of his bed. James tries to lighten the mood by busting Vinnie's balls. "Bro, who would have thought losing an ear would have made you better-looking?"

"Are you kidding me right now?" Wes asks. Vinnie glares at James too. "Tell me about this Russo thing, Vinnie."

Vinnie tries speaking with a raspy voice, but James interrupts him. "Wes, it's best if you don't get involved."

Wes replies. "You've been talking out your ass all night, James. You busted through my door with Vinnie beat to shit, asking for help, and you don't want me *involved*?"

James's head drops. Wes continues. "You know I'm right. Not only did you bring this trouble to my home, but one of Russo's men found me and Caleb in his house."

"What the fuck were you doing there?" James asks.

"Trying to find you two."

"Nobody asked you to."

"And yet here we are."

James looks away. Wes continues. "I'm trying to help you. Not jam you up. But for me to do that, I need to know what happened." Wes asks Vinnie, "Bro, what exactly did you two do at Russo's house?" Wes leans in to Vinnie's good ear and whispers, "Did you kill him?"

Now James snaps at Wes, "No, motherfucker, we didn't! And you need to quit asking before someone hears you and actually thinks we did."

Wes doesn't back down. He has never backed down to James. "Then tell me what the hell happened."

Vinnie throws James a *Should we?* look. James gives him a conceding nod. Vinnie explains, struggling for every word. Growing impatient, James stops Vinnie by raising his hand. James says to Wes, "Look, man, we did rip off Russo. The fat fuck had it coming, always yelling at us. And yeah, we smacked him around a little to get him to open up his safe ... " James and Vinnie share a look. James continues. "But he was alive when we left."

Through a groggy voice, Vinnie says, "Yeah, Wes, he was."

Wes takes a moment to look at his two childhood friends. James knows he's trying to recognize any bullshit they might be shoveling his direction. "What was in the safe?"

James and Vinnie exchange another look. Finally, James speaks cautiously. "Dope and cash."

Wes's body freezes. His face tightens. He tries to bring his voice under control. "How much was there?"

A pained smile surfaces on Vinnie's face. "A lot."

Wes isn't impressed. Instead, he shakes his head and asks, "Where is it now?"

James laughs in his face. "Why would we tell you?"

"You're right, I don't want to know. But you realize, this isn't some bar beef. Russo worked directly for the Professor, which means you not only ripped off Russo, but you also stole from the Professor. You both are fucked."

James stands for a moment and eventually sits down slowly in a nearby chair. He stares off into space.

"James, what are you looking at?" Wesley asks.

James blinks rapidly a few times before coming back to reality. A smirk on his face. "I was feeling hungry." He asks Vinnie, "You want some tacos, bro?" Vinnie nods with exhaustion. James tells Wes, "Let me take your car and I'll go pick up some food."

"Sounds like a good idea. Especially since you got Maggie pissed off at me."

"I know, man. I'm sorry about that."

"I hope you are. I was supposed to have sex with her later." The mood in the room lightens.

"Don't want to hear it, Wes."

"Not sure if you care, but your sister likes me when I take her from behind." A weak burst of laughter leaves Vinnie.

Hurrying out the door, James says, "You're fucking sick, Wes." Vinnie and Wes laugh.

In the hospital parking lot, Wes gives James his car keys. "We'll figure all this out, James."

"Yeah, I will."

On his way back into the hospital, Wes stops for a moment to let a tan Crown Victoria sedan pass in the parking lot.

CHAPTER 30

Having enough of Wes's sanctimonious, self-righteous bullshit, James forgoes the tacos and develops an exit strategy. Trying to find the motivation and courage to run, he contemplates his childhood with both Wes and his sister. Indignation fuels James's escape plan. *Who do those two think they are? We all grew up in the same shithole town. And now they walk through life as if they don't know what it's like to be poor.* As James's internal rant continues, he finds a plan of escape formulating.

He decides he needs to leave town for at least a couple of days. Maybe two weeks at the most. James settles on heading to Baker, California, to lie low for a while. Until Vinnie gets better. When Vinnie recovers, James will come back and get him. *But what about the dope and cash we have now? With Vinnie in the hospital, I wouldn't be a good friend if I didn't secure Vinnie's half of the rip. This would be irresponsible. And God forbid those two crazy country fucks get Vinnie's half. All of this trouble will have been for nothing.*

Once inside his house, James stuffs a snub-nosed .38 in his pants and grabs a small backpack off the floor. He rummages through the bedroom closet, exposing the dingy carpet. James pulls at the corner of the carpet, revealing a makeshift safe underneath. He unlocks the safe revealing a three-foot-deep metal box attached to the bottom of the floor.

One benefit of living in a trailer is that it's lifted off the ground. This allows all sorts of things to be hidden and secured. A tweaker buddy of James's came up with the design and built it out. James usually uses the hidden space for some other type of contraband. But tonight, the hidden floor safe is filled with fifty thousand dollars in cash and more cocaine than James has ever seen.

James stuffs his portion of the load into his backpack. He goes into Vinnie's room. He digs through dresser drawers. No dope, no cash. "Okay, Vinnie, you're playing it smart." He looks under Vinnie's bed, pulling out old shoes and dirty bath towels. Again, nothing. "What the fuck, Vinnie?"

He glances at a clock in the room. It's been almost thirty minutes since he left the hospital. Picking up the pace, James goes through Vinnie's closet. He starts hurling clothes out, frantically looking for Vinnie's portion. Again, James comes up short. Enraged, he starts grabbing boxes on the shelf and dumping their contents. Nothing but old pictures, some glass pipes, and a few porno mags fall out. "You stupid motherfucker! I bet you gave your cut to some cock tease at the bar. Fuck!"

Knowing times is short, James gives up on the search. Hurrying into Wes's car, he considers which route to take to the small, desolate town. He can either drive through Vegas on the I-15 or take 372 toward Shoshone. There is also a back road to Tecopa that leads to Baker. He decides the back road to Tecopa in the middle of the night is safest and less populated.

CHAPTER 31

E ARLY THE NEXT MORNING, James is halfway through the back road leading from Pahrump to Tecopa, California. It is still dark and hazy outside before he notices the fuel tank is only a quarter full. *What the fuck, Wes?* James kicks himself in the ass for not having a better exit plan. He should have been on the road earlier, but he stopped by some female's house for a last-minute hookup. *Didn't want to leave town without getting my dick wet one more time. Finding some chick in Baker, California, to have random sex with is going to be a tough task.*

But instead of doing his thing and leaving, James ended up falling asleep for a couple of hours before waking up in a panic and rushing out of town. And like everything else in James's life, his self-punishment is short-lived as he focuses his attention on his next steps.

The morning sun etches its way up from the east when James's getaway car finally dies and rolls to a stop. *You're a dummy.* Talking to himself, he hears his father's voice telling him to *quit being a pussy and keep moving.* Motivated by this mantra, he grabs the backpack and gun off the front seat and trudges up the deserted highway road.

Within minutes, the early-morning sun is completely in the sky and the temperature reaches the nineties. He looks ahead. His eyes fixed on the endless road. It splits the desert landscape like a black slithering snake with two yellow stripes running along its back.

Not five minutes into his trek, James feels sweat and dust clinging together on his shaggy face. Thick white paste forms in his mouth as if smoking a bowl of high-end weed.

Damn, what time is it right now? Seven-thirty? Fatigue and desperation start to set in. He knows this highway is not traveled much. But he tries to reassure himself any decent, red-blooded American who lives in the area will pass by soon and offer to give him a lift.

Four miles into his morning marathon, a tan Crown Victoria with dark limo-tinted windows makes its way down the road toward him. *Finally.* He's suddenly conscious of his youthful, hobolike appearance. Straightening himself up and raising his thumb in the universal sign for hitchhiking, James prepares. He tries not to raise his hand too fast, an attempt to avoid showing desperation, but with enough pep to convey he has a valid need. He paints on a smile to match his hand gesture, hoping to avoid looking deranged or threatening. Rather, his aim is to communicate the look of a youth in trouble.

The vehicle approaches from the same side of the road he's walking on, veering as it slows down its approach. James stands there like a fast-food statue waving to potential customers. The vehicle comes to a crawl as James attempts to look through the dark window tint, not seeing even the shape of a human. He keeps his boyish smile steady, waiting for the Crown Vic to stop.

But it doesn't. Instead, it picks up its pace and continues past him.

"Fuck me," James says, losing the shit-eating grin. But he sees the bright glow of brake lights from the vehicle. A surge of relief rushes through him. Casually, he strides up to the vehicle, his grin back on display. The Crown Vic is now moving in reverse, meeting James halfway. *Keep it cool.*

The vehicle comes to a stop next to him. There is a long, awkward moment when James stares at his reflection in the window tint. Finally, the window lowers, unveiling an attractive woman in her forties. Her smiling face is smooth except for a few subtle lines around her red-painted lips. Her bright blue eyes are accentuated with big, natural eyelashes. Two full breasts excessively fill a low-cut black tank top, immediately drawing James's eyes down to them. Unintentionally, he lets his gaze linger longer than it should, attempting to determine whether they're fake or not. It doesn't take him long to decide they are in fact natural.

James quickly adjusts his gaze back to the beautiful face in front of him. He notices the black baseball cap she's wearing over her auburn hair has the letters *NRA* embroidered. Not wanting to appear like a lustful teenager, James quickly looks at the driver.

The man seated behind the steering wheel, also wearing a matching NRA hat, looks to be a little older and a little more worn than his female companion. With peppered black hair, the man is wearing aviator sunglasses, a cigar hanging from his mouth. He's also smiling, but more to himself, staring ahead. His demeanor is less friendly than the woman's and invokes a feeling of uneasiness in James. But the cool air-conditioned breeze mixed with the odor of a fine cigar rushes out of the window onto James's face. The lady speaks with the remnant of a southern accent. Most of it sounds washed out and more collegial.

"Hey there, stranger," the woman says.

"Hi. Thank you for stopping."

"Of course." A small dose of seduction escapes her tone. "Where you headed?"

"I'm headed to Baker to visit my girl," James says as he reaches his hand out to her. "My name's Jessie," he lies, attempting to be clever with a little wordplay.

The peculiar woman looks at his extended hand curiously. Without taking it, she says, "Nice to meet you, Jessie. I'm Amber, and this is my husband—"

"Look," the man says, interrupting her, "Jessie, is it?" His tone is accusatory as he takes a long pull from his cigar. His gravelly voice showing a command presence with more twang than the woman's.

"Yes, sir."

"Well ... *Jessie* ... we don't normally pick up hitchhikers."

James keeps up the ruse of a young man in need. Speaking with a boyish tone, he says, "Oh, sir, I'm not a hitchhiker. My car ran out of gas a couple of miles back."

"That black Honda I saw back there?" he asks, chuckling at James's plight.

"Yes, sir," James says through gritted teeth.

"And now you need a ride?"

"Yes, sir."

The man chuckles again. "Sounds like a hitchhiker to me."

James's fake smile fades. With his mouth hanging open, he's at a loss for words. He mentally scrambles on how to save the situation while also holding back everything he wants to say to this sarcastic fuck.

James finally finds some luck when Amber says, "Oh, stop it, baby. Let's give the kid a ride."

After a long moment, the old man delivers a heavy, heartfelt laugh. "Of course we will, sweetheart. I'm just breaking his balls a little."

Amber joins him in his laughter.

James relaxes and throws in some nervous laughter of his own.

"Well, hell, Jessie," the driver says, "I can't very well argue with a pretty little face like that, now, can I?" The driver pulls his sunglasses down, revealing cold, dark eyes. "Besides, my wife is a sucker for a young man with broad shoulders."

The couple continue to laugh. James, instead, fakes an embarrassed smirk. After the laughter dies down, Mr. Aviator Sunglasses stuffs his cigar back between his teeth.

"I guess we're going for a ride," the man says, offering his hand to James. "The name's Lee ... Lee Walker."

Lee smiles bigger now. Taking his hand, James notices a tinge of yellow near the gum line of his otherwise pearly whites. "Thank you, Lee."

"Hop in, son."

James complies with the direction, getting in the backseat. Once he's seated, Amber rolls up her window with a coy smile on her face. The three speed off in a plume of dust and gravel.

James estimates that the drive to his remote hideout in Baker, California, will take one hour. *That's enough time.*

"You folks from Vegas?" James asks.

Lee straightens himself up in his seat, puffing out his chest like a politician standing at a podium, giving an acceptance speech. "No sir, Jessie. We are from the proud state of Oklahoma."

"Oh yeah?"

Lee continues. "Oklahoma is the home of Mickey Mantle and Garth Brooks."

"And don't forget Reba McEntire, honey," Amber says.

"Oh yes, sweetheart, you're right," Lee says, patting her on the thigh. "Ol' Reba. The only ginger in the world who can turn my head other than you."

Again, the couple laugh with an odd pitch in their glee.

James's discomfort continues to grow. He checks the revolver still firm in his waistband. "What brings you to Pahrump?"

"We have some business to tend to, Jessie," Lee says, eyeing him in the rearview mirror.

James blocks out the old man's rambling, plotting his next steps.

This is going to be easy work. Plus, they put me in the backseat, giving me their backs. He knows he needs to make his move before getting off this two-lane back road. But he needs a little more time. "My buddy works at the Golden Nugget Casino. He's always talking about a steak and egg special. Supposed to be the best in town."

Lee flashes his bright smile at James in the rearview mirror. "Hell, that's mighty white of ya, Jessie. I think we'll do that."

James chuckles to himself, amused by the off-colored compliment. Looking out the car window now, he recognizes several natural landmarks. With forty-five more minutes before reaching Baker, James decides it's time to make his move.

CHAPTER 32

H AVING GARNERED ALL HIS strength, James mentally rehearses his next steps. *Pull your gun. Tell the old man to pull over. Leave the keys in the ignition. When they get out, take their wallets. If they give you any shit, give them bullets in the face. Now man the fuck up and get this done!*

James waits another minute until Lee sets his gaze back on the road. When he does, James reaches for the gun under his waistband. The vehicle bounces, driving over a shallow pothole in the road, causing James to fumble his grip. He glances back up at the couple. Both are still unaware of his movement. Quietly, with his head down, James slips the black .38 revolver from his pants. He starts to pull the hammer back but stops. A large, cold piece of metal presses hard against his forehead. James looks up to confirm what he already knows.

His eyes cross, trying to focus on the abnormally long gun barrel leading from his forehead to a pair of steady female hands. His eyes refocus on Amber casting a seductive smile and bedroom eyes to match. Embarrassment and fear flood James's veins like they did when his grandmother caught him looking at an old *Playboy* magazine from his grandfather's stash.

James tries to compose himself. But he can't because Amber starts making a gesture with her mouth. Like a dentist beginning an annual cleaning, Amber drones out, "Ahhh."

What the fuck? Confusion engulfs James's brain like a raging river. Amber helps him regain his focus with three rapid bumps to his forehead with the chrome tip of the pistol. With her mouth open and head nodding, James mimics her gesture. Amber forces her pistol deep into it his mouth.

James can hear the grinding sound of metal and enamel converging. Past his teeth, the barrel slides along the roof of his mouth. The insertion comes to a gentle halt, short of making James gag. Amber playfully moves the pistol around in his mouth. Painfully guiding the movements of his head. James can only let out a slight whimper. Amber bites her lip and smiles.

In the rearview mirror Lee is smiling at James too. James's hand is still on his revolver. But all thoughts of escape dissipate. Lee gives James a beckoning gesture, reaching back behind his shoulder.

"Nice and easy, now, son."

James moves as slow as pond water. Reluctantly, he raises the revolver. Lee toys with him by tapping the brakes on the car. This causes James's arm to flail. Lee and Amber mockingly react to his jerking movement caused by the brake check.

"Bang!" Lee says jokingly.

Amber lets out a loud, demented cackle that melds into a moan of pleasure.

James finally relinquishes the gun with no more hesitation.

"There we go," Lee says. "Boy, I tell you what, Jessie. You have got to be one stupid son of a bitch to pull a gun on two people wearing 'NRA' in huge gold letters on their fuckin' foreheads." Lee laughs at his own assessment.

He continues his dissertation. "That dime piece you have in your mouth right now is a chrome-plated Desert Eagle .50-caliber hand cannon. Yes, sir! If Amber were to pull that trigger, I imagine it would blow your brains about five miles back to where we found you."

James starts shaking his head frantically.

"What can I say, Jessie?" Lee's voice lowers into a giddy, perverted growl. "My wife likes 'em big."

Amber roughly moves the pistol up and down. James's head is forced to follow. "Yes, I do, young man. Yes, I do." Her movements afford James another dose of pain in his mouth.

"Now," Lee says, "if you got any more pistols in your pants, I suggest you give 'em up."

James manages to squeeze out a sound from deep inside his stomach. Through the little space left between the inside of his mouth and the barrel lodged deep inside it, James exhales a gargled "No."

Lee smiles. "Okay, good. Now, I'm gonna get Amber to take that thing out of your mouth. And you are gonna sit back and behave." Lee puffs on his cigar and blows a big plume of smoke. "Do we understand each other?"

James answers with his eyes and a little shake from the muscles in his face. Amber helps him respond by forcing his head up and down several times.

"Good," Lee says, patting Amber on the thigh. "Okay, baby."

She pulls the barrel out, enjoying every second. Once it's completely removed, James coughs erratically. He takes a couple more deep breaths. The taste of copper from his blood is also present.

Lee and Amber look at him, amused by his uncontrollable hacking.

Motherfuckers. "Please—"

Lee cuts James off. "No one said you could talk, Jessie."

James submits. The muscles in his neck and jaw twitch as they try to get back to their normal position. He wipes his mouth and the built-up moisture around his eyes.

"Do you like classical music, Jessie?"

James sits in silence.

"Boy, I sure do," Lee says, punching at the buttons on an outdated car stereo.

A melody rises in the air to a comfortable decibel as the Crown Vic heads toward Amargosa.

I'm fucked. This is the couple that cut Vinnie's ear off. He panics, contemplating his options. *I can try to appeal to the woman by crying.*

James curses this idea. *Are you fucking stupid? That crazy bitch jammed a pistol down your throat.*

He considers another option. *I can try to play tough. But these two don't seem to be afraid of anything. Shit! Think, stupid!*

Finally, he settles on a third option. *Hold your ground without challenging theirs. That might earn their respect. Let them know you fucked up and are willing to take on the consequences.*

James likes this strategy. He tries to be optimistic, pumping himself up. *Time to man the fuck up and not be a bitch. Who knows? Maybe I can work for them when this is all over.*

The Crown Vic hums down the roughly paved road, Lee giving no care to its suspension or paint job. Lee and Amber sit as calm as a family driving home from Sunday church. While James sweats like the whore who sat next to them in the pew.

A few minutes later, the Crown Vic slows down. James knows exactly where they are. The world-famous pupfish pond, in the shallows of Devil's Hole. People come from all around the world to see this giant hole in the ground. Back in the '60s, people used to scuba dive in the water, which is supposed to be bottomless. But some divers never came up, so going in the water became an illegal act. There are also some rare, endangered fish that were discovered in the pond. Tourists come to the location trying to catch a glimpse of the fish. But today, there are no visitors.

As they come to a complete stop, Lee turns off the vehicle and all goes deathly silent.

CHAPTER 33

The Golden Nugget is one of the better casinos in Pahrump, Nevada. Located on the corner of Highway 160 and Route 372, it catches all traffic coming in and going out of town. Whether from California, Las Vegas, or northern Nevada, the Golden Nugget is seen from every direction. When it comes to modern amenities, it has its typical buffet, steak house, and poker room, where Wes works as a dealer.

Usually, Wes is happy to come to work. The hours are steady, the days are predictable, and the pay is decent when the tips come in. Another perk to the job is not getting shot at in a Third World country while sleeping in a dirt hole. And he enjoys the handful of regulars who come in and play. Most of them are at least thirty years his senior and appreciate Wes for his military service. Unlike many of the twenty-somethings living in the small town who struggle to wake up before noon. A couple of the gamblers prod him for a blood-and-guts story from time to time. He sometimes obliges if the guy's a good tipper.

But today, Wes isn't in a good mood. Having James and Vinnie show up the way they did last night put everything in motion. He barked at Maggie before rushing Vinnie to the hospital. This earned him a first-class ticket to the living room couch when he got home. But what brought his shitty night full circle was James never coming back with tacos or his car. Wes didn't enjoy having to explain to Maggie how her degenerate brother stole their vehicle.

James leaving his keys in the ignition of his work truck is the only luck Wes had last night. In James's haste bringing Vinnie to Wes's house, he forgot to take his keys and lock the door to his old truck. Because of this error, Wes got himself to work rather than calling in.

Wes drags his feet through the casino to the poker room. He scans the casino floor, eyeing all the early-morning gamblers pumping their hands on the slot machines. *Maybe I should work for Sean.*

When he figures out what table he's working today, he tries to adjust his attitude before interacting with the customers. *Last night was a cluster fuck, but today I need to make money.* He contemplates the Russo rip and what happened to Vinnie's ear. *Shit is getting real, and I want nothing to do with it.*

Wes prepares his table by counting chips, checking the card-dealing machine, and buttoning up his gold-sequin vest. He reminds himself that a card dealer's attitude affects the game. If the dealer is shitty, so are the players. And that's not good for business.

Settling in behind his table, Wes puts on a fake smile. He overhears three of his regular gamblers discussing the politics of horse racing. The cocktail server brings him a cup of coffee, which he's grateful for. Especially after not getting a lot of sleep last night. Between trying to explain himself to Maggie through a closed door and tossing around on the couch, flipping through the television to distract his mind, a good night's sleep hadn't been in the cards.

The pit boss today gives Wes a nod, signaling him to start the first game.

Wes broadcasts to the table, "The game is Nevada Lowball," as he deals the cards. From the first card dealt, Wes feels his slump kicking in. Usually, he's more tentative. But today he's operating on muscle memory. *This is going to be a long fuckin' day.*

A few bets are made, a few cards tossed, and before long, he's dealing the river card. "All right, boys, here comes the river," Wes informs the group, flipping the last card over.

Chris, a short, pudgy Asian man seated next to him, jumps up in grand celebration. "That's what I'm talking about, baby!"

Wes is not in the mood today. *Relax, Chris. You won twenty dollars.* But he reminds himself he has a job to do. So, like with everything else in his life, Wes leans forward in the saddle. With as much enthusiasm as he can muster, he announces, "Winner. Jacks full of aces." The other men grumble, throwing their used cards back to the center of the table. Wes privately joins their grumbling. *You got what's coming to you, James.*

CHAPTER 34

L EE AND AMBER HOP out of their Crown Vic and take in the hot summer air. Lee opens the rear passenger door and holds it like a polished New York chauffeur.

"Here we are, sir."

James hesitates, trying to find any remaining confidence left inside himself.

Lee waits patiently, enjoying the moment. "Come on, son. Get some fresh air."

James doesn't move. But to his relief, Lee wanders away from the open door. James watches him saunter around. Amber puts on a pair of her own dark, mirrored sunglasses. Lee smiles at her. They take each other by the hand and stroll the perimeter of the protected pond like vacationers, enjoying the majestic views of the vast desert scenery.

Enough of this bullshit. James takes a deep breath before pushing himself out of the car. He tries to put a casual look on his face and to move with some courage, walking to the front of the tan sedan. He struggles to act nonchalant.

Lee meets James at the front of the car. James digs his feet into the dirt. *Don't fucking move an inch. Show him you're not scared.*

Lee pulls out another cigar and lights it with a DuPont lighter. The universal *ping* sound comes from the high-end lighter followed by a soft flame. Lee toasts the fresh tobacco hanging from his mouth.

James watches the cigar closely. *Ask him for one.* Lee picks up on James's perceived interest. He smiles and pulls another cigar from his front pocket and stretches it out to James. *Let him offer it to you first.* James waits for verbal permission.

"Go on, Jessie, take it. They're authentic Cubans. Smooth and delicious."

James's plan to bond with Lee is beginning to work. James nods and reaches out, calmly taking the cigar with great care and putting it in his mouth. Another metallic *ping* fills the air and now a soft flame is headed toward James's face. *Don't let this motherfucker burn your eye out.* James is careful not to flinch. The flame touches the end of the cigar and James puffs on it until the tobacco at the tip is fully lit.

"Beautiful country, ain't it?" Lee asks.

James takes a long drag on the cigar, his hand shaking with adrenaline. "The desert?" he asks. *Is this going to be my last smoke?*

"I love the desert," Lee says. "Deep expansive valleys. Beautiful vanilla skies. And if you're lucky, a small body of water like this one with nobody around for miles. Can't beat it."

Nobody around for miles. Lee's words echo in James's head. He says, "Looks like a bunch of dirt to me."

"Oh, come, now, Jessie. You have to learn to appreciate your surroundings a little more," Lee says as he takes another puff from his cigar, enjoying the smoke as it dances around in his mouth and out of his nose.

Watching Lee smoke like a pro, James becomes overtly aware he's holding his cigar awkwardly. He checks the ember to ensure that it is still lit.

Lee says, "That's the problem with you kids these days. You never see the little things, life's little pleasures."

James has nothing to say. *Sounds like my pops.* And in that moment, he notices the silence. No classical music. No pounding of rocks on the vehicle's floorboard. No spine-tingling cackles. Only silence.

James takes the moment to subdue his anxiety and to find a little courage. "What are you going to do with me?"

Lee's joyous face drops at the question. "Now, why would you wanna go and ruin a moment like this with talk like that, Jessie? Relax and enjoy the view, son."

Hopeful thoughts flood James's mind at Lee's philosophical words. *I might get out of this. This old man isn't so bad. He wants to teach me a lesson.* James also finds hope in the fact that they didn't kill Vinnie. *If that were their plan, they would have done it when they had him.* James finally relaxes and joins Lee in the moment. They both gaze out over the horizon.

Beyond the ledge are multicolored rocks, dirt, and Joshua trees, as far as the eye can see. The wind whistles. The faint crunching sound of gravel causes James to look over at Amber, who is off in her own little world, wandering about the pond's edge, giving the two men some privacy.

"Look here, Jessie, I'm going to be candid with you." He takes a puff from his stogie. "My wife and I aren't exactly law-abidin' citizens ourselves. And I would like to think your motives weren't all bad." Lee continues sampling his cigar the way a wine sommelier would approach a new vintage. "The way I see it, you panicked. And from one outlaw to another," Lee says with a wink, "I think I might be able to look the other way."

James mouth opens slightly. *He's going to let me go.* He snaps it shut as he holds Lee's gaze, attempting to convey a sense of humbleness and appreciation.

"I'm going to keep your gun, though."

James makes sure not to interrupt the moment this time. Lee continues. "But after this here cigar, I think we can go our separate ways."

James is at a loss for words. Struggling to mimic Lee's ease, he asks, "You would do that?"

"Absolutely!" Lee says. "We're a rare breed, you, Amber, and me."

The idea of an outlaw community creates a dysfunctional and somewhat nostalgic feeling in James. He knows exactly what to say: "Well, thanks, Lee. That's mighty white of you."

Lee appreciates the retention of one of his more endearing comments. The two exchange looks of amusement and respect as they continue to puff on their cigars. They return their gazes to the horizon.

Amber sashays across the desert floor toward Lee and wraps one arm around his neck, nuzzling his back.

Comfortable with the situation, James moseys away from the couple toward the pond's edge. *They're going to let me out of this.* Grateful, James points toward the bottom of the pond. "These pupfish have been around for centuries."

"Oh, I'm aware. Hell, son, I would do less time for killing you than I would taking a few of these little fishies and putting them in my pond."

What the fuck? Why is he still talking about killing me?

Lee notices James's reaction and laughs it off. James does too.

With his finesse for handling the cigar continuing to improve, James takes more mature puffs off the Cuban treat. *I am one lucky son of a bitch. I played it right.*

James's internal celebration is cut short. Behind his head, the metallic sound of Lee pulling the hammer back on his .44 Magnum snatches every ounce of hope from him. The afternoon sun burns his skin again. He's completely petrified. Too afraid to turn around, too afraid to speak.

"Well, son, I think our time together has ended," Lee says, like a thankful guest having to leave after a fine dinner.

James's voice, on the other hand, is filled with the type of betrayal one might feel finding out the love of your life had been sleeping with your best friend. "I thought you said you were going to let me live?"

With a chastising tone, Lee says, "No, I don't remember sayin' anything like that."

Panic sets in. "What? Yeah! You said we would go our separate ways!"

"Well, yeah, you're right. And we will. Amber and I are gonna go to the natural hot spring south of where we found you." After a dramatic pause, Lee says, "And you ... well ... your lifeless corpse is goin' to be these here fishes' food for the next century or so."

James's eyes swell with tears. He drops his cigar to the ground, mumbling incoherently. His breathing becomes heavier.

"Don't worry, son. You're gettin' off light ... James," Lee says, smirking.

James's face drops at the mention of his real name.

"'Jessie James,'" Lee says. "Bet you thought you were pretty fuckin' clever, didn't ya?"

Hopelessness sets in for James. He knows the next words will be the last he ever hears.

"The Professor sends his regards."

Overwhelmed, James screams in terror, "I saw who … "

Lee pulls the trigger.

A stabbing pressure like James has never felt before shoots through his head. He feels the splash of water slap his face milliseconds before going dark.

The water in the prehistoric pond settles around James's floating body. The little pupfish converge on the corpse.

Standing near the pond's edge, Lee looks upon his work. He stares at his reflection in the water. His chin high and his revolver still in tote. Amber meets him at the edge and takes his hand. She lifts herself up on her toes next to Lee's ear like a child wanting to tell a secret. "Honey, do we want young James to float away?"

"I don't suppose we do, my love. With this place being the Devil's Hole and all, I suppose we could expedite his meeting with Mr. Lucifer himself." Lee raises his gun and places five strategic shots in the back of James's body. Two in the upper left, two in the upper right, and one in the middle.

After the bullets rip into James's body, the remaining air in his lungs gurgles out, forming bubbles rising to the pond's surface. The Oklahoma couple watch the body sink beneath the surface into the dark water for another moment. More prehistoric pupfish swarm James's body, attaching themselves to his face in the bloodstained water. "Hot damn, these little critters are hungry!" Lee says.

"I guess I would be too. Eating algae for the past million years," Amber says.

Back at their Crown Vic, the Professor's dope and cash are displayed on top of the hood. Lee's face tightens. "There's less than half here," Amber says, disappointment in her voice.

"Damn, sweetheart, this really chaps my ass." Lee trails a circle in the dirt, taking off his hat and running his hand through his hair.

"Are you thinking about Gary?" Amber asks.

Lee waits to answer. "I can't help but think that, to his final breath, Gary stood by his son. And how much of a piece of shit his son actually was? If you ask me, taking both James's and his father's lives is like smoking a fine Cuban cigar while drinking a diet pop. A plain waste."

Amber puts her arm around Lee's side, offering him comfort.

"The upside to all of this is, Gary no longer has to live with the shame of his son." Lee says.

"You're a good man, honey."

He pulls Amber close into a firm hug. "You know what I'm thinking? Lee asks.

"That the kid was too much of a flunky to have planned this himself."

"Exactly. Seemed like he started to give a death bed confession."

Lost in thought for another moment, Amber breaks the silence. "I'm getting hungry. Should we head back and grab some breakfast at the casino?"

"That's a fine plan. And after breakfast, how about we play a couple of hands?"

CHAPTER 35

AT WES'S TABLE, THE trash-talking and boisterous jubilee goes on for about an hour before everyone leaves except Chris. Wes takes a pause to nurse his coffee when an older couple with racks stacked two high, full of chips, sits down at the table. They're an attractive couple, though odd, with matching black hats embroidered with gold NRA lettering. For the town of Pahrump, this look isn't as uncommon as people might think. Everyone has a gun, and everyone loves shooting them. Even the local pastors like to sling some lead from time to time.

"How's the action this morning?" the woman asks with too much excitement in her voice for 9:00 a.m.

"Doing all right," Wes replies. "The game is Nevada Lowball."

The woman's companion, whom Wes guesses is her husband, smiles a toothy grin, apparently liking the sound of the game. "Nevada Lowball? That's a new one for me," the man says.

Wes explains the game to the couple. "It's quite easy. Each player is dealt four cards, like Omaha. Everyone discards, with the small and big blinds' discards becoming the two-card flop.

Two more community cards follow as the turn and the river. Blinds and betting are like Hold 'Em."

If one had to explain the game to a non–poker player, players are usually dealt their pocket cards first (cards only they get to see). There's usually a round of betting, essentially making an educated guess (based on odds and what cards are left in the deck) of what kind of five-card hand you might have by the end of the deal. After that round of betting, the first round of community cards comes out (cards laid out faceup on the table for each player to use to make a hand in combination with their pocket cards). More betting, and the final dealing of the community cards and betting, with the last card being called the "river" card, as in "the last chance to catch a hand downriver."

The difference between Nevada Lowball and other games is each player discards two of their four pocket cards, which isn't that different from some games out there, except the small blind (the person next to the dealer) puts in the smallest automatic bet to keep the money rolling and the big blind (the next player and next biggest bet) each choose a card to place in the middle, either to screw the other players or to continue to play their discard in the community cards. Essentially, each time you are the small or big blind (which moves around the table), you are able to somewhat dictate the start of the community deal. Whether you throw something of value or something worthless in the middle, no one will know until the river.

As Wes finishes his brief explanation, the man confirms his understanding. "Sounds easy enough. The discard flop is interesting."

Wes continues. "Brings a new dynamic to the game. The small and big blinds can disguise their hand by putting a bluff in the middle or their weakest card in. Either way, they try to lowball the rest of the players. And with the blinds always moving, every player gets a chance to lowball."

"Where did you get this game?" the man asks with a toothy smile.

Chris speaks up, pointing at Wes. "The kid created it. The bosses upstairs liked it so much they put it in regular rotation."

Wes glances away, sheepish about the compliment. The couple picks up on it. The woman smirks at Wes as she says, "My Lord, you must be a really smart kid. I bet you play chess too."

"Yes, ma'am, I do."

The man sitting next to her sends his own compliment with another toothy smile. "A thinker ... I like that."

"Well, thank you ...," Wes says. "I didn't catch your name, sir."

"The name's Lee. And this is my lovely wife, Amber," he says, motioning to his lady, who smiles seductively at Wes.

Wes opens his hands in a welcoming gesture. "Shall we play?"

Lee nods his approval, pulling out a cigar.

Wes is shuffling the cards when he hears a distinct metallic sound. He looks up and sees Lee lighting his cigar with a DuPont lighter. Wes leads with the formalities of the game. "All right. Blinds are ten and twenty."

Lee settles into his seat, blowing a cloud of smoke from his cigar. Amber straightens herself up like a secretary preparing to type a memo. "That's my kind of action," she says.

More formalities from Wes. "Place your blinds, please." He deals four cards each, facedown, to Chris, then to Lee, then to Amber. Everyone discards and the small and big blinds' cards go in the middle, facedown. It's up to Amber to call.

"I call," she says, smiling at Wes. She throws a couple of chips at the center of the table.

Wes points to Chris first. "Action's to you." Then to Lee sitting behind a thick cloud of cigar smoke. "And to you, sir, check or bet?"

Lee glances at his cards with a stoic eye. He throws his own chips on the center of the table.

"I think I'll raise," Amber calls without hesitation.

Chris glances at Lee, being more than a little serious.

Lee stares at Wes, smiling as smoke swirls around his head.

Chris finally speaks. "I'll call you, Mr. NRA."

Lee breaks his stare with Wes and shoots back, "Good, a little action."

"Three-way action. Let's see the flop," Wes announces, flipping two cards over on the table and nodding at Chris. "Action's to you." Chris places a large bet. Amber lets out an exaggerated exhale, throwing her cards on the table in front of her.

"Please wait for your turn to act," Wes says. Playfully sheepish, Amber takes her cards back, appearing to be amused by Wes's parentlike correction. He motions to Lee. "Action's to you, sir. Call, raise, or fold."

Lee's demeanor changes immediately. He locks eyes with Wes again. The hair on the back of Wes's neck stands up.

"I never fold," Lee says in a serious tone. He quickly returns to his smile, leaning back in his chair.

The nervous feeling in Wes leaves as fast as it came. *What the hell was that? I haven't felt that in a long time.*

Lee makes the call.

Now Amber folds her cards in proper poker etiquette, smiling at Wes the whole time.

What the hell is it with these two? "Let's see 'em, gentlemen," Wes says.

Lee flips his cards over, revealing trip aces. Chris scoffs and mucks his cards.

"Winner, three of a kind. Aces," Wes announces, pushing the winnings to Lee.

Chris is clearly pissed off. He hops up from the table and barks at Wes, "That's some bullshit, Wes! I feel bad for your wife."

Wes deflects the comment with a grin. "So do I."

Chris storms off.

Wes starts gathering up the cards when Lee asks, "Now, why would he say that about Maggie?"

Did he just say my wife's name? It only takes a millisecond for the nervous feeling to return before Wes can process what he heard. He plays it cool. But his question to the couple is now direct. "Where did you folks say you were from?"

The couple smile as Lee says, "The fine state of Oklahoma." He extends his hand out and says, "It's a pleasure to make your acquaintance, Wesley."

Wes doesn't take his hand.

Old couple from out of town ...

Kind of country ...

Shotgun and a revolver ...

NRA hats ...

My shit radar is going off ...

A thousand thoughts race through Wes's mind before he finally sees it in both of their faces. *Ah, there it is.* That look a man gets after he's killed so much that any sense of fear is utterly depleted. Where the guilt of taking another man's life is gone and it becomes second nature. Some of the teenage Somalis Wes fought against in Mogadishu had the same look at such a young age.

The three stare at each other for a moment. Wes can feel a scowl growing on his face. Lee and Amber continue smiling at him.

Lee finally breaks the silence. "It's obvious you're smarter than Vincent and James."

Wes's heart beats faster as adrenaline rush into his hands, making them tingle. He plants his fingertips on the poker table's surface to keep them from visually shaking.

Lee continues. "Unfortunately, I have only been able to retrieve half of what was taken."

Without conscious thought, Wes shifts his foot forward, taking a subtle fighting stance.

"That's why you're going to help us. Because you're a good friend ..."

"And a good husband," Amber says with her ever-present seductive tone.

"That's right. And a good husband." Lee scratches his head. "Do you understand the butterfly effect theory?"

Wes remains silent. His eye flitting around the table. He hears what Lee is saying. But can only think about how to kill him right where he stands.

Giving his scientific dissertation, Lee points at the various objects around the poker table. "Let's take your heavy coffee mug for example. It would do a number against the side of my head. But Amber would shoot you in the temple."

Amber makes a shooting gesture at Wes with her hand.

"There's the pen you have in your pocket. It would require several punctures in my neck to do any actual damage. But you're not in range to do that before Amber again shoots you in the temple."

Another gesture from Amber.

"And of course you're thinking about grabbing my wife by the hair because you think she's the weaker of the two of us. But what you don't realize is she actually enjoys having her hair pulled."

"I really do," Amber says.

"Plus, when you do, I'll shoot you in the temple." Lee makes his own hand gesture.

Wes doesn't move or respond.

"The only constant denominator in all these scenarios is Maggie, your dear bride, getting informed today that her husband was killed on the job. And then, because she is so riddled with grief, she ends up taking her own life, with our assistance, of course."

Wes feels his jaw flexing. And his face burning hot.

"You see ... butterfly effect," Lee says.

These motherfuckers are two steps ahead of me. And they don't give two shits about killing me or Maggie in public. Fuck me! They have me by the balls.

Lee continues. "So, what you're going to do now, son, is retrieve the rest of my package from your pal Vinnie and bring it back to me."

Okay, I get more time, but then what? Wes gestures his acknowledgment.

Lee reaches into his side pocket and pulls out a sandwich-sized zip-lock baggie. Inside the baggie, a chunk of something slides around in dark, thick liquid. Lee throws the baggie on the table like tossing chips in for another bet. He says, "I'm assuming your first stop is to the hospital to speak with Vincent. I promised to give this back to him after I found James."

Wes examines the inside of the baggie by holding it up and squeezing it. *What the fuck is this?* It only takes Wes a second to recognize it. *This crazy bastard handed me Vinnie's ear! Right here at the table! This is too much. I'm out of my league.* Wes's courage dissipates. "Where's James?" he asks in a defeated tone.

"To tell you the truth, Wes, James and I, well, we went our separate ways."

Lee gathers up the rest of his chips and says, "We'll need the rest of our package by ten o'clock tonight, Wesley. That gives you twelve hours. The casino here has a five-ninety-nine steak and egg special that starts at eleven. We'd like to try the special, so if you don't mind, let's wrap this up on time."

They offer Wes a last look, now sauntering away. Lee says over his shoulder, matching the noise of the casino, "The rest of it, Wesley. Or trust me ... you'll regret it."

What am I going to do? Make Vinnie tell you where their shit is. What about Maggie? The gravity of Lee's last comment shoves Wes into a sprint out of the casino.

Samantha, a cocktail waitress, steps in front of his path, stopping him in his tracks. Her face filled with concern. "Are you okay, Wes? You're pale and sweaty."

Wes tries to make an excuse on the fly. "Uh ... Maggie's sick and I have to get to the hospital."

Samantha throws him a weird look, almost seeing through his bullshit. Wes takes off again, not giving her a chance to ask any more questions. He yells over his shoulder, "Can you tell the boss?"

She yells back, "Yeah. Send my love."

CHAPTER 36

WES RUNS TO JAMES'S work truck that he used to get himself to the casino. He fumbles with the keys and Vinnie's bloody ear, trying to gather his thoughts. He contemplates going straight home to get Maggie so they can run. He decides against it, at least for the time being. Until he knows exactly what's going on. *What am I going to tell Maggie about her brother? He's probably dead.* His heart grows heavy as he thinks about this, but hardens a bit as he remembers James put this entire thing in motion. But Wes knows, regardless of who's at fault, if something happened to James, it would destroy Gary, and that would destroy Maggie.

I need to go see Gary. That's the next best step. If James is alive, he would go to the shop and get his dad's help. If he isn't there, I can get Gary to take Maggie and then help unfuck this thing. Wes settles on his plan of action, hoping not to get killed in the process.

Wes speeds toward Gary's cabinet shop.

Within five minutes, he's in front of the tin building. He notices the front door swinging loosely. *That's not normal.*

Reaching for the handle, he hears Sean's voice in his head telling him to "Get the hell out of the fatal funnel." Wes hasn't had to worry about the dangers of standing in a doorway for years. But he's thinking about it now. He takes a moment to gather his wits. With violent energy, Wes bursts through the door, pushing it hard against the inside wall, making sure no one is waiting in the blind spot for him.

The door slams, rattling the entire shop. *I'm an idiot. Entering the shop like I'm on a fire team ready to engage enemy troops.* Reevaluating his situation, he knows he has no rifle and no squad and can't do much if there is an armed threat. *Calm down, Wes.*

Entering the shop, Wes scans the front area for anything unusual. Everything appears to be in order. Until he glances over at one of the workbenches. He sees what looks to be Gary. But something about him doesn't look right. He's sitting in a chair, his head and body leaning to the side in an abnormal position with one of his hands on the bench. *What the fuck is wrong with him?* "Gary!" Wes receives no response. Moving closer to his father-in-law, he notices some sort of dark, dried paint or varnish on the floor around Gary. *What the hell?*

Getting closer, Wes now can see broken glass scattered in with the dried paint. His subconscious mind knows what he's looking at. This triggers the odor the conscious part of his brain now remembers. Another half second and Wes registers what's in front of him.

Horror and anguish fill his heart when he sees the dried blood matted in Gary's hair on the back of his head. Upon reexamination, Wes realizes it's not varnish on the floor but Gary's blood. *What the hell happened?* With full comprehension of the scene, the odor of Gary's dead body rushes up through his nose, into his mouth, and down his throat. The smell causes his face to contort in revulsion to the rotten aroma death brings with it. It has been a long time since Wes has been in close contact with the smell. Most of the dead bodies he dealt with in Somalia were fresher. And, though mangled, they didn't have the same stench a body has being dead for a day, baking in summer heat.

Wes struggles to bring his thoughts under control. He looks at Gary's body with a more technical eye. The skin has turned yellow and purple, caused by the remaining blood pooling on the bottom side of Gary's face. The area where his right eye used to be is now a ripped hole of bone, meat, burnt flesh, and dried blood.

Wes notices a pressure building in his chest. A concoction of deep sorrow and confusion explode inside him. The emotion erupts out of his body in the form of heavy crying. Wes's body heaves with the pain of losing this father figure. Through tear-filled eyes, Wes notices the broken glass on the floor is Gary's whiskey bottle. *Did they kill him while he was taking his last drink?* While fighting off shock, Wes looks closer at what used to be Gary's hand.

Smashed in the vise, it is almost indistinguishable. Only his fingertips and short fingernails are reminiscent of a human hand, protruding from a ball of smashed meat held together by dry blood.

What am I supposed to do now? Standing on weak legs in the middle of this horrible mess, Wes commands himself to stop crying. He considers his next steps. He knows he needs more intel and assets to help him navigate this shit show. *I need to get Maggie and get to a safe place.* Staggering over to Gary's office, he wipes any remaining moisture off his face and sits down behind his desk. He grabs the phone and dials.

The phone rings only twice before Wes hears a raspy voice on the other end. "This is Sean."

"They killed her dad."

"Wes, is this you? What did you say?"

"I said your boss killed Maggie's dad!"

"What are you talking about, brother?"

Unable to control his tone now, Wes yells and spews hate into the phone. "Those two Oklahoma fucks! The old man and his wife! They came to my job and basically told me they killed my buddy James. And they fuckin' threatened me and Maggie!"

"Holy shit."

"I didn't have nothing to do with this shit, Sean!"

"Wes, relax, I know."

Wes continues to lose his shit on Sean, crossing a line now. "Fuck you, Sean! Are you part of this? Are you coming after my family?"

For the first time in a long while, Sean barks back at Wes. "What the fuck did you say to me, Wes! Did you just ask me if I was coming after your family?"

Then silence; neither of them speaks.

Wes can hear Sean gathering his thoughts and picking his next words more carefully now. "I'm not going to bullshit you and say this is some coincidence. Yeah, your two friends ripped off Russo, and it looks like they killed him too. And those two you met earlier are most likely here because the Professor sent them. But asking me if I have anything to do with hurting your family," Wes can hear some kind of emotion in Sean's voice, "you need to readjust your shot group."

Is Sean about to cry?

Sean's voice softens. "That … it bothers me … that you would think I could do that to you, Wes. I thought things were different between us."

His words and his tone knock Wes down a few pegs. Guilt saturates Wes for even suggesting such a thing. "Sean, I literally walked in on my father-in-law having been shot in the face with his hand smashed in a vise. What the hell am I supposed to do?"

Sean's voice tightens back up. Wes hears his old platoon sergeant beginning to issue orders. "First, I'm sorry for your father-in-law. Now, you need to man the fuck up and lean forward in the saddle. I'll call my boss and tell him you weren't involved. That should help slow-roll this thing with these two country fucks. What I need you to do now is go talk to your other dumb-ass friend and find out where Russo's stash is. We need to return the Professor's shit as quickly as possible. If you can get your buddy to tell you where he put the stash, that should buy you some goodwill with the Professor."

"Maybe we should call the police."

"Don't do that," Sean warns. "If you do, there's no coming back from this. They'll most likely put it on you."

"What do you mean?"

"I mean, you worked for Russo. And you and Caleb were in his house the other night. You need to stay away from this as much as possible."

"But I need to hide Maggie."

"Do that. But go talk to your friend first and call me and tell me what he says. Any information he has is going to buy you more time. I'll let my boss know you're working the problem and to call his dogs off for a bit."

Both men sit for a moment, quiet on the phone, settling the plan in their heads. Wes breaks the silence. "And you wanted me to work for this guy?"

"Yeah, after this, I might need to find new employment myself."

"You should. I'll call you when I get something ..." Wes pauses, appreciating Sean's help. "Thanks, Sergeant."

"No problem—out," Sean says, hanging up the phone.

Wes leaves the shop, locking the door behind him in case Maggie swings by unannounced like she usually does. *It would ruin her if she found her father in this condition.* And it would damn near drive Wes toward suicide if he found Maggie in the same way. *Fuck you, Vinnie—you better have something.* He hops into the old work truck and speeds off to the hospital.

CHAPTER 37

G RIPPING THE STEERING WHEEL of the old work truck tightly, Wes races toward the hospital, where Vinnie is still recovering. Wes glances down at the digital clock on the dashboard. It reads 10:45 a.m. The panic Wes has been wrestling with all morning resurfaces. Now he regrets spending as much time as he did at the shop. *How am I supposed to navigate walking onto a scene where my father-in-law has been tortured and murdered?*

Pulling in to the hospital, the front end of the truck slams into the driveway of the parking lot. The old shocks underneath the raggedy truck frame scream as the front end dives into the asphalt. Wes slams the truck door closed and sprints to the hospital entrance.

Once inside the main lobby, Wes transitions into a speed walk. Trying to avoid drawing any attention while still moving with a purpose. Wes finds Vinnie's room and goes inside.

Vinnie is lying in bed watching TV. Wes quietly closes the door behind him. Vinnie notices Wes and sits up with a bit of excitement. Vinnie appears to be doing a lot better. Even with the giant white bandage wrapped around his head, covering the area where his ear used to be. He also sounds more coherent.

"My man, did you finally bring—"

Wes interrupts Vinnie's greeting. Taking aim at the bandage, Wes slaps the cloth target as hard as he can. All the hate, anger, and fear Wes is feeling are transferred from his hand to Vinnie's mutilated injury. Vinnie screams in agonizing pain, clutching his ear as he rolls to his side.

"What the fuck, Wes!"

Wes's body floods with rage, disconnecting from any conscious thoughts. He grabs Vinnie by his face with both hands. Fingers dig into the meat under Vinnie's jawline. His thumbs pushing into Vinnie's orbital bones.

Vinnie tries to fight back by squinting. But Wes is on him like a pit bull locked onto a tire, training for a fight. He knows he has a good grip on Vinnie's face when he finally feels the mush of his eyeball under his thumb. Wes takes a moment to enjoy his emotional relief by dishing out some physical pain himself. A response to the shit he has faced all morning.

Wes tightens his grip with his left hand and grabs Vinnie around the throat with his right. The pressure on Vinnie's face and airway gets tighter by the second. Vinnie attempts to wiggle free but fails. All he can do now is grab on to Wes's wrist.

"They came to my job and threatened Maggie, you stupid fuck," Wes says through gritted teeth, saturated with blind savagery.

Vinnie responds with a gasping air sound.

"And they killed Gary," Wes says.

Vinnie nods in acknowledgement as his face changes from red to blue, filling with panic. Wes holds Vinnie in place for a few more seconds before coming back to his senses and releasing him. When he does, Vinnie slams himself back against the bed, sucking in air like he'd been held underwater.

He coughs, mucus and spit running from the sides of his mouth. Vinnie wipes his face, and his breathing returns to normal. Fear mixed with sorrow fills his expression. Wes gives him a moment to collect himself and to process the update.

"Is Gary really dead?"

"Yeah, they tortured him and shot him in the face."

Vinnie shakes his head. "Is Maggie okay?"

"For now. But they want their shit back. And they think I can do that."

"We need to talk to James," Vinnie says, worry in his voice.

When Vinnie mentions James, it reminds Wes of the little baggie Lee gave him. Wes pulls out the bloody bag with Vinnie's ear. He drops it on Vinnie's lap. "They told me to give this back to you."

Vinnie picks up the baggie and looks at it for a moment before recognizing what it is. A tear runs down his face. "James is dead."

"You think?" Wes asks sarcastically. Vinnie keeps staring at his ear in the bag, moving it between his fingertips.

"Put your fucking ear down!" Vinnie complies, tossing it on a nearby hospital tray. "Where's their stash?" Wes continues.

"I don't know."

The answer comes too quick for Wes's liking.

Wes smashes a fist into Vinnie's stomach. Vinnie folds over in the bed, trying to catch his breath again. Wes is now towering over him. "They said they're going to kill me and Maggie if they don't get the rest of their shit back. So quit playing games and tell me where the dope and cash are."

Vinnie regains his breath, this time with some anger in his eyes. Wes notices. Offended at Vinnie's reaction being anything but submissive, Wes grabs him again and pins the side of his head to the bed rail, exposing the white bandage covering the missing ear.

This time Vinnie tries to throw a half-ass punch at Wes. Unfortunately for Vinnie, he has no leverage to throw an effective anything. Vinnie's legs and arms start to flail. He finds himself helpless.

With his head under control, Wes makes a tight fist, rubbing, grinding, and pushing his knuckles deep into Vinnie's wound. With a controlled but furious rage, Wes tries pushing his fist into Vinnie's brain through the stitched area where the ear used to be.

"Where the hell is their shit, Vinnie!"

Blood soaks through the white bandage and onto Wes's hand. Vinnie's screams loud enough to snap Wes out of his violent trance. With more clarity now, Wes worries, only for a moment, that somebody may come into the room. Wes brings his bedside interrogation to a close and releases Vinnie. Tired and exhausted by the pain, Vinnie doesn't move. He can only slump back into the bed, holding his bloody wound.

"Where is it?" Wes asks again, a little winded himself.

Through tears of pain and the frustration of being stupid, Vinnie confesses. "You know Kelsey from the bar?" Wes nods. "She has an old RV in the back of her property. My half is in there."

"Does she know it's there?"

"No, I stashed it while she was at work."

"Who else lives with her?"

"Just her kid, but he's usually with the grandmother or at school."

"What's the address?" Wes asks, getting anxious at the thought he might get out of this after all.

"I don't know the address, but it's on the corner of Hardy and Corbin. You can't miss it. The house is a bright blue double-wide, and the RV is in the back."

Wes grabs the phone seated on a small table near the bed. He calls Sean.

"This is Sean."

"He said their shit is in an old RV on Hardy and Corbin."

"Off of Charleston Parkway?"

"Yeah. He said some girl and her kid live there. But the girl is supposed to be at work and the kid at school."

"Okay, Wes, go get Maggie and call me back at fourteen hundred."

"Got it." Wes hangs up and then turns back toward Vinnie. "You better not be bullshitting me, or I swear to God, Vinnie, I'll cut your nose off and bleed you like the fat pig you are ... nice and slow."

A look of true shock flashes across Vinnie's face. Wes has never said anything like that before. But no one has ever threatened him and his wife. Let alone murder one of his family members.

Everything is happening so fast, to Wes he's beginning to lose his ability to think logically. He rushes out of the room. *If the shit ain't there, I'm going to come back and kill him.* He jumps into the old truck to go retrieve Maggie.

CHAPTER 38

WHAT THE FUCK HAPPENED? Vinnie thinks after Wes storms out of the room. Since they were kids, Wes has never acted that way toward him. And outside of playful childhood wrestling matches, Wes has never raised a fist to him, let alone say he'd kill him. Trying to gather up any self-respect he has left, Vinnie lies to himself, *If I weren't so beat down, I would have punched Wes in his mouth for disrespecting me the way he did.*

At the surface level, Vinnie has always thought Wes's love for James's sister has been overboard. Frequently over the years, Wes has chosen to be with Maggie more than his guy friends. If someone were to ask Vinnie his thoughts on their relationship, he would say Wes is pussy-whipped. Grabbing the baggie with his rotting ear, Vinnie is seething now. *Fuck you, Wes, and your uptight wife.*

Needing to get out of this situation, Vinnie contemplates his next actions. Before he does, he needs to clean his conscience. He makes excuses about how he got involved in the first place and blames James for everything. *I can't believe James is dead?*

Vinnie frets. *I have to get the fuck out of this hospital right now.* Vinnie knows, when Wes or the Oklahoma couple come back, he won't be able to talk himself out again.

He looks down at his body. *I'm only wearing a hospital gown with paper-thin pants. And I don't have access to a car right now. If I can get to the parking lot and steal someone's ride, I can get the hell out of Pahrump with my cut.* With everything Vinnie has gone through, he's not leaving town without it.

Struggling to get moving, Vinnie pushes himself off the hospital bed, feeling pain in every joint of his body. A side effect of getting the shit beaten out of you and made to trudge five miles through the desert afterward.

Vinnie's bagged ear is still mind-fucking him too. Besides the physical pain, Vinnie still hasn't come to grips with his ear having been cut off like a scene in a shitty horror movie. A genre of film he will never watch again. Every time he looks at the bloody package, it makes his stomach turn and puts his brain into a frenzy. *I don't know anyone who has lost an ear. Let alone got it back in a sandwich baggie.* Vinnie considers what to do with the dismembered body part. The damn thing looks dead, so getting it reattached is out of the question. He contemplates taking it home and putting it in some sort of jar so he can tell a good story about it. *That's fuckin' stupid.* He quickly disregards the idea. This damn ear is a reminder of how stupid he had been for helping James. *What do I do with it now?* He decides to throw his body part away. He wraps the baggie several times in toilet paper and tosses it in the trash.

With every turn of his head, pain races deep into where his ear used to be. And with Wes driving his knuckles into the tender area, he opened up the stitches, causing the wound to bleed and ooze puss and blood. There is also a rotten odor coming from the injury. The stench reminds Vinnie of the infections he would smell in his pit bull's ears after having them cropped.

I can't deal with those two old rednecks again. They scared the shit out of Vinnie, and he wants no part of them. *I'm better off running.*

Having decided what to do, Vinnie scans the empty hospital room for the shirt and pants he came in wearing. He only finds his shoes, covered with dust and a few drops of his blood. As he bends over to put his shoes on, dizziness falls on him like a ton of bricks with the strength in his legs almost giving out. He stops to regain his balance for a moment. *What the fuck? This is worse than being drunk.* The vertigo is so bad he fights not to throw up. The doc told him this would probably happen. Wes driving his fist into the side of his head didn't help either.

Recalibrating his steps and balance, he carefully bends over and scoops up the raggedy Chuck Taylor tennis shoes under his arm.

Opening the heavy door quietly, Vinnie peeks down the hall in both directions. A few rooms down, a good-looking nurse with curly dark hair and tight-fitting scrubs pushes a cart filled with the same type of clothes she's wearing. Vinnie waits for the nurse to step into one of the rooms, leaving the cart in the hallway. Moving toward the cart, he notices his legs beginning to work again, but the dizziness doesn't let up.

Sneaking past the room the nurse entered, he catches a glimpse of her. She's bent over the bed, pulling on the sheets, making sure they're straight on the mattress. *Nice butt cheeks.* After his quick glance, he checks out the supply cart left in the hallway. He finds two stacks of faded green scrubs. He grabs a set, not wasting time to check the sizes, and continues down the hallway, ducking into a public bathroom.

Finding an empty stall, he enters the small space, latching the door behind him. He collapses on the toilet seat, dropping the scrubs and shoes on the floor. Vinnie notices he's breathing hard. *There's no way I'm this tired from a short walk.* "You need to get your shit together," Vinnie says, stripping off the one-piece hospital gown. Thankfully, they left him in his underwear, so he doesn't have to free-ball when he escapes the hospital. He puts on the scrubs and shoes, takes a deep breath, and stands up. He goes over to the sink and gives himself a once-over in the mirror.

He's shocked at what he sees. His face is painted with bruises and scuff marks. And now with only one ear, his head appears flatter than it was. Even with the bloody gauze wrapped around it. *I look like dog shit.* He runs the water in the sink. Cupping both hands, he catches the water, bringing it to his dry, thirsty mouth. His nerves settle. His breathing coming back to normal.

He splashes water on his face and starts scrubbing the dried blood off his neck. Residuals left over from the wound's leakage. As he is finishing his birdbath, an old man waddles in toward the urinal. He doesn't notice Vinnie, who stays in place until he can hear the old man beginning to piss. The liquid splashing against the porcelain tells Vinnie it's time to go.

Moving past the old man, Vinnie notices he's wearing some sort of ball cap. Vinnie stops for a second, contemplating his missing ear and the blood-soaked bandage covering the area. *Fuck it.* With the old man in midpiss, Vinnie snatches the ball cap off his head like a high school prank. The old man doesn't move an inch. He's only focused on making liquid, slowly. Not until Vinnie puts the stolen ball cap on and is pulling on the bathroom door does the old man mumble something feeble.

Vinnie makes it to the hospital's waiting area with little trouble. The room isn't full. A young couple sits in the corner watching two little boys push toy trucks around on the floor. There is also an elderly woman sitting in a chair; she's about the same age as the old man whom Vinnie took the hat from. Her bent and wrinkled hands twitch as she pushes and pulls pink and white yarn with long metal crochet hooks. No one notices Vinnie, let alone cares that he's leaving. For the first time in his life, this is a good thing.

He escapes through the automatic glass doors.

CHAPTER 39

"MOTHERFUCK!" NOT HAVING SEEN actual daylight for a couple of days, Vinnie's vision is stung by the sun. Plus, the heat from the parking lot asphalt beats against his face without mercy. He knows he needs to steal a car. And that he's going to need some sort of tool, like a screwdriver, to crack open the ignition. Scanning the parking lot, he sets his eyes on an old gray Buick Century station wagon.

Making his way across the parking lot, Vinnie peers through the window to see if there's anything in the cab that will help him get the Buick started. Down on the floorboard he spots an old, greasy toolbox.

There has to be something in there I can use. He first considers busting the window open with his elbow. But he feels physically weak. Plus, he doesn't want to break or cut anything else on his person. He settles on searching for a baseball-size rock from the desert landscape underneath a nearby tree. He's confident he can throw it through the glass. Before he can find a rock, he hears a harsh, familiar voice yell out his name.

"Yo, Vinnie, what's up with you?"

Fuck me. Vinnie's heart pounds hard as he turns around to the voice.

Across from him, Caleb stands a few cars down. His tattooed arms, red hair, and freckles are hard to miss. *I don't need this GI Joe motherfucker getting shitty with me over Wes right now.* Expecting his encounter not to go well with Caleb, Vinnie musters up all the strength he can find. *I've got one punch to knock him out. If I don't, he's going to smash me, bad.*

Fortunately for Vinnie, when he gets completely turned around, the look on Caleb's face tells him he doesn't know about the beef between him and Wes. Instead, he's staring at the top of Vinnie's head with a goofy look on his face.

"You fought in Korea?" Caleb asks.

"What are you talking about, Caleb?"

He points to the hat on top of Vinnie's head. "Yeah, your hat says you're a proud veteran of the Korean War."

Without thinking, Vinnie takes the hat off and looks down at it. Embroidered on the front of the hat are a bunch of military ribbons with the words "Korean War Veteran" in gold letters.

"What the fuck, Vinnie?" Caleb says, staring at the side of his head with a disgusted look. "What the hell happened, man?"

Embarrassed and a bit scared, Vinnie quickly comes up with a story to explain his ear. "Yeah, it's pretty fucked-up. Me and this girl from the bar were doing our thing and I guess her moans got too loud and her fuckin' dog pounced on me."

"You shitting me?" Caleb asks, not completely convinced.

"On my mother's grave. I guess because I was on top of this broad, the dog thought I was hurting its owner, so it literally gnawed my head."

"That's crazy, bro. You're lucky he didn't clip an eye."

"Yeah, you're right. Some old vet saw my head and asked if I wanted his hat to cover my ear, so I took it."

Caleb shakes his head in astonishment.

"So, what brings you down here?" Vinnie asks, trying to change the subject.

"I heard Wes and Maggie are down here."

Can I please catch a break? Vinnie thinks. Faking concern, he asks, "Where did you hear that?"

"You know that cocktail waitress that works with Wes, Samantha?"

"The one with the big ass?"

"Yeah. I go in to play a few hands with Wes, and Sam tells me he ran out in a panic because Maggie is in the hospital."

Without even thinking about his next words, Vinnie blurts out, "Oh, I understand now."

"What?"

"I saw both of them leave a few minutes ago. They weren't clear why they were here. They said Maggie wasn't feeling good."

"Well, shit."

"Yeah, I told them I would catch up with them in a few, but when I got to the parking lot, I realized James took my ride." *I can't believe this shit is coming out of my mouth right now.* Vinnie knows he's on borrowed time. Sooner or later, Caleb is going to hear the real story from Wes and Maggie.

"Well, damn, Vinnie, I can't leave you out here looking like a bloody Korean War medic. Let me give you a ride and we'll go see Wes together."

"Nah, that's not necessary."

"I insist," Caleb says, smiling, but his tone is now more direct.

Before Vinnie can say anything else, he spots Lee driving through the parking lot at a distance, staring right at him, with a cigar dangling from his mouth.

Fuck! Leave with an old friend or lose my other ear? Vinnie considers his options. He shakes his head and accepts the ride from Caleb. "I appreciate it, man. Do you mind if we make a quick stop? I need to pick something up."

"Not a problem."

Once they're inside Caleb's rough-looking pickup truck, Caleb starts in on him. "Wes told me about you and James ripping that guy off."

"What are you talking about?"

Caleb raises his tone. "Don't fuck with me, Vinnie. Me and Wes went over to the guy's house to figure out what was going on."

"You went to Russo's house?"

"Yeah, and I choked a motherfucker out after he hit Wes in the back of the head with a—"

Flashing headlights interrupt Caleb. He looks up. In front of his truck, a tan Crown Vic sits idling with Lee and Amber inside.

Vinnie squirms in his seat. Caleb notices his uneasiness. "Let me guess, Vinnie, they're here for you?"

"Yeah."

Caleb laughs. "And I bet they're the ones who fucked your ear up?" Vinnie only nods, eyes getting watery. "You better tell me right now if you have their shit. If you lie, I'll throw you out of this truck."

"I do."

"And we're going to get it, right?" Vinnie is slow to answer. "You and James sucked Wes into this. You better decide right now if you're going to help Wes and yourself."

Another moment and Vinnie concedes. "Okay, I'll take you to it."

Caleb nods in acknowledgment and moves his truck past the Crown Vic.

Vinnie tries leaning back as far as he can in the truck's bench seat, attempting to hide behind Caleb's body. Turning his head in the opposite direction, Vinnie hears Caleb ask in a pleasant tone, "Can I help you, sir?"

At the sound of the responding voice, Vinnie fights not to piss himself. "As a matter of fact, you can, son. I noticed my friend Vincent get into your truck. I wanted to see if he got the gift we sent him."

Still facing the opposite direction, Vinnie feels Caleb turn toward him.

Vinnie quietly responds, "Yes."

Caleb turns back toward the sedan. "He said he did."

"You know, Vincent never said what happened."

Caleb smirks. "He was ... mauled ... by ... a dog."

Lee and Amber look at each other, letting out a chuckle. "Well, I hope Vincent is okay. I'd hate to see what the dog would do if he didn't get his bone back."

"Yeah, I agree."

Lee and Caleb stare at each other for an awkward moment. Lee breaks the silence. "Well, I'll let you two get back to it." He then turns to Vinnie. "We'll be seeing you soon, Vincent."

The Crown Vic and the truck pull away in opposite directions.

"That motherfucker is going to kill you. If I were you, I would run," Caleb says.

CHAPTER 40

Z IPPING DOWN A RURAL two-lane road, the black Porsche appears out of place. Behind the steering wheel, Sean continues to mentally navigate this cluster fuck of a situation. *Wes is a good kid. But the friends he keeps are total dipshits. I wish he would work with me. This would make this whole thing easier.*

And though the Professor told Sean not to get involved, Sean considers giving both of Wes's friends a dirt nap. *What could he say if I showed up with the dope and cash and got rid of his two problems?* Would his initiative be rewarded? Or would the Professor only worry about Sean disobeying orders? *He likes to keep me on a leash. So did Russo.*

Sean considers Lee and Amber Walker too. With them in town and Wes saying his friend is missing, it's pretty much a done deal. *Fuck him, he had it coming, that mutt dog.*

Sean met the Oklahoma couple once. When he first started working for the Professor as a driver, he was tasked with driving Lee and Amber to Arizona and staying with them for a couple of days. During this time Sean discovered Lee to be a Vietnam tunnel rat turned lawyer turned "fixer." And his wife, Amber, well, a sex-crazed killer. The two men exchanged war stories over glasses of whiskey and took a liking to each other. They never became bosom buddies, but each had a surface-level respect for the other's battlefield experiences.

Pulling up to the corner of Hardy Street and Corbin Lane, Sean spots the blue double-wide Wes told him would be there. In the back of the property, an old run-down RV sits by itself. *So far, so good.* The only problem Sean sees right now is the car in the front driveway. *Somebody is probably home.*

Sean considers a couple of options on how to navigate this challenge. He can walk back to the RV, grab the goods, and leave. *But if the owner comes out and catches me leaving their yard with the packages, they'll probably call the cops. Or worse, confront me, thus making it a physical confrontation.* The other option is to knock on the door and give her some bullshit excuse about why he needs to be in her backyard. *But she'll see my face, which isn't good either.* He contemplates his options for a moment and goes with number two.

Sean strolls up the gravel driveway, knocks on the door, and waits. There is no answer. *Maybe I'll be able to get back there with no problems.* He knocks once more time. But now he hears movement inside the mobile home. *Of course.*

The door slings open. A tall, thin Mexican-looking woman stands in the doorway. The first thing he notices are her breasts and nipples protruding through a translucent tank top. The woman doesn't try to cover them up. *Damn.* She's also wearing black shorts that could pass as underwear. Long, slim legs jet out from the black shorts. He looks at the woman with a smile and notices she's groggy. On what could be a pretty face if done up, heavy eyelids struggle to open. Her hair, though messy, is long and curly. Not a bad-looking woman, if you ask Sean.

"Hello, ma'am, I'm with Valley Electric. We believe something is wrong with your meter."

Sean doesn't know much about electricity. He had an uncle back in Michigan who worked with electrical meters for his local electric company. Uncle Dave ran a bit of a racket with the meters. He would modify them so they didn't spin as much while recording usage. This resulted in a smaller electrical bill for the business. In turn, the business would give Uncle Dave a little monthly kickback from the savings. He never took an amount that would raise any eyebrows. Only enough to cover his weekly bets at the track and a little booze. The kicker to this little scheme was a rubber washer. All he had to do was stick a little washer in the sprockets of the meter and the friction would slow the spinning down.

With limited knowledge of electrical meters, Sean continues his story to persuade this lady to let him in her backyard.

"Like what?" the woman asks in a half-asleep tone.

"To be honest, ma'am, it looks like we've been charging you too much on your bill."

This wakes her up more than Sean likes. "How's that?" she asks.

"Well, there might be some damage to the line running to your meter. I was hoping you would give me permission to come onto your property and take a look. We think the damage is somewhere behind your RV."

"Really? We don't have any power connected back there."

"I'm sure you don't, ma'am. It's probably coming from the property line. All I need to do is get back there and verify there's no exposed wires and run a few tests, and I'll be done."

"Go ahead," the woman says, not giving a shit again.

"Thank you, ma'am. I'll let you know what we find."

With a slight nod, Sleeping Beauty steps back into her house and closes the door, and Sean heads to the back. Moving toward the RV, he notices old and new dog shit all over the ground. Even the dirt smells like piss. *Disgusting.*

The door to the RV is facing away from the main house, which is good. This helps conceal Sean's entry into the run-down recreational vehicle.

He turns the door handle. It's locked. "Not a problem." He pulls out a small pocketknife and pries at the door latch. With little to no trouble, the door releases. Sean goes inside.

The interior space looks like your typical RV. In front are two giant seats for the driver and passenger. In the middle, a small stove, sink, and kitchen table. Along the ceiling are wooden cabinets. And in the back, a small square room with a twin mattress. But instead of the recreational vehicle being clean and comfortable, it's more of a shit box. Extremely dusty, musty, and unwelcoming. Scattered throughout the RV are random boxes and five-gallon paint buckets filled with all sorts of miscellaneous crap.

"Fuck me," Sean says. He doesn't have time to politely go through everything. Instead, he grabs the first box and dumps it on the floor. Old books and baby clothes fall out. Sean's temper grows. He dumps one of the five-gallon buckets. Nails, screws, and other hardware pieces fall to the floor. "Fuck!"

Sean takes the next ten minutes dumping all the boxes, all the buckets, and going through every drawer, cabinet, nook, and cranny. Every unsuccessful dump chips away at his patience. He doesn't find any dope or money. At this point, Sean is only thinking about killing Vinnie himself. *Who cares what the Professor says?*

In a final desperate attempt, the last thing Sean checks is the mattress. He flips it upside down and cuts the old thing open. Sean would be happy to find a five-dollar bag of weed or even a rusted quarter. But he finds nothing. *This cocksucker lied to Wes. Which means he lied to me. Fuck it. I'm going to kill this kid myself.*

Exiting the RV, he storms through the backyard, dodging piles of dog shit covering the ground like Russian land mines in Afghanistan. He hears the back door to the blue mobile home open. In his peripheral vision, he can see the skinny woman come out. He doesn't look at her. She yells at him. "Did you find the problem?"

He yells back over his shoulder, not stopping. "Yeah, I did. There's too much dog shit back here. Clean up your yard, you nasty bitch."

Getting back to his Porsche, he hears some sort of indiscernible noise come from the woman's skinny neck. He starts the engine, slams the transmission into reverse, and steps on the pedal angrily. Gravel rocks kick up as the sports car aggressively backs out. Sean slams the transmission into drive and speeds off. Driving away, he sees the skinny collector of dog shit standing in her front yard flipping him off.

CHAPTER 41

WES PULLS UP TO his house and rushes inside. He hurries down the hallway, calling for Maggie. She must have heard the panic in his voice because she popped her head out of the bedroom as soon as he started calling to her. Seeing his shoes still on, Maggie says, "Wesley, your shoes!"

"Fuck my shoes!"

A stunned and hurtful look falls on Maggie's face.

Wes corrects his tone. "Look, sweetheart, this shit with your brother is worse than I thought. We need to leave, and we need to leave now."

"What are you talking about, Wes?" Maggie says, fear in her voice.

Gently, Wes takes Maggie's face with both hands. Calmly but quickly, he says, "Maggie, please, do what I say. Get a bag and grab a few things for a couple of days. There are people who want to hurt us because of James. Now they think I had something to do with it."

"What ... how?"

Growing impatient and exhausted, Wes releases her face. "I don't know. Taking Vinnie to the hospital. Going to the Russo house. Who fuckin' knows!"

"You only put up cabinets," Maggie says.

"No, Maggie. Me and Caleb snuck back in the house the other night."

"But why?"

"I was trying to figure out how to help your brother. But we're part of it now. That's why I need you to pack your stuff so we can leave in the next few minutes."

Wes hurries over to his nightstand and grabs his Glock 17 Gen3. He press-checks the pistol, making sure there is a round in the pipe. He grabs two magazines loaded with nine-millimeter ammunition. He stuffs the pistol into his waistband and throws the magazines into his makeshift go bag. He catches Maggie staring at him with watery eyes. Before he can say anything to her, the phone rings. Wes rushes down the hallway and picks it up. "Yeah?"

Sean's voice is on the other end. "That motherfucker lied to you. There's no dope or money in the RV."

"Son of a bitch."

"Look, Wes, head out to my place in Crystal."

"You want me to take Maggie to a brothel?"

"There's a VIP suite separated from the rest of the house. I already let Valentina know you were coming."

"Who the hell is Valentina, Sean?"

"She's the madam working right now."

"Doesn't the Professor own those brothels?"

"He does, but he doesn't run them. He doesn't visit any of them either. Hell, he doesn't even know who works them.

Crystal is your best bet. You and Maggie get out there and wait for me. When can you be there?"

"Another five minutes here and twenty minutes to get to Crystal."

"Perfect. I'll call you in the room when I get out there myself. Should be within the hour."

Wes hangs up and sees Maggie staring at him from down the hallway. "Who was that, Wes?"

"It was Sean. He's got a place set up for us in Crystal to lie low. Are you ready?"

Without saying a word, Maggie marches outside and gets into the old work truck. Double-checking the locks to the house, Wes follows. He keeps his head low, knowing where he's taking his wife.

Once they're out of town and on Route 160, tension pulsates off Maggie. Every fidget, every breath, every sniffle worsens as they travel through the barren desert. He tries to comfort her by putting his hand on her thigh, but his gesture is met with a quick swipe of her own.

Every mile marker they pass is a punch to Wes's stomach. He hasn't told her about her father. And he doesn't know when he should. He's afraid of how she's going to react when he does. But right now his only priority is keeping Maggie safe. At least until he can figure this mess out with Sean's help. Wes is confident his old platoon sergeant will come through and plead their case to the Professor. At this point, he's their best chance.

Twenty minutes later, Wes and Maggie arrive at the only road leading them into this dump of a town. *What a shithole. I can't believe people come all the way out here to get laid,* Wes thinks. Entering the dilapidated town, Wes notices a run-down dive bar with several motorcycles in the front. A few overweight biker types stand around the bar's dirt parking lot, not paying much attention to their arrival. He makes a left turn at a sun-bleached sign. It reads Love Patch Brothel, with a giant red arrow pointing the way. *Could the sign be any bigger?* Wes's face begins feeling hot with embarrassment. Maggie looks up at the sign too. This elicits the first words from her since leaving their house.

"Are we going to a brothel?" Maggie asks, irritation in her voice.

No, sweetheart, we're going to be hiding at Disneyland.

They drive past three red single-wide mobile homes stitched together. On display in front of the building is a giant, half-naked Las Vegas showgirl mannequin. Behind the statue is another giant sign that reads Adult Fun All Night Long. *What the hell? Are people who pay for sex blind too?*

"Real classy place." Maggie says.

Wes remains silent.

They finally get to their destination and park. Wes looks over at Maggie and says, "I have to get a key from a girl named Valentina."

"Valentina. How exotic!"

"Do you want to come in with me or stay in the truck?"

"I bet you're excited to go in there."

"Of course not. Sean said—"

Maggie doesn't let him finish. She gets out of the work truck and slams the door shut behind her. Wes takes a moment to gather his thoughts before joining his wife outside. The two walk to the front of the brothel.

The entrance appears to be secure, with a hard metal security door. At to the door is yet another blaring sign that reads Ring Bell for Service. Next to the sign is a red button connected to an intercom speaker. Wes looks at Maggie, who is scowling back at him.

"Ring the bell, Wes."

He follows her instructions. The sound of a fire bell comes from inside the building.

Next, a sultry voice comes over the intercom speaker. "One moment, please. We're getting the girls ready."

Oh shit, they're going to bring out the girls.

The top of Wes's head is on fire.

"This should be fun," Maggie says.

About a minute later, the security door opens and a good-looking blonde in her thirties, wearing a scanty red dress, greets them. "Welcome. Please come in."

Maggie enters the brothel first. Wes drags his feet as he follows.

When they get inside, ten women in lingerie stand in line in front of the married couple. Most of them look to be Wes and Maggie's age. But all of them are different colors and shapes.

Wes tries his best not to stare too long at one girl. Most of them are rough-looking. One woman catches Wes's eye. Not because she's attractive. But because he can see her red wig slipping off her forehead, revealing short blond naps of hair. None of the women are physically fit. The skinny ones have saggy muscle tone. The heavy ones also sag. All of them hide their bodies' imperfections behind cheap, silky material.

Nervous and trying to carefully pick his words, Wes says to the only good-looking woman in the bunch, the blonde who let them in, "We're looking for Valentina."

Her eyes widen. She asks, "You're Sean's friend?"

"Yes, ma'am."

Valentina says to the ten girls on display, "They have business with me, ladies. Thank you." The line of half-naked hookers dissipates. Some jet off to their rooms while others meander away, chatting with each other. The last few hang around, flashing seductive looks at Wes and Maggie. Wes's skin crawls.

Pointing toward some sort of disco-looking bar nearby, Valentina guides the two of them over. Most of the bar is painted shiny white, accented by clear lighting that dangles in nearby corners. All the tabletops are mirrored, and the entire floor is covered in gray shag carpet. Wes notices Maggie taking in the scene. *If she ever gets booked to cater an orgy, she's definitely going to use the '70s porno carpet.*

The three sit at a private area of the bar. Valentina pulls up on the top part of her dress.

I guess she doesn't want me looking at her boobs in front of Maggie. Once settled, Valentina offers each of them a drink, her sultry performance now gone.

"No, thank you," Maggie says, more relaxed than before driving into Crystal. Wes also declines the offer.

"Sean tells me you're an old army buddy of his," Valentina says, handing Wes a brass key and a business card with her name on it.

Wes takes the items. "Yes, ma'am."

"Well, your room is behind this main building. There's a couple of parking spots next to it. You can't see the room or parking area from the main road. It's all out of sight and exceedingly discreet."

"Thank you, ma'am," Wes replies.

"Please stop calling me 'ma'am.' You're making me feel like my mother. Just Val, please."

"Sure thing, Val."

Val guides Wes and Maggie toward a side door leading to the front parking area. Before passing through, Maggie addresses their host, "Val, do you mind if I ask you a question?"

Oh shit, Wes thinks.

"Sure, sweetheart."

Maggie continues. "You are so much prettier than the other girls. Do you do the same type of work?"

A quick burst of laughter comes from Val. "Well, thank you, honey, but no, I don't." Val now leans in closer to Maggie. "I only keep these skanks in line when Sean is gone." Both ladies share a genuine chuckle together. "If you two get bored later on, I can give you a tour."

Wes leaves Maggie no time to answer. "No, thank you. I appreciate the offer."

Val gives Wes and Maggie a polite nod and closes the door behind them.

Once in front of the suite, Wes pushes the brass key into the doorknob, unlocks the latch, and takes a deep breath. *I can't deal with any more freaky sex shit.* He pushes through.

Inside, he looks around. *Thank goodness.* The space looks like a normal hotel suite. There's a living area with a couch and television. In the corner sits a desk with a phone. Separated from the living area, the bedroom has a king-size bed covered in a thick brown quilt. Inside the bathroom, multicolored tile set in a diamond pattern cover the walls and shower.

Wes shuts the door behind them. A little of the tension subsides, but not much. Maggie washes her face in the bathroom sink. Wes turns on the air-conditioning and plops down on the couch. He tries to take a moment to relax before Sean calls.

CHAPTER 42

V INNIE'S DEMEANOR IS OVERTLY nervous as he rides in Caleb's truck. It appears to Caleb every street they cross, Vinnie's head darts around like he's looking for someone. Especially after running into the older couple at the hospital. When they pass a couple of cars, Vinnie throws his head back like he's trying to hide. "You all right?" Caleb asks several times. Vinnie can only nod.

As he turns his truck onto a desolate side street, something hard smashes his rear end, throwing both young men forward in the cab. Caleb quickly glances behind him. It's the Crown Victoria from the hospital. "What the fuck, Vinnie! It's that old couple."

Vinnie turns around to look. He screams at the top of his lungs, "Drive, Caleb! Drive!"

Hearing the fear in Vinnie's scream, Caleb takes his cue and punches the gas. The truck lunges. Within seconds, both truck and sedan are traveling over sixty miles an hour on a two-lane road. With both windows down in the truck's cab, the wind coming in makes it hard to communicate, but Caleb tries. He yells over the noise, "This old bastard wants you bad."

"Shit, here they come, man!" Vinnie says.

Within moments, the Crown Vic is neck and neck with the truck, driving in the oncoming lane. Caleb sees Amber with her long red hair blowing wildly in the wind, pointing a shotgun at him.

Lee, who is driving the sedan with an excited smile on his face, leans forward. He shouts over both vehicles' screaming engines, "Looks like we got a good old-fashioned car chase!" He tells Amber, "Blow 'em a kiss, baby."

Amber smiles, charges the shotgun, and lets off a round. Caleb ducks as the top of the truck's door frame smashes, shredding the cab's headliner.

"Holy shit!" Caleb says.

"They're going to kill us, man!"

"Be cool Vinnie!"

"How the fuck am I supposed to be cool when they almost shot your head off?"

The Crown Vic increases its speed, pulling up farther ahead. Amber is now hanging outside her passenger window. *She has a good grip on her shotgun, but nothing for precision shooting,* Caleb thinks. She steadies the business end of the shotgun at the truck's windshield. Another round flies at the truck. Caleb jerks the truck to the left. The blast smashes the middle of the truck's windshield. Instinctively, Caleb eases off the gas, creating space between them and the tan sedan.

"What the fuck, man!" Vinnie yelps again like a little bitch. "That almost hit me!" He jerks an imaginary steering wheel in front of him, "Turn away from the bullets, man! Turn away."

His gesture makes Caleb laugh out loud. But he notices bits of broken glass in his own mouth. *I guess that was pretty fucked-up—my bad.*

With the Crown Vic now in front of the truck about fifty yards, Caleb points to the glove box and tells Vinnie, "Open it." He does.

Waiting for Vinnie to get the hint, which he doesn't, Caleb tells him, "Give it to me." Vinnie reaches inside and pulls out a black Glock 19. "Hold on to it," Caleb orders. He jerks the wheel to the right, making a hard turn down another desolate street. The tires squeal and smoke. *I have to get the driver.* He steers the truck into the oncoming lane, holding his position.

On cue Vinnie says, "You're on the wrong side of the road!"

Grabbing the pistol from him, Caleb says, "I know, Vinnie! Shut the fuck up and keep your head down!" Caleb brings the pistol close to his lap.

With a quick glance behind him, Caleb sees the Crown Vic turn onto the same street. And like Caleb wanted, the sedan is coming up the right lane. He slows the truck down a pinch so the sedan can catch up.

"Why are you slowing down?" Vinnie asks, panic in his voice.

The Crown Vic pulls up to the passenger-side window of the truck. Lee shouts at Caleb with a smile, "Damn, son, your truck is holding up pretty good." He pats the top of his steering wheel. "Doesn't Ford make great vehicles? I love my Crown Vic."

Caleb grins. He shouts back, "Yeah! They do!" And with the speed of a snake, Caleb lifts his pistol, points it out the passenger-side window, crossing Vinnie, and takes aim on Lee.

In an instant, Lee's eyes open wide, his smug smile disappears. He slams on his brakes. Caleb lets off five or six rounds.

The sounds of snapping bullets, breaking glass, and screeching tires ring out.

Vinnie howls with Caleb shooting around him. The brass casings from the Glock eject, peppering Vinnie's chest. *Maybe that will back them off, but probably not.* Caleb's assumption is right.

The Crown Vic speeds back up to the truck and once again the two vehicles are window to window. Caleb notices Lee is steering with his left hand and holding a large chrome revolver with his right.

Again, Lee yells to Caleb, this time with disgust in his voice. Lee asks, "Was that a nine-millimeter? Pussy round if you ask me."

Lee launches a round through the driver-side door of the truck. It enters the cab, hitting the rearview mirror, which explodes all over Caleb and Vinnie. A through-and-through hole is left in the windshield where the mirror used to be. The noise alone from the heavy revolver causes Caleb to flinch and duck his head.

Without looking up, Caleb can hear Lee, "That's a forty-four, you little shit. In Oklahoma, we call it a man's gun."

Caleb pops back up into view with his Glock pointing out the window. But Lee has already backed off. He is now in the blind spot of the truck. Completely out of Caleb's field of fire.

Another loud explosion from the revolver rings out. The rear window to the truck shatters. The explosion of more glass forces Caleb and Vinnie to drop their heads again. With their heads down, another gunshot followed by the sound of a loud pop is heard. The truck starts to drag on the road, veering to the right. *He shot my tire out. Fuck!*

Caleb smashes the brakes, quickly pulling the truck over. When it comes to a complete stop, he bursts out of the truck, pistol up, searching for a target. *I'm not dying in some metal box.* When he gets his bearings, he sees the Crown Vic still traveling up the road. He waits for a moment, watching for brake lights, but never sees them. The tan sedan continues driving before taking a side street several miles up.

Caleb wanders around his truck, examining the damage. He looks over at Vinnie, who is damn near petrified in the seat. He has broken glass all over him.

Vinnie looks back at Caleb, fear and relief on his face.

"No more bullshit, Vinnie. Where's their stuff?"

"Just take me to my grandmother's house," Vinnie says, lips quivering. "That's where it's at."

Up the road, Lee pulls his Crown Vic over. Having shot the tire out of Caleb's truck and watching it drag to the side of the road thrilled him. Lee and Amber let out a full belly laugh, staring at each other like they came off a roller coaster. "Gosh damn, woman, that was fun!" Lee says.

"Poor Vinnie was so scared. Especially when the front windshield exploded in his face," Amber says, still chuckling,

"Amber, my love, you are a downright surgeon with your shotgun."

"Well, thank you, honey."

Lee hops out of the sedan and moves around his prized possession. He counts five bullet holes on the driver's side of the vehicle. One lodged in the front fender. *No real damage.*

Two more bullets penetrating through the front door into the seat, barely missing him. *That one was close.* And one through the back door into the backseat. Whistling, Lee says, "Woo-we! That ginger boy had a little fight in him. Has to be prior military."

"What do you expect, darling? Us redheads are dangerous," Amber says.

"Yes, you are."

"I wish we could have finished," Amber says, pouting playfully.

"You and I both. But we have a meeting, and we can't be late. We'll be wrapping this up real soon."

CHAPTER 43

WES HASN'T HAD HIS eyes closed for five minutes when Maggie asks him. "So, are you going to tell me the entire truth now, Wesley?"

I can't blame her. I'd freak out too if she ran into the house telling me to grab a handful of things so we can hide in the back of a brothel in the middle of the desert.

Opening his eyes, Wes pats the open spot on the couch next to him, signaling her to come sit down. She does. "No questions till the end, okay?" Wes says.

Maggie agrees.

He takes a deep breath before recounting all the events leading up to them going into hiding.

Halfway through his explanation, Maggie interrupts. "This is a joke, right?"

He politely puts a finger up as a reminder to their "no questions" agreement. "I asked you to let me finish, and no, Maggie, this isn't a joke."

"Fine," Maggie says.

Wes presses forward. "The couple showed up at the casino this morning and sat at my table." His hands shake. His throat tightens. "These two motherfuckers sat right there in front of me and played a hand. Then the old man told me he only got half of their shit back from James before going their 'separate ways.' After that, they said they were going to hurt you if I didn't get the other half back from Vinnie."

Wes is almost in tears, thinking about life without Maggie.

Maggie's face softens for the first time. She caresses the side of his face. "You're not lying."

"No, Maggie, I'm not. These sick fucks cut Vinnie's ear off, brought it to the casino in a plastic bag, and threw it on the table in front of me. They didn't care one bit if anyone was watching. And the way they were talking ..." He takes a pause. "I really think they killed your brother."

Tears run down Maggie's face. Wes gives her a moment to process all the information. Through sobs, she asks, "Why are you involved? You didn't rob anybody."

"No, I didn't. The only connection I can think of is your dad sending us to Russo's place for the install job. And from that, they're connecting me with James and Vinnie."

Hearing this, Maggie asks about her father. "Is my dad in trouble, Wesley?"

Wes can't hide his reaction for long. Tears well in his eyes now.

Maggie can see something is wrong. Through her own tears, she commands the answer. "Tell me, Wes."

One contraction of sorrow escapes the inside of Wes's chest. For the man who had been like a father to him. He brings himself under control and says to his wife, "Your father is dead, Maggie. They killed him."

A stunned look forms on Maggie's face. Wes can see her mentally processing this statement. After making sense of what she's heard, Maggie cries heavily.

"How do you know that, Wes?" she asks through deep moans and tears.

Wes grabs her close and pulls her into his embrace. Her head rests on his chest as water continues to exit her face. They hold each other for a moment, crying in each other's arms for their father.

But suddenly, Maggie bolts straight up to her feet. Her face still wet. But all crying ceased. Wes stares at her, confused by her reaction.

She snatches the truck keys off the desk and heads for the door.

At first, Wes tries to gently stand in Maggie's way. But this doesn't deter her. "Get out of my way, Wes! I want to see my dad."

"You can't, baby; it's too dangerous. We need to stay here."

"Fuck you, Wes! I'm going to see my father! Where is he?"

Her little frame gets heavier with every push against Wes toward the door. Her persistence causes him to grip her tighter by the arms. He tries not to hurt her.

Realizing she can't get to the door, she kicks at his shins and starts biting his hands.

What the hell, Maggie! Wes has never seen his wife like this before. She isn't letting up with her attacks. One of her bites is painful enough to cause Wes to release one wrist.

With her free hand, she whales on Wes with a hammer fist, not realizing she is holding the truck keys.

Wes does his best to block and dodge. "Please, Maggie, stop. It's not safe."

Not relenting with her untrained strikes, she yells, "I don't care! I want my dad!"

Nothing Wes is doing is working.

The phone in the room rings.

The sound distracts Wes. He looks at the phone for only a moment. Before he can look back at Maggie, jagged metal keys crash down on his face. The strike hitting both his upper cheek and the side of his nose. Pain surges through his face. He sees black for a moment. Instinctually, he grabs Maggie hard by the arms. Roughly and violently, he swings Maggie around, smashing her into the wall, knocking the air and the fight out of her body.

Oh shit! I didn't mean to, baby.

Ringing phone.

Not completely back under control, Wes pins her arms against the wall and pries the keys from her hand.

The married couple are nose-to-nose now. Panting in each other's face. Again, Wes pleads with her. His tone mixed with anger and sorrow. "Please, Maggie, stop!"

Ringing phone.

Wes slowly lets Maggie's arms go. Her posture loosens in defeat.

Ringing phone.

Lethargically, Maggie staggers past Wes. Slowly, she lies down on the bed, her back toward him.

The phone continues to ring. Wes finally picks it up. Somberly, he answers, "Yeah?"

Sean's voice is on the other end. "I'm here."

"Did you talk to him?"

"I did. He said he'll meet you at the opera house in Amargosa."

"In Amargosa? Why out there?" Wes asks. Energy finally coming back into his voice.

"I don't know, Wes. He likes to have his meetings out there."

"Okay. What time?"

"Sixteen hundred."

"All right, I'll be out in five minutes."

"Roger that."

Wes hangs up the phone. He's exhausted and regretful for what happened. "Sean set up a meeting with his boss at four. It sounds like we'll be able to work this out. I need you to stay here until I get back."

"If you get back," Maggie says.

"Sean is going with me, so I should be good." Wes heads toward the door. "Are you okay?"

Maggie doesn't respond.

Wes chokes down tears. Through a cracked voice, he asks, "Is the baby ... okay?"

"I hope so."

Her response amplifies the shame Wes is already feeling.

"I love you, Maggie."

She doesn't respond.

"I'm going to fix this."

Still nothing. Wes leaves the suite, closing the door behind him gently.

CHAPTER 44

O UTSIDE, SEAN IS WAITING by the old work truck, smoking a cigarette. He offers Wes one.

Putting the cigarette in his mouth, Wes hears a loud metallic *ping* sound. A soft flame shoots from a high-end DuPont lighter guided by Sean's hand. Wes places the cigarette in the flame and takes a deep drag. "I haven't smoked a cigarette since Africa," Wes says.

"I don't blame you. This is some deep shit you're in." Something on Wes's face draws Sean's attention. "What the hell happened to you?" he asks.

"Maggie got pretty crazy when I told her that her dad is dead."

Sean shakes his head remorsefully. "That's understandable."

"So, what's the plan after we get to the opera house?"

Sean shakes his head again, taking his last drag on the cigarette before throwing it to the ground. "You're going out there on your own."

Wes panics. "Alone? I can't go alone; I don't even know this guy! And what about Maggie? I have to keep her safe."

"Look, Wes, this is probably your best chance. The Professor doesn't meet with just anyone. You're lucky even to be meeting with him in person. He's guaranteed you safe passage, so those two crazy country fucks won't be bothering you. And between you and me, I don't think he believes you had anything to do with it. I told the Professor you're a working stiff and have always steered clear of any illegal activities. He only wants to assert his power, and if you offer to help find your buddy Vinnie, which shouldn't be too hard, he'll give you a pass."

"You think so?" Wes asks.

"I know so. Look, it's awful what happened to Maggie's old man." Sean makes the Catholic sign of the cross, touching his forehead, heart, and then left and right shoulders. "As things go for your fucked-off brother-in-law, we can only assume he won't be found. And I say good riddance to the cocksucker. Putting you in the middle of this. We'll find Vinnie and the shit he stole and put a beating on that one-eared freak."

"That's all it takes, huh?" Wes asks, still doubtful.

"Pretty much."

"What about Maggie?"

Sean looks back at the front door of the suite. "What about her? I'll stay here until you get back. I've got a little paperwork to deal with, anyway."

Wes contemplates all the information for a moment. Taking a final drag from the cigarette, he unlocks the door to the truck.

"Wes, I know you've got a lot going on right now. Are you sure you don't want to crew up with me? It could help with your sit-down with the Professor."

"I sincerely appreciate everything you've done, Sergeant. But I don't want to make a commitment I can't keep. Especially with Maggie being pregnant now."

Sean freezes at the announcement. Something sad sweeps over his face. But finally a grin emerges. He hugs Wes. "Congrats, brother."

"Thank you."

Sean holds his young soldier by the shoulders for another long moment. He opens the truck door for him. Wes hops in.

"Are you strapped?" Sean asks.

"Yeah, of course."

Sean shakes his head and reaches out. "Give it to me. You don't want to go up there with a gun. If they search you, which they will, and you have a gun with you, they'll take it as a threat and will shoot you on the spot—trust me."

Reluctantly, Wes hands his Glock to him.

"Now get out of here," Sean says. "Get back on 160, go west on 372, and ride for thirty minutes over the California border. You'll run smack dead into the opera house."

Wes nods. "Got it," and drives away.

CHAPTER 45

TWENTY MINUTES AFTER THEIR skirmish with the Oklahoma couple and a hasty tire change, Caleb and Vinnie pull up to a fashionably designed stick-built home. The house has a redbrick facade, natural green grass, and a concrete driveway. "This is your grandmother's house?" Caleb asks.

"Yeah," Vinnie says, hopping out of the truck and heading toward the side of the house.

Who would bring heat to their grandmother's home? thinks Caleb as he follows Vinnie.

They go into the backyard through a side gate.

This is nice, Caleb thinks, scanning the immaculate outdoor space. A large built-in pool encircled by decorative concrete sits in the middle of the yard. Behind the pool is a small house about the size of a double-car garage with white French doors and several rosebushes in the front.

"Who lives there?" Caleb asks, pointing to the small structure.

Seeming to still be out of it, Vinnie says, "Uh … no one. My grandmother uses it to throw parties in the summer. It helps keep the mess in one area."

Caleb nods in appreciation.

They continue toward the main house, coming to a covered patio area. Built within the patio is a giant outdoor kitchen. There's a large, shiny grill, a refrigerator, and a pizza oven all covered in Spanish tile. For added entertainment, mounted to one wall is a television surrounded by outdoor seating. "Your grandma's house is nice, bro."

Vinnie doesn't respond. Rather, he opens one of the steel doors under the grill and pulls out a key hidden inside.

At the back door of the main house, Vinnie lets them in. A beeping alarm chirps. Vinnie punches the code on the keypad, turning the system off.

They walk through the kitchen area and into a large, open living room.

"Hang out here. I'm going to jump in the shower real quick."

"The fuck you are, Vinnie," Caleb says, irritation in his voice. "You said you were going to show me what the fuck is going on. It's time. And you better not hold back."

Defeated, Vinnie nods in agreement and trudges down a hallway into one of the back rooms. Caleb can hear what sounds like a closet door opening and a few boxes rustling around. Another couple of seconds and Vinnie comes out with a blue laundry bag over his shoulder. The bag appears to be full. But not with clothes.

Back in the kitchen, Vinnie plops the bag on top of the table with a thud.

"That doesn't sound like laundry," Caleb says.

"It's not."

They stare at each other. Vinnie's hand still on the bag.

He doesn't want to show me. Caleb can see it in Vinnie's face. This causes Caleb to second-guess his decision to know. He gathers his confidence.

"Come on, man, show me what this is all about," Caleb says, overwhelmed with curiosity.

Saying nothing, Vinnie takes a deep breath. He dumps the bag onto the kitchen table.

Five bundles of green paper fall out with two brick-size packages wrapped in brown paper.

Caleb stares at the contents sprawled out on the table. It takes only a second for him to recognize the bundles of cash. He remains calm. He grabs one of the brown packages and examines it carefully. It's relatively heavy but firm.

"Cocaine," Vinnie says.

"What the fuck, Vinnie!"

Vinnie matches his volume, thumbing the cash bundles. "I know."

"How much cash is here?"

"Fifty K."

Caleb's eyes jolt to Vinnie, who has a smirk on his face.

"So, exactly how did you get all of this?"

Vinnie pulls a chair out from under the kitchen table and sits down. Caleb does the same.

"Me and James ripped off some guy we were installing cabinets for. Originally, it was James's idea, but my dumb ass got involved."

Caleb's thoughts immediately go to Wes after hearing about the cabinet install.

Vinnie continues. "The only reason they're going after Wes and Maggie is that Wes took me to the hospital." Vinnie's eyes then narrow on Caleb. "And because you and him went to the Russo house."

Dread and anger fill Caleb's chest. Dread that Wes and his wife are in real trouble. And anger that Vinnie and James got the two of them sucked into this.

My boy isn't the best gunfighter. He's good enough on high ground with a squad-size element. But taking on two killers by himself while trying to keep Maggie safe ... he might really be fucked.

The kitchen becomes still. Worried now, Caleb touches the pistol tucked in his waist. "Did you smoke this Russo guy?" he asks cautiously.

"No!" Vinnie says.

"What about James?"

Vinnie shakes his head. "Honestly, I don't know, man. We left together, but James went back. But I never saw him kill anyone."

Makes sense, Caleb thinks. "Yeah, seeing how scared you were today, James would be the one to pull a trigger."

Vinnie snaps back, rage seeping from his words. "Look, Caleb, I know you're supposed to be a badass sniper and all, but those country fucks cut my ear off."

Continuing with his sarcasm, almost lecturing Vinnie like a child, Caleb asks, "So, why did they take your ear?"

"To make a point, I guess."

Caleb shrugs. "You can't blame them. So James has the other half?"

Fear creeps into Vinnie's voice. "I don't know anymore. I know he did, but I think they killed him."

"What are you going to do now?" Caleb asks.

"Take this dope and money and get out of town."

Another surge of anger races through Caleb. "The hell you are, Vinnie. You ain't leaving town and expecting Wes to eat this shit sandwich."

For the first time today, Vinnie tries to act like a man in charge. He hops up out of his chair, his chest puffed out. This doesn't faze Caleb. *What a joke!*

"They took my ear, and you expect me to leave empty-handed? Fuck you, Caleb! I'm sorry about Wes and Maggie, but those two are on their own."

Another dose of rage stabs Caleb in the chest. Now his voice rises. "Sit the fuck down, Vinnie, and quit talking tough! You're a bitch! I know it and you know it!"

Vinnie doesn't back down. Instead, he grabs the dope and cash and tries stuffing it back into the blue laundry bag.

Caleb pulls his pistol from his waistband and points it at Vinnie's face. "Sit down."

Vinnie complies, shrinking back into the kitchen chair. "What are you going to do, Caleb?"

"Oh ... I got a plan."

CHAPTER 

FINISHING A QUICK BUSINESS call, Sean ponders Wes on the road alone and why Maggie is understandably upset. Looking at his watch, he decides it is time to check in on her.

At the suite, he knocks on the door, trying not to be too loud. Maggie opens it. Her precious face is splotchy, her eyes, swollen and red.

Attempting to be charming, he says, "Hey there, beautiful."

A slight smirk escapes Maggie's face as she rolls her eyes in embarrassment. "I look like trash, Sean." Then a confused look. "Weren't you supposed to go with Wesley?"

"He wanted me to stay here and keep an eye on you. Especially with everything that's happening."

"Honestly, Sean, I don't know what's really going on. Can you tell me anything?" She asks, her voice shaky.

"Of course. I don't think we should discuss this out here in the doorway."

Maggie nods in agreement, opening the door wider.

Closing the door behind them, Maggie says, "Thank you so much for helping us. I know Wes trusts you very much."

"It can't be easy for you, having to hide behind a brothel."

"That's putting it lightly, Sean." They both chuckle for a moment. Maggie sits herself at the foot of the bed. Sean takes a place on the couch.

"So, what questions do you have? I will answer them the best I can," Sean says.

"Wes said my brother and Vinnie robbed some guy, and that's why there are people after us."

Not wanting to get into the complexities of the situation, Sean keeps his answer simple. "Yes, this is true, Maggie."

"Wes said he thinks my brother is dead because he stole drugs and money from some man he did a job for."

Sean takes a deep breath, choosing his words carefully. "I don't know for sure ... but yes, most likely he has been dealt with."

"Dealt with!" Maggie says. "What does that mean?"

Sean lowers his tone and says somberly, "You and I both know what that means."

Maggie continues to cry. "What about my dad?"

"I don't know much about your dad's situation, but—"

Sean pauses as he hears a car pulling into the rear parking spot outside. He pulls back the drapes. A tan Crown Victoria is parked. Sean looks back at Maggie and says, "I know who can answer that for you."

CHAPTER 47

W ES IS ABOUT FIFTEEN minutes from the old opera house past the California-Nevada border. Over and over, he rehearses in his head what he wants to say to the Professor. He takes into account the Professor is older and won't take kindly to a twenty-five-year-old kid running his mouth at him. But nobody respects a rollover either.

I appreciate you making time to speak with me.

Sean said you're reasonable and fair.

If my brother-in-law stole from you, I understand why you dealt with him.

Wes also considers what he'll say if the Professor wants him to kill Vinnie. Wes isn't sure if he's willing to commit to that. *I'm willing to help you find Vinnie.*

But if anything were to happen to Maggie or their unborn child, Wes knows in his heart he would burn the entire valley down and die doing it. *Sir, with all respect, I'm not a tough guy, but if someone comes after my wife, I'd be put in a corner.*

A healthy dose of fear remains with Wes too. A feeling he has always been familiar with. But with no gun and no backup, *I'm a lamb going into the lion's den.* If he were back in Mogadishu, he would at least have some white phosphorus or high explosive rounds. *I'd flatten this opera house with the Professor inside.*

But he's not in Africa, and he doesn't have a gun, let alone artillery or mortar rounds. So now he has to rely on his brains and wit.

Enough of the dramatics. I need to stay focused on my task. I'm going to have this meeting and be done with all *this bullshit.*

Wes also considers leaving Pahrump if he can get out of this unscathed.

It's about 3:50 p.m. when Wes pulls into the run-down opera house. Giving the property a quick scan, he notices a small diner occupied by a few patrons on the south end of the parking lot. Connecting the diner to the actual opera house are twenty hotel rooms. Each marked with its own metal number hanging off the door. Wes observes little movement from the rooms. There are two cars parked in the otherwise empty lot. None of them look like anything a crime boss would drive. *Employee vehicles?*

Wes considers positioning the truck closer to the opera house itself. He dismisses the idea. He doesn't like being in the direct line of fire. The other disadvantage would be having little space to maneuver if need be.

The middle of the abandoned parking lot, where he would have zero cover, is completely out.

His last option is parking closer to the diner. God forbid this meeting takes a shit on Wes with bullets raining down on his head. But if it does, he'll need to get off the property fast. His chances will be better using the walkway and brick pillars to cover his egress. *I'm better on foot than stuck in the truck.*

After parking near the diner, Wes gets onto the concrete pathway that follows all the hotel rooms to the opera house. The concrete is old, cracked, and weathered, as are the old stucco and paint on the walls. Moving down the pathway, Wes watches every door and window for movement. He sees none. Concerned about the time, he picks up the pace and makes it to the main entrance of the opera house.

The door handle reminds him of those you'd see on an old church, where you press down with your thumb and push. But when he does, nothing budges. "Fuck me," Wes says. He knocks. No response. "What the hell, man?" Getting desperate, he hurries around the building, looking for another entrance.

Every step he takes, Wes's tactical bearing unfurls. He scrambles to find a way in. Eventually, he comes across another door on the north end of the building. It's a typical door with an ordinary doorknob. Wes turns the handle. It gives way with a little squeak. He edges in.

Immediately, he notices a light inside the opera house about twenty feet in front of him. He stumbles at first on a staircase three steps high. Finally, he gets his footing, heads up the short staircase, and ends up on a wooden floor. He traverses slowly toward the light and makes out what looks like costumes hung from metal racks. Many of the costumes are fluffy and colorful. Looking left, Wes finally figures out that he's on the backstage of the opera house. Now oriented to the inside of the building, he follows the dark, heavy curtains to the center of the stage. Getting past the curtains, he sees the entire opera house in all its glory.

At first glance, it reminds him of the old movie theaters on the marine base his grandfather used to take him to. Red folding chairs, row by row, line the inside of the house. Low-accent lighting shoots from the side walls, illuminating odd paintings of old English royalty looking down at him. If he weren't here to negotiate for his and Maggie's life, this would be an interesting place to check out. But because of the context of the meeting, the painted royalty staring down on him makes the whole situation worse. *Is this why the Professor wanted to meet here?* Wes decides to plant his ass at center stage where he can see all the exits and still be visible to anyone who comes in. *All right, motherfucker.*

CHAPTER 48

I N THE PRIVATE PARKING area of the Love Patch Brothel, the tan Crown Victoria sits idling.

Still inside the suite with Maggie, Sean looks at his watch. *Wes should be in Amargosa by now.* With a calm demeanor, he signals for Maggie to come outside.

With a confused look, Maggie doesn't move.

In the parking lot, Sean can see Maggie looking at him through the door's threshold. He beckons her to follow him. "You want to know what happened to your father. I can show you if you want."

Hesitant, Maggie agrees.

Exiting the suite, she and Sean move toward the Crown Vic, where the Oklahoma couple are standing, both displaying their own sadistic smile. Lee introduces himself to Maggie with genuine enthusiasm.

"Well, hello there, Maggie. It's nice to see you again." He points to Amber, who is next to him. "And you remember my wife."

It doesn't take long for Maggie to remember meeting the two at her father's shop. *These two animals killed my dad.*

Smiling now, Sean watches Maggie's eyelids flutter and her stance sway. She finally straightens up and points at Lee. "You're the one who killed my father!"

Lee lowers his head a little, kicking at the gravel under his boots. He takes his black cowboy hat off his head and puts it on his chest. "Well, Maggie … yes … I did. And let me say, it wasn't one of my prouder moments. He was a fine man. A good strong man."

"*We* … killed her father, honey," Amber says, reminding her husband it was a joint effort.

Apologetic, Lee turns toward his wife. "Why, yes, sweetheart, you are correct." He turns back toward Maggie. "My wife and I did, in fact, take Gary's last breath."

"You son of a bitch!" Maggie screams at Lee.

Lee corrects her. "Whoa, young lady. My mother was a saint. And besides, if you want to slice this pie evenly, your dipshit brother killed your father by being a thief."

"And you know where James is?" Maggie asks.

Lee and Amber look at each other and laugh. This time Amber speaks. "Oh, sweetie, he's better off where he is."

"Where is he?" Maggie asks, yelling and almost hysterical.

Amber directs a question at Sean. "What do those Italian mobsters say?" Sean shakes his head, not knowing the answer. She continues. "Something about fishes?"

Realizing what Amber is referring to, Sean offers his answer. "Oh, sleeps with the fishes." He turns toward Maggie, who is shaking with rage and fear, staring back at him in shock. "What this lovely lady is saying is, your brother is sleeping with the fishes." Sean lets out a genuine snicker, thinking Amber's comment is funny. His laughter grows. "The thing is, Maggie, the only fish I've ever seen in Pahrump are the ones in the aquariums inside the Terrible's casino."

Now Sean addresses the entire group. "Can you imagine getting yourself a little buffet on a Sunday morning, and you look over and see this head floating around inside the glass aquarium?"

Everyone except Maggie bursts into deep laughter. Sean continues. "His face would be all bloated and chewed up by the fish." Everyone except Maggie laughs wholeheartedly.

Maggie attempts to run back toward the suite. But Sean is quickly on her, catching Maggie by the top of her hair. His fingertips grab on to her scalp, yanking her backward and dragging her toward the Crown Vic. She screams in pain, kicking. "Where do you want her?" Sean asks.

Lee, pops open the trunk to the Crown Vic and says, "Inside if you don't mind fine, sir."

Sean lifts Maggie up by her jaw and tries to press her into the trunk. But she offers unexpected resistance. Sean answers her defiance with a hard punch to her stomach. She folds over his fist, air rushing from her body.

She looks up at him, tears in her eyes. Through wet sobs and snot-filled sniffles, she asks, "Why are you doing this, Sean? Wes trusts you. He loves you!"

"Fuck you, Maggie, you pretentious little shit. Wes has always had his head so far up your skinny ass that he forgot how to be a man. Busting his balls every time he called you when we were overseas. What kind of woman does that? I'll tell you what kind, Maggie ... a selfish one. And now he doesn't want to work with me because it will upset you."

Sean grabs her by the throat and squeezes. Maggie gasps for air. "Now get in the fucking trunk."

Not wanting to experience any more physical punishment, she follows his orders and falls back into the Victorian tomb. Sean slams the trunk lid closed.

Lee doesn't appreciate that. "Whoa! Have a little respect for my vehicle, sir."

"It's obvious he has mother issues," Amber says.

Sean doesn't respond. Instead, he gives Lee a piece of paper with a phone number on it. "This is the direct number to the suite. He should be back within the hour."

Lee takes the paper. "Well, nice working with you again. Hopefully, someday the Professor will gift you with one of his high-end lighters too. Seems like you've about earned one."

"Maybe," Sean says. His jaw clenches ever so slightly.

The Crown Vic starts to drive away when Valentina comes out of her office and calls to Sean, "Someone is on the phone for you."

CHAPTER 49

K EEPING VINNIE AT GUNPOINT, Caleb digs through his own wallet. He finds a business card for the Love Patch Brothel. Sean always said that if Caleb needed to get a hold of him fast, call there first. So he does. Once he's on the phone, the other end rings twice before a seductive-sounding woman answers. Caleb asks for Sean. She takes his name and tells him to wait a moment, putting Caleb on hold.

Another minute, and Sean asks, "Caleb?"

"I'm with our jerk-off friend who has a bunch of cash and a couple of bricks of dope."

"Where are you right now?" Sean asks. His tone is urgent. Subconsciously, this doesn't resonate well with Caleb.

"South end of town," Caleb says. "Look, Sean, some old man and woman chased us down in my truck and we dumped rounds at each other about an hour ago. Then my dipshit friend said they want to hurt Wes and Maggie too. So I figured I'd call you to come grab their shit, get it back to your boss, and smooth things out for Wes."

"That sounds like a solid plan of action. I'm coming right now. Shouldn't take me more than thirty minutes," Sean says, his voice calmer now. This calms Caleb too.

Caleb gives Sean the address and they hang up. After the call, Caleb looks over at Vinnie, still sitting in the chair, defeated. Caleb relaxes his posture by placing the pistol to his side. Not wanting to let his guard down too much, he keeps Vinnie at a safe distance. *In case he makes a last-ditch effort to run with the dope and cash.*

Vinnie asks, "And what about me, Caleb? What happens to me?" The question stirs up a bit of sympathy in Caleb.

"Hopefully, my buddy will work things out for everyone."

Vinnie chuckles. He, James, Wes, and Caleb all grew up together. And Vinnie has always been kind of the follower in the group. And yes, Caleb knows how squeamish he was during all the shooting. *I wouldn't, but most people would probably freeze up after having their ear cut off, chased in a car, and shot at.* Having fought in Mogadishu himself, Caleb knows most Hollywood movies portraying combat are bullshit. And most people will never have to deal with the harsh reality of war.

The problem here is, though, Caleb loves Wes and Maggie. And he and Wes came up through the ranks together. They have dealt with a lot worse than a couple of rounds shot from a sedan. *If Vinnie asks questions where my loyalty lies more, it will always be with Wes.* Caleb and Wes have gone through and have seen too much together. *Vinnie can piss up a rope for all I care. Especially if he's willing to throw Wes under the bus.*

CHAPTER 50

S ITTING ON THE EDGE of the old wooden stage, Wes struggles to stay focused on the task at hand. Over and over, he rehearses in his head everything the Professor may say or ask.

This opera house itself is eerily quiet. Wes is not wearing a watch, so he doesn't know the exact time, but he estimates he's been at the opera house for at least ten minutes. *Where the hell is he?* Assuming the Professor is being fashionably late because he is the boss, Wes grows impatient.

But something else is nudging his intuition. In his uneasiness, Wes asks himself a thousand questions.

Are the Professor's goons waiting for me to come back outside?

Is this some sort of psychological power move?

Am I even in the right place?

I have to be. There's only one opera house in the middle of the desert.

While he is analyzing his thoughts in silence for several more minutes, the sound of the opera house's front door opening interrupts Wes. The metallic sound of the lock and hinges reverberates inside the old theater space. A jolt of adrenaline pumps into Wes's heart as he quickly slides off the stage and onto his feet. He takes a confident but nonthreatening stance and waits. That moment of anticipation feels like a lifetime to Wes before an older-looking woman, in her sixties, makes her way through the front door.

Long, stringy gray hair hangs on both sides of the woman's narrow face. Round, silver-framed glasses rest firmly on the bridge of her pointy nose. A *jingle* sound coming from bells sewn to her sky-blue cotton shirt follows the woman now moving down the carpeted path.

She's carrying a cardboard box in one arm and using the other to close the door behind her. *That doesn't look like somebody I should be meeting.* The woman enters the theater. She doesn't notice Wes standing at the front of the stage until she is halfway down the red-carpeted entrance. The old woman's head jolts up, startled at his presence. But she relaxes quickly, finding Wes nonthreatening.

"You're not supposed to be in here," the woman says with a polite tone.

"I apologize, ma'am." Wes hesitates to tell the woman why he is there but decides to. He opts to do so in case the Professor is trying to test him through some type of ruse. "I'm supposed to be meeting somebody in here at four p.m."

"And who might that be?" the old woman asks.

Again, Wes hesitates as he tries to decide how much to say. "A gentleman." More hesitation. "The Professor."

The old woman squawks, her voice sounding confused. "Professor? This isn't a college, so there aren't any professors here. Once in a while, we get a high school teacher who comes out here with their classroom on a field trip, but we haven't had one since February."

Confusion and panic flood Wes's body as he processes everything the old woman said. "Do you know what time it is, ma'am?"

The woman looks at a humble silver watch hanging from her wrist. "It's four-thirty."

Wes's stomach convulses and tremors. "Is there a phone I can use?" he asks before his nerves affect his speech.

"Yes, there's one in the back office." She continues down the slanted walkway toward the side of the stage. She waves at Wes to follow. He does, his legs tingling with adrenaline.

When they get to the back of the stage, the old woman guides him to a small office door hidden behind more costumes. She opens the office door and pulls a string. The room goes bright with the help of one lightbulb mounted on the wall. Under the lightbulb, a phone hangs underneath. The old woman tells Wes, "When you're done, please turn off the light and go out the front."

"Yes, ma'am."

The old woman drops the cardboard box she's carrying and strolls out. Wes gives her a second or two to clear the area before he picks up the phone. Quickly, he riffles through his pocket and finds the business card Valentina gave him. Wes dials the number. The phone rings and the familiar sultry female voice answers, "Love Patch."

"Valentina, it's me, Wes, Sean's buddy."

"Hey there, Wes. What can I do for you?"

"Can you connect me to my room, please? I need to speak to my wife."

"Sure thing, hon."

The phone rings again. With every unanswered second Wes feels a stab in his stomach. Moments later, Wes hears Valentina's voice again. "She's not picking up."

"Can I talk to Sean?"

"Oh, I'm afraid not, hon. Sean left about a half hour ago."

"He left!"

Valentina responds with a confused tone, "Uh … yeah."

"Okay, thanks." Wes slams the phone receiver back onto the cradle. He sits for a moment to make sense of everything that has transpired since he left Maggie and Sean at the brothel. And finally, it makes sense to him. He yells at himself, "Fuck me! He set me up! Why!"

Pissed off, scared, and not thinking straight, Wes rushes out of the office. Busting through the front door into the dirt parking lot outside, he takes a half second to scan the area before sprinting over to the truck parked by the diner. He throws himself inside, starts the truck, and smashes on the gas, heading back toward Pahrump.

Before getting out of the parking lot, Wes slams on the brakes and considers his route. *If I go through Pahrump, I'll hit traffic and stoplights and all sorts of shit.* He figures he can get back to the brothel quicker by taking back roads through Amargosa. *The roads are empty, and I can drive faster.* Having recalculated his route, he smashes on the gas pedal again. He turns the old work truck to the left and starts heading north toward the heart of Amargosa.

As he speeds down Highway 127, the deserted road allows him to get the old work truck up to a hundred miles an hour. He feels every little dip in the road. At some moments, the entire truck bounces off the road as it roughly races back to the Love Patch.

He gets back to the brothel in under eighteen minutes and parks hastily. Wes rushes into the suite to find Maggie is gone. His heart drops. Frantically, he scans the room for any signs. He notices Maggie's bag is still on the dresser, as is his. He reads a message written on the mirror with Maggie's lipstick. "Wait for his call."Wes staggers over toward the phone, slowly sits down on the couch, pulls the phone onto his lap, and decides.

"I'm going ... to kill ... all of them." Wes repeats the mantra several times, solidifying his conviction for blood and revenge. Now convinced of what he needs to do, he considers how he's going to do it. He quickly concludes he'll need another gun, since Sean took his. *Hell, I'll need several more guns.* And there is only one man he knows who has an arsenal fit to go to war with. *I need Caleb.*

Wes pages him with the number Caleb gave him and Sean while they were at the range earlier in the week. He waits several minutes for a call back.

Finally, the phone rings. He answers it, snapping the receiver to his head. But it's not Caleb.

CHAPTER 51

S ITTING ON THE EDGE of a king-size bed with a lit cigar in his mouth, Lee holds the hotel phone to his ear. Half-undressed, wearing only a white tank top undershirt and boxer underwear, his entire body has a light layer of sweat. Like someone who just finished having sex. His hair is also slightly disheveled. The smoke from his cigar finds its way out of the room through a cracked window at the foot of the bed.

Listening to the phone ring on the other end of the line, Lee waits patiently for Wes to pick up. Slight anticipation grows in Lee, like he's getting ready to tell a joke.

When Wes finally picks up the phone, Lee, being the gentleman he is, attempts to relieve some pressure off Wes's shoulders. He offers the young man a hearty Oklahoma greeting. "Hello there, Wesley."

Wes doesn't skip a beat, asking, "Do you have Maggie?"

Lee expected this. "Of course I do. And let me tell you, she is one spitfire."

Even though Wes's question came at him rapidly, to Lee, Wes sounds to be relatively calm. *There's something to this kid.*

He considers the reasons a man in this situation would be this composed. Either he's a talented actor, has the product, or is prepared to die.

In past jobs, Lee has dealt with all three types. Men trying to bluff, buy, or fight their way through negotiations. None of them have ever deterred the final results the Oklahoman has executed. It always ends with Lee and Amber being present for the last bit of oxygen their targets use.

Maybe because Lee hasn't had to fight a worthy adversary in a while or he needs to prove something to himself being the ripe age of fifty, he hopes Wes is willing to fight. *The kid has balls and is willing to die trying to get his wife back.*

"Let me talk to her," Wesley says.

"That's going to be impossible right now, young man." Lee looks at Amber across the room, sitting next to Maggie.

Wearing only a short black silk robe, Amber picks at Maggie's hair. With her hands and mouth bound with tape, Maggie hardens her posture, glaring at Lee, only allowing one tear to run down her face. Lee continues. "But let me assure you, son, your little wife is doing fine. Her and the missus are having some gal time right now."

"If I don't get to speak to her right now, I'm going to take the drugs and money to the police!" Wes says.

Lee breaks out into laughter. "You go and try that, son. These Podunk cops will arrest you before you get through the front door." He keeps laughing. "Besides, did you find our product?"

Silence from Wes.

This angers Lee. "I didn't think you did." He continues to chastise Wes. His tone now direct. "So here's what you're going to do, you limp-dick Gen Xer. You're going to come to our hotel at ten p.m. And either you're going to drop off what belongs to me and get your wife back, or you're going to come pick up your wife … in the fucking Dumpster. It's up to—"

"Fuck you, you country bumpkin motherfucker," Wes says. "I do have your shit, and I will see you in a few hours. But we're meeting on the dry lakebed."

Taken aback by what Wes has said and how he said it, Lee sits for a moment. *I love this kid.* He feels a smirk emerge from his face, his faith restored in the young fighter.

Lee shouts to Maggie, "Whoo! Your husband has some fire in his belly. I like it. He had me thinking for a minute he's your average Joe."

Maggie lets out a muffled scream.

"You see, Wesley, she's alive. Like I said." *This proposal sounds juicy.* "And why would I meet you at the dry lakebed?"

"It's secluded and wide-open. There's nowhere for either of us to hide."

Lee takes a moment to relight his cigar.

"That's what I thought." Wes says. "You're too fuckin' old to go toe-to-toe. Even with that old crow you call a wife."

Oh, you little shit. I'll cut your tongue out. Lee looks at his wife. Her beauty and skill calm him. "Nose-to-nose? I like your style, Wesley. Be there at ten."

"You're going to be there at eight," Wesley says, boldness in his voice.

Lee jerks up straight. "At dusk! My favorite part of the day."

"Yeah, I don't want you to miss your steak and egg special at the casino."

"Wesley, you sly dog. Two hours before the deadline. And on a dry lakebed at dusk. I never pegged you as having a flair for the dramatic."

"It's called getting it done." Wes takes a pause and then asks, "Oh, Lee, did you hear that?"

"Hear what, Wesley?"

Click. The phone goes silent in Lee's ear without saying another word. Lee laughs again. "I'm going to have to remember that one."

CHAPTER 52

F OR THE PAST THIRTY minutes, Vinnie has been compliant. Sitting at the kitchen table of his grandmother's house. This compliance has come with its own challenges, though. Vinnie has tried to debate why he should be let go. But every time he says something, his efforts are met with a stern "Shut the fuck up" from Caleb. But this hasn't deterred Vinnie's attempts to verbally spar with Caleb about the cash and dope. Vinnie has even played the emotional card, reminiscing a little about their childhood together. This trip down memory lane might have been the only thing that garnered a laugh or two from Caleb.

With minutes away from Sean showing up at the house, Vinnie asks for mercy one more time. Caleb tries to explain what type of leader Sean is. Feeling a little sympathy for Vinnie, Caleb assures him he will ask Sean to help smooth things out with the Professor. Not only for Wes but for him too. *Maybe this will shut him up for a while.*

A few more minutes pass before Sean pulls up in the front driveway. He knocks at the door.

Caleb gives Vinnie a "don't mess around" look before letting Sean in. When he opens the door, Sean is a little more amped up than usual. He automatically looks around Caleb, inside the house.

Caleb side steps and lets Sean enter the home. Sean looks at Vinnie sitting at the kitchen table and sneers at him. Sean's eyes then dart at the cash and dope stacked on the other side of the table. He twirls the brown bricks and thumbs through the cash.

Sean looks at Vinnie. "I remember you, you cocksucker. Your friend with the big mouth wanted a job." Vinnie lowers his head, avoiding eye contact. Sean continues, moving closer toward Vinnie. Vinnie's uncontrollable shaking in his seat causes the wooden chair to audibly clatter on the kitchen tile floor. "And this is how you get my attention?" Sean asks, placing his hand on Vinnie's chin, pushing it a little to the side so he can get a better look at the missing ear. Sean snickers. "Well, it looks like you got *somebody's* attention."

"Sir, Caleb said you ... you might be able to smooth this all out with the Professor, if I tell you the truth," Vinnie's says.

In a flash, Sean slaps Vinnie where his ear used to be. Vinnie howls in pain, grabbing his wound. His head collapses on the table.

Caleb also flinches at seeing the pain. *Damn, Sergeant.*

Sean is now towering over Vinnie with his infamous knife hand one inch from Vinnie's nose. "You aren't my soldier and weren't in Africa with us, so you can go fuck yourself."

Observing Sean's demeanor continuing to intensify, Caleb attempts to deescalate the situation a bit. "Is there anything he can do to earn some goodwill with either you or your boss?" Caleb asks.

This does the trick. Sean raises himself up and saunters around the table and stands next to Caleb. To Vinnie, he says, "Yeah, there might be something you can do."

Vinnie sits up straight in the chair, eager and desperate. "Tell me, sir. I'll do anything you want."

Sean's tone softens. "That's good. I'm glad to hear that." He pulls Wes's Glock 17 from behind the small of his back. He takes aim at Vinnie.

Vinnie squirms in his seat. Sean continues. "What you can do is stop breathing for us." And without missing a beat, Sean dumps a volley of shots into the face and body of Vinnie.

Vinnie's body twists and bends as hollow-point bullets strike his person, pushing his head back and causing his body to go limp. Vinnie's body doesn't fall to the floor. Rather, it slides into a slouch, remaining in the chair as his arms fall to the side. Within seconds, one can hear dripping blood hitting the kitchen floor.

Shocked at what he witnessed, Caleb yells through ringing ears, "Why the hell did you do that, Sean?"

Sean gives Caleb a look like Caleb is stupid. "Really?"

"What the hell, man? You didn't have to do that shit in front of me."

Now irritated, Sean asks, "Have you lost your stomach for this type of work?"

"What?" Caleb asks, almost insulted by the question. "No, but there's the legal side of this shit too."

Sean tries to calm his young soldier. "Caleb, does anyone know you're here?"

"No."

"Then we're good." He sets the pistol on the kitchen table next to the pile of dope and cash. He sits down at the table and inspects the inventory in more detail.

While Sean counts the money, Caleb gets a page from the same number he used to get a hold of Sean at the brothel.

"Who paged you?" Sean asks.

"I don't know. It looks like the same number I used to call you."

Sean stops fingering the cash. He looks up at Caleb solemnly. The two stare at each other awkwardly for a moment. Something in Caleb's head screams at him: *Get off the X.*

Another half moment passes before Sean leaps to his feet. The kitchen chair underneath him flies back across the floor. Slamming his hand down on the black pistol, Sean whips it up at Caleb and begins shooting at him.

Caleb dives behind a pony wall separating the kitchen from the living room. He lands hard on the carpet. His pager flies off his waistband. He can hear Sean's footsteps coming his direction. *Start moving.* Caleb gets to his feet. He pulls his own pistol. *Fuck, not enough time.* Knowing he can't turn around and get a good shot off on Sean, Caleb runs toward the sliding glass door directly in front of him. He shoots the glass three times.

The rounds penetrate the door, causing the glass to crack. Caleb then runs through the sharded glass. He tries to move through it as fast as possible, covering his face with one arm and the back of his neck with the other.

Making it through, Caleb hears several more shots ring out. Snapping sounds race past Caleb's head as he clears the door.

With his face still covered and being disoriented from the initial attack, Caleb knows he's outside somewhere in the back-yard, but not exactly where. He continues to run to get out of

Sean's line of fire. He smashes hard into what feels like the corner of the steel grill with his hip. The impact and momentum of his movement throw Caleb to a full spin, like he's a professional quarterback deflecting tackles. Losing his balance, he continues propelling forward. *Where the fuck am I?* He doesn't know exactly—not until the last second. He's about to fall face-first into the pool.

Caleb's body smacks the blue pool liner resting on the surface of the water. When his body lands, he falls to the deep end of the pool. The water creates a vacuum, causing the liner to collapse in around him. The liner wraps Caleb's legs and arms tightly with the rest of the blue plastic falling on top of his head. The plastic cuts off all sound, air, and light. Caleb can hear the muffled sounds of gunshots overhead. Panic sets in as his entire body continues to get tangled in the thick liner. His body sinks to the bottom.

CHAPTER 53

S EAN ARRIVES AT THE Calvada Meadows Airport thirty minutes after leaving Caleb dead in the pool. The blue laundry bag filled with the dope and cash hangs over his shoulder. Sean strolls over to a 172R Cessna airplane parked on the private runway. Standing in front of the aircraft is Sean's flight instructor, Harold Thach. A short, stubby man in his sixties, with white hair and a creased pink face to match.

He greets Sean with a handshake. "You know you don't need to take me with you anymore. You've had all your hours for over a month now."

Sean smiles. "Come on, Harold. You know if I'm gone more than an hour, you'll have the air force on my ass."

Harold lets out a hearty, old-man laugh. "I wouldn't call anyone for at least two hours."

I know. And since I need three hours to reach my destination, you're coming with me.

The two men board the small plane. Sean, in the primary seat. Harold copiloting.

Sean runs through the typical preflight routine, and within minutes the Cessna is up in the air, heading south.

For thirty minutes, Harold and Sean make small talk. Sean puts the aircraft into autopilot mode. Harold says, "I thought you wanted to fly today."

"I got something for you. A going-away gift."

"For me?"

"It's like saying farewell at the end of school."

Harold perks up. "Oh, I see. That's very nice of you."

"Let me get it," Sean says, slipping out of the pilot's seat and squeezing to the back.

Harold places his hands on the control yokes, a content look glowing on his face.

In the backseat, Sean pulls the drawstring cord from the dope-filled laundry bag. He coils the ends around each of his hands, crisscrossing them to make a big loop with the cord. *That'll get over his thick head.* He glances up at Harold, whose hands are still on the yoke.

Like a spring-loaded trap, Sean throws the loop over Harold's head and around his neck. Harold's hands jerk the yoke as he brings them to his throat. The plane jolts in the air but autocorrects. Harold's attempts to get his fingers under the cord are futile. As he realizes this, panic sets in on the old flight instructor. His eyes bulge from their sockets. His face turns a dark blue. Fear and suffocation wheeze from his mouth. His body thrashes around in the seat, hands still digging at his throat until, finally, they stop. His arms and body go limp.

Letting go of the cord, Sean gets himself back to the front. He unbuckles Harold, unlatches his door, and tries pushing the old man out.

The door opens only about an inch. "Fuck," Sean says to no one. *I need to descend and reduce my speed.* He gets behind his yolk, drops the altitude and speed of the plane, and resets the autopilot. Bracing himself against his own chair, Sean leg-presses Harold's body with both feet out the door. The door opens more, but not enough. Harold's upper torso is hanging out of the aircraft. But his lower body won't let go. "What the fuck, man?" *He's probably caught up on something.*

Sean gets an idea. Taking the autopilot off, he brings the plane back to a higher altitude. Once there, he banks the plane toward Harold's side and the dead body slips more. Sean straightens the aircraft and repeats the maneuver two more times. This time the movement is jerky. Viewing the plane, the left wing might look like it's swatting at a fly.

Finally, on the last bank of the plane, Harold's body dislodges from the cab. Falling at a speed of a hundred and twenty miles an hour, Harold's body smashes into a desert mountaintop. *That was fuckin' insane! The old man held on to the end.*

With Harold's door still open, Sean banks the plane toward his side. This time using gravity and momentum to slam the door shut. He gets this done on the first try. Leveling the plane for the last time, Sean laughs out loud. *I pulled it off. I fuckin' pulled it off! There were a few hiccups. But hey, I adapted, improvised, and overcame. It's my time to enjoy life now.* "Fuck you, Uncle Sam. And fuck you, Professor." The plane increases speed as it continues its trek south.

CHAPTER 54

T HE DRY LAKEBED IN Pahrump, Nevada, is on the far south end of town off Homestead Road. To get to it, one must drive by two Victorian-style brothels before accessing several dirt roads to the lakebed. Once you're on the lakebed, the first thing you see is flat, crusted dirt. On the moonlike surface, small sage bushes extend from ankle-high dirt mounds scattered along the surface. This flat, barren scenery runs for miles in every direction. The area is so expansive one could drive a hundred miles an hour for several minutes in any direction before having to slow down. Except for major holidays, when only a few locals visit, the lakebed usually remains deserted. As it is tonight.

As much as Wes wants to see his old platoon sergeant dead right now, he still adheres to many of the performance standards Sean has drilled into him while serving under him. One of those lessons being "If you're on time, you're late."

Wes parks about five miles in from the main road. He orients the truck's nose to the east, with his back against the falling sun.

Inside the old work truck, Wes sits, fighting back sporadic jitters caused by the adrenaline slowly filling his body. He struggles to clear his mind of the many thoughts running through his head right now. With everything he's considering, getting killed is at the bottom of the list. Instead, Wes is reflecting on the loss of Maggie's father. *He was the salt of the earth. Going after him was completely unnecessary.*

Wes fights his guilt.

I'm the reason Maggie was abducted.

I trusted Sean too much.

Not now—head in the fight, Wes.

He considers his wife being stuck with those animals for the past few hours. Subjected to who knows what. Wes's confidence level for getting Maggie back safely has fluctuated all day. The one thing Wes knows for sure is that by the end of tonight, they'll be back together. Dead or alive.

Needing to stretch his legs, Wes gets out of the truck. He dumps every thought of losing tonight out of his mind. There's only one direction, and that's forward.

As he waits for the 8:00 p.m. mark, a warm but light evening breeze blows against Wes's face. It calms him. He looks down at his feet.

For the first time since leaving the casino earlier this morning, Wes notices he's still in his work shoes. The once highly shined footwear is now scratched, scuffed, and covered with dust. His white casino button-down shirt has been pulled out for hours, and the mandatory gold-sequin vest abandoned when he and Maggie first got to the Love Patch. *You don't look much like a hero, Wes.* "Hell, I don't feel like one either."

From the main road, Wes can hear the sound of a revving engine. He looks and sees the tan Crown Victoria racing his way. Barrels of thick dust shoot into the air, the vehicle speeding in his general direction.

Wes reaches into the truck and flashes the headlights, signaling his position. He pulls out a black sports bag. The Crown Vic adjusts its course toward him, still moving fast. Wes drops the black bag on the desert floor about thirty feet in front of the truck. He takes a step back.

Arriving in the area, the Crown Vic drives a circle around Wes and his truck twice. Wes looks inside the vehicle for any signs of Maggie. But he doesn't see her. He only sees the old man and his bitch wife. *Where's Maggie?* Not seeing his wife replaces any remaining doubt with a righteous, burning anger.

Finally, the Crown Vic comes to a stop fifty feet in front of Wes with the trunk facing him. More dirt and dust kick up. The engine turns off.

The Oklahoma couple exit their vehicle like they're celebrities being welcomed by paparazzi. Amber is toting a black shotgun with a polished wooden forestock and rear stock. With a wicked smile, she puts herself to the rear of the Crown Vic, near the trunk.

Lee, also smiling, strides out a few feet next to her. A cigar hangs from his mouth. His intense eyes watch Wes. On Lee's hip, a chrome-plated revolver hangs with pride from a worn leather holster. The old man greets the young one.

"Evening, Wesley."

For some unexplained reason, hearing those words from Lee helps dissipate any remnants of fear and doubt Wes has left in his body. It's showtime, and Wes is ready to perform. The familiar feeling of being relaxed but alert covers Wes. *I haven't felt this way since deployment.* This state of calm usually came when the battlefield was about to get hairy and he knew he might go night-night for good. It didn't happen all the time. Only in situations so awful, even a bad decision is the best decision to be made. And right now Wes is in that state of mind.

"Where's Maggie?"

Lee points at the black sports bag resting in the dirt between them. "Does that belong to me?"

"Yeah. Now where's Maggie?"

Amber taps the trunk lid with the butt of her shotgun. She says, "Maggie, Wesley's here and he wants to see you."

Frantic pounding and muffled screams come from inside the trunk.

"Open the fucking trunk!" Wes says.

"Oh, I don't think so. Maybe we should handle some business first," Lee says.

"Everything you asked for is right here. Now let my wife go."

"That's not the game we're playing, Wesley."

This old piece of shit is baiting me. But into what?

"What do you have in mind?" Wes asks.

Lee chuckles, raising his arms up in the air in a gesture of appreciation. He looks left and right, and says, "Well, considering this ... grandiose setting you've chosen"—Lee glances at Amber—"not to mention the particular time of day ..." Now back at Wes. "...I say we have ourselves a good old-fashioned draw." He slaps the side of his revolver and says, "Just like in the Old West."

This guy is absolutely crazy. Wes tries to buy some time to think. "How are we supposed to have this 'draw' if I don't have a gun?"

Lee laughs. "Now, Wesley, don't bullshit me. I've been a lawyer for almost twenty years. I know when somebody is lying to me." He signals for Wes to lift his shirt up by pulling on his own.

Wes endures another blow to his ego, raising up his shirt.

Lee raises his eyes too. His shit-eating grin grows bigger with Wes exposing the gun tucked in his waistband. Lee's blissful face contorts into a scowl.

"Is that a damn Glock in your pants, son?"

Wes nods.

"I bet it's a nine-millimeter too, ain't it?"

Another nod from Wes.

Lee says. "Put your gun where you need it. I don't want you crying about not getting a fair shake."

Taking his time, Wes removes his button-down shirt, leaving him in a white undershirt. Lee continues berating him.

"You young folk don't have any regard for American-made firearms ... plain disgusting." Lee readjusts the cigar in his mouth. "It's a damn shame you're going to die with that plastic junk in your hand."

Wes tries to protest. "I'm not doing this."

Amber responds to this by opening the trunk of their Crown Vic. Inside, Wes can see Maggie. Her hands and mouth taped. When Wes and Maggie make eye contact, Amber points her shotgun at Maggie. Seeing only Wes and not the barrel of the shotgun, Maggie tries to jump out of the trunk.

Wes raises his hand to her. "Stop, baby, no."

Looking defeated and betrayed, Maggie slides back into her luxury car tomb. Wes tells her, "Sit tight, sweetheart, I'm gonna get us out of this." Looking back at Lee, Wes says, "And if I don't do this?"

Smirking, Lee replies, "If you don't do this, Amber there is going to shoot precious Maggie with her shotgun at point-blank range. Thus splattering her face, head, and neck all over the inside of my trunk. After that, because Maggie will have ruined my trunk, I'll have to give my car to a junkyard and have them smash it up into a little box ... with Maggie inside."

"You're a sick fuck—you know that?"

The odd couple laugh. "We've been told as much," Amber says.

Figuring there's no way out, Wes takes a few slow steps to the side, clearing himself from his work truck and lining up with Lee. "Two on one—that doesn't seem fair."

In a lower, sympathetic tone, Lee says, "It's not going to matter."

Both men shuffle their feet in the dirt, making sure they're good and dug in. Their stances are similar to what they would be at the range training reflexive fire drills.

Wes looks at Lee who still has his shitty grin on display. But his cold eyes are locked tight on Wes. Having only watched old cowboy movies, Wes isn't sure about this type of gunfighting etiquette. So rather than asking what to do next, he nods, letting Lee know he's ready.

A deathly calm washes over Wes, and the earth stills. The air goes stiff and silent. Wes listens to his own heartbeat, slowing to a steady pace in his chest. Nothing exists except this moment. Wes can hear Amber's foot shift ever so slightly in the dirt. He can even hear her gun click from the tightening of her grip. The night's first star comes to life and twinkles in Wes's peripheral vision. His own breath echoes in his head. He inhales deeply, holds, and releases his breath.

Lee says to Wes, "Call it, son."

Upon his order, Wes casually raises his non–gun hand, showing two fingers, and says, "Two."

With enough time for Wes to see, Lee's face changes almost unnoticeably from determination to confusion. Wes takes this microscopic moment in time to step off the X to the right.

Two rounds snap off, almost simultaneously. Both rounds rip through the stillness of the air, missing Wes's head by centimeters.

The first round came from Lee's American-made .44 Magnum.

The second round from a .308 Winchester located three hundred yards to Wes's rear. Also American.

As the echo of the competing guns fades, Lee flinches as a red liquid mist splashes across his face. Looking like he's in shock, Lee raises his hand and wipes his cheek. He inspects his fingers. Smeared blood covers his fingertips. Lee turns toward a humming, bubbling sound coming from his wife.

Amber, barely standing with her knees locked, lazily holding her shotgun now, looks over at Lee. The upper-left side of her face and head hangs from shattered bone and torn meat. With her left eye gone and her upper jaw stripped of its teeth, she looks to her beloved husband as blood and other bodily fluids drip from her wound. Her body twitches like she's trying to walk toward Lee. But her mangled, malfunctioning brain won't let her.

Lee goes to his wife and grabs her by the shoulders, lowering her to the ground. He caresses her hair and rocks her in his arms as if she were a baby. He mumbles something to her Wes can't hear. Wes thinks he can hear Lee sniffle, as if he were weeping.

Amber breathes her last gurgling breath. Lee lays her down gently and stands to face Wes. Whatever sadness he felt a moment ago is replaced with an unbridled rage, seen only in his eyes.

Lee then squints, peering past Wes.

Wes doesn't follow his gaze but only smirks as he watches Lee figure out what he already knows is there.

Out in the distance, a sage bush comes to life, standing up. It starts walking toward the two men with a rifle, still up, tracked on Lee. The bush eventually falls to the ground, revealing Caleb.

Starting at a low volume, Lee laughs to himself, half maniacal, half pained.

"It's over, Lee," Wes says.

Lee's laughter gets louder as his face hardens. He readjusts his grip on his revolver ever so slightly.

"Don't do it ... just lay it down."

Lee's laugh becomes louder and louder, mixing with the whistling sound of the wind. "I told you before, Wesley ... I never fold."

He raises his gun at Wes, almost halfheartedly.

Wes, with his Glock already pointed at Lee, puts two controlled rounds into him. One round in the chest and the other in his throat.

Lee falls to his back, bleeding profusely, gripping his neck in a futile attempt to stop the blood gushing through his fingers.

Wes stuffs his gun back into his waistline, grabs the black sports bag, and brings it over to Lee.

Standing over him, Wes says, "Should've left it alone, old man." Wes tips the bag over to show Lee its contents. Old newspapers, a *Reader's Digest*, and a couple of *Playboys* empty onto the dirt next to him.

Lee grabs at some of the paper debris and gargles a frustrated yell.

Wes says to him with a smile on his face, "When you put a bluff in the middle, it's called a Nevada Lowball."

Lee's eyes go wide with rage. He gargles one last time and dies.

"What the fuck is wrong with you?" Caleb asks, catching up to the scene.

"What?"

"Don't wait so long to pull your gun next time. I was going to have to dump him too."

Caleb and Wes share a moment of silence as they hug. "There can only be one motivated killa," Wes says to Caleb.

"You're damn right."

CHAPTER 55

T HE CELEBRATION BETWEEN WES and Caleb is cut short with Maggie still inside the trunk of the Crown Vic. Before Wes can get to her, Maggie is already halfway out. The two men help her the rest of the way. Wes reaches for the tape on her mouth. "Let me pull this off." She nods at him with an impatient acknowledgment.

Wes grabs the edge of the tape and deliberately removes it. Maggie takes in a deep breath of air, throwing her arms around Wes's neck. She accidentally bumps his face because of her bound hands. Wes and Maggie embrace for a long moment, kissing each other hard.

Maggie pulls her arms back over Wes's head. Wes looks at Caleb. "You have a blade?"

Caleb reaches into his back pocket and tosses him a multi-tool.

"Don't move, sweetheart." When her restraints loosen, she rips off the remaining tape stuck to her wrist.

Maggie hugs Wes again. "I'm so glad you're okay, Wesley."

Caleb asks, "What about me? Gingers need love too."

Wes and Maggie snicker. Maggie wraps her arms around Caleb's neck. She pulls his head down toward her face and kisses him on the forehead, looking deep into his eyes. "Thank you so much, Caleb, for keeping Wesley safe. I will always be indebted to you."

Caleb's eyes almost begin to water.

Wanting to avoid seeing Caleb cry and feeling a bit emasculated by his great shooting, Wes jokingly interrupts the moment. "Kept me safe? You mean I kept him safe. I was the one up in the front."

Maggie plays along with the young men's banter. She wipes Wes's face and fixes his hair. "Yes, Wesley, you were incredibly brave," she says to him like he was a child who scraped his knee.

She then scans the dry lakebed and sees the two bodies of her captors lying on the crusted surface. Maggie staggers over to the dead Oklahoma couple. Wes tries to stop her by gently pulling on her arm. "You don't want to see that," he says.

She pulls from Wes's grip and stands above the carnage, staring at both bodies, which continue to water the dried surface with their blood. Wes can see Maggie's gaze is odd. More curious than mortified. Wes then looks at Caleb who seems to notice the change in Maggie's demeanor too.

Casually, Caleb moves over next to Wes. He leans in close. "Is she okay?"

Wes doesn't respond.

After another awkward minute of Maggie staring at the bodies, she returns over to their small huddle. "Can we go home now?" she asks.

"Yes, baby, we can," Wes says. He opens the truck's door for her. Getting in, she leans her head back against the bench seat. "Give me and Caleb a minute, sweetheart." She nods in acknowledgment.

Standing over the two bodies, Caleb asks, "Are we making a statement?"

Also, staring at their work, Wes says, "Yeah, a loud one."

Wes and Caleb lift Amber up first and toss her inside the trunk of the Crown Vic. Lee goes in next on top of his wife. Both men pause at what they see.

Lee's and Amber's faces lie next to each other like they're posing for a portrait.

"That's fuckin' creepy, bro," Caleb says.

Wes looks too, captivated by their final resting position. He eventually breaks the silence. "I don't have a gas can."

Caleb smirks and says, "I have an idea." He ejects five shells from Amber's shotgun onto the ground. He gathers the shells and a few pieces of newspaper from the sports bag. "Tear the paper into six-inch squares and set them on that asshole's chest. Make sure to bend the paper into a bowl shape," Caleb says.

Wes does as he's told.

With Wes having finished making the paper bowls and placing them strategically on Lee's chest, Caleb follows. With the pliers from his multitool, Caleb begins disassembling the shotgun shells. First he cuts open the plastic casing and pours the lead pellets into the trunk. Little metal balls can be heard rolling off Lee and Amber's corpses, falling to the bottom of the trunk. Caleb then pulls out a plastic piece, or the "wad," from the shell casings. Behind the wad, dark gunpowder is revealed. Carefully, with each open shotgun shell, Caleb pours the leftover gunpowder into the paper bowls staged on Lee's body.

Caleb instructs Wes, "Twist the paper up so the powder doesn't fall out."

Wes goes to work on his assigned task.

Once complete, Caleb refines the placement of the powder filled bowls inside the trunk. He says to Wes, "Go grab some of those magazines and stuff them in the trunk underneath their bodies."

"What are we doing here, making a bonfire?"

"Exactly," Caleb says.

Smiling, Wes grabs a couple of the old magazines. One of them being the September 1988 issue of *Playboy* featuring Madonna and her hairy armpits. *Disgusting*. Wes rips the pages out, balling them up and stuffing them in every pocket of open space inside the trunk.

When Caleb approves of the final setup, he asks Wes, "Do you have a lighter?"

"No, man." But Wes remembers. *This dead fuck in the trunk always smoked cigars*. He rushes to the front of the Crown Vic and looks inside.

Right there, sitting in plain sight, is a glass jar filled with light brown cigars. Next to the jar is Lee's fancy DuPont lighter. Picking the lighter up, Wes notices the weight of the object.

He glances on the floorboard and sees a black backpack. He rips it open. Inside, he finds several bundles of cash and two brick-size packages wrapped in brown paper and plastic. Wes grabs the pack.

Outside the cab, Wes holds the high-end accessory and the backpack for Caleb to see.

"Hell yeah, that's what I'm talking about," Caleb says. "Wait, is that the dope and cash?"

"It is."

Caleb grabs the pack and stares at the contents inside. "We can run, brother. Me, you, and Maggie."

We can. Hell, we might have to. Wes contemplates his options. After a long moment of thought, he says, "No, brother. This is what got everyone into this situation to start with."

Caleb nods in agreement. "You're right. Let's burn these motherfuckers down and go."

Wes tosses the backpack in front of the sedan and far enough away so it won't catch on fire but will be found.

Wes flips the top of the lighter open and a loud, metallic *ping* rings out. Identical to the lighter Sean had earlier in the day. *Interesting.*

Wes lights the gunpowder packets placed in the trunk. Black chemical smoke billows out. Within a minute, the entire trunk is up in flames. The smoke causes Wes to reflect on his grandfather sharing with him how he ran a flamethrower in the marines while fighting the Japanese on Iwo Jima. *And now I will never forget the smell of burning human flesh.*

With little effort, the trunk is now a furious fire. The two men watch it until the flames are full throttle and pushing into the backseat of the Crown Vic.

"Enjoy hell, motherfuckers," Wes says to the burning Oklahoma couple, feeling vindicated.

They leave the trunk lid open, making sure the fire has enough oxygen to burn.

Wes and Caleb run back to the work truck. Maggie is watching the scene herself. Wes expects to see a terrified look on her face, but he doesn't. Instead, she looks more like a college student listening to a world-renowned guest speaker.

Caleb throws his rifle into the bed of the truck and hops in next to Maggie. The three take off. By the time they're back on the main road, they can only see a bit of the flame. But there's no missing the black smoke in the air. Even being miles away now.

Wes takes a couple of back roads, trying to avoid anyone else wanting to kill them. The trio isn't on the road two minutes before Maggie starts asking questions.

"So, who's going to tell me what happened?"

"With what exactly?" Wes asks, trying to avoid the conversation.

"How did you two pull this off? They were dangerous people."

"We're even more dangerous," Caleb says, arrogance in his voice.

Knowing they're not out of trouble yet, Wes says, "We were more lucky than anything."

Maggie continues to push. "So, tell me."

CHAPTER 

Two Hours Earlier

S TILL UNDERWATER AND TWISTED up in the plastic liner, Caleb panics, sinking to the bottom of the pool. His frantic movements are a blessing and a curse. A blessing, by distorting his exact location from Sean, who searches for him from the surface. And a curse, by pulling Caleb to the deep end of the pool, wrapping up his limbs.

Only by sheer luck does Caleb get his hand into the tight, wet denim pocket of his pants to retrieve his multitool quickly. Frantically, he cuts at the plastic liner. With large pieces of the plastic floating to the surface, muffled gunshots ring out. Piercing holes appear in the liner with every successive shot. Caleb holds his breath for another minute until his ribcage begins to convulse, trying to preserve the last bit of oxygen.

I need air. Not able to hold his breath any longer, Caleb's head breaks the water's surface. He gasps. Still sucking in oxygen, he swings his head left and right. Sean is gone. The only traces of him left are the nine-millimeter brass casings around the pool's edge.

Caleb pulls his tired body out of the water. He goes back into the house. Before entering, he dips his head through the broken sliding glass door. He spots his pager. Securing the communication device, he eases into the kitchen. *Oh shit!* Vinnie's dead body, slumped in the chair, startles him. "Forgot you were here."

Finding the phone, he calls the number on his pager. Wes picks up on the other end.

"Caleb?"

"Brother, what the fuck is going on?"

"Sean took Maggie. Or someone Sean is working with took her."

"That motherfucker tried to kill me."

"What?"

"Yeah, he shot Vinnie, then you paged, and that's when he came at me."

"Holy shit, man. Vinnie's dead?"

"Yeah, real dead."

"Are you good?" Wes asks.

"Pretty much."

"I'm not asking you to get involved, Caleb, but I need to borrow a gun. These two country fucks have Maggie. I got them to meet me at the dry lakebed at twenty hundred."

"I'm not letting you go out there by yourself, Wes. How long will it take for you to get to my house?"

"About thirty minutes."

"Good. It's about to be a Mogadishu reunion," Caleb says, excitement in his voice.

Thirty minutes later, the two men are inside Caleb's home. Knowing Wes is most familiar with Glock pistols, he gives him a 17, identical to what Sean took from him earlier. Wes double-checks the ammo in the gun and straps two more magazines to his back.

Wes takes a couple of practice draws from his waist, getting his rhythm back,

Caleb secures his rifle, checks his ammo count, and pulls out a ghillie suit he uses for hunting coyote. Wes looks at him. "You're thinking overwatch?"

"Roger that. You call the targets, I'll knock 'em down. Business as usual."

The two young men grab their gear and jump into Wes's work truck. They take a power line road running predominantly on the outskirts of Pahrump to the dry lakebed from the west.

When they get approximately one mile from the exchange site, Wes drops Caleb off on the side of the road. They shake hands before Wes is back on the move.

It takes Caleb about twenty minutes to get within four hundred yards from where the exchange will take place. When he arrives, he spots Wes's truck parked in the position they agreed to. Caleb moves another two hundred yards closer to his final position, using a moderate stalking pace. Once in place, he adjusts his ghillie suit and rifle. With a few clicks to the scope, Caleb fine-tunes his optic based on the distance he is from Wes. He chambers one round into the rifle. Putting his eye close to the scope, Caleb exhales, flattening his body into a still position. From this point out, it is the discipline of the sniper to wait for its target. If one is patient and self-controlled, one will be rewarded with a kill.

"So, your plan was to bluff your way through?" Maggie asks.

"That was only the setup," Caleb says.

"When I figured out what happened, I decided I'd do anything to get you back." Wes says.

Maggie puts her hand on her husband's face. "Or get yourself killed trying."

"Pretty much, sweetheart," Wes says, eyes moist. Stuffing his emotions down, he continues. "Thankfully, I had the power of the ginger or things would have been worse."

Caleb nods in approval.

The three sit in silence for a few minutes, traveling the back roads.

"I want to kill Sean," Maggie says in a low voice. Almost talking to herself.

"You and I both sweetheart," Wes says.

"Put me on that list too," Caleb says.

"No, Wesley," Maggie says, much louder now. "I ... want to kill Sean."

Wes and Caleb exchange uncomfortable glances at each other.

What did she say? Wes thinks. Everyone agrees Sean needs to die. But Wes doesn't enjoy hearing his wife talk this way. He attempts to derail her train of thought, holding on to any sweetness she has left. "Maggie, please, don't say that."

Maggie balks in his face with an almost crazy cackle. "I watched you burn two dead bodies in the trunk of a car. And now you're going to tell me you don't like what I'm saying?"

Wes looks at Caleb for support. Caleb looks back at him with a *Can you blame her?* look. Wes tries to explain to Maggie, "You don't want to do something like that. It's a heavy burden to bear after you do."

Maggie turns in her seat, facing Wes. She screams at the top of her lungs: "Don't you tell me about heavy burdens! Those motherfuckers killed my dad, my brother, and … our baby!" Her face is now red and swollen and dripping with tears.

Dreadful pain shoots through Wes's body. "What do you mean 'killed our baby'?"

With venom, she says, "I've been bleeding, Wes. Ever since Sean punched me in the stomach and threw me into a trunk."

Wes's brain and hands go numb. This is the first time since Maggie was taken that he's heard exactly what happened to her.

Caleb leans his head against the passenger-side window. His eyes fill with tears.

They drive a few more miles in silence before Wes pulls the truck over. He brings Maggie over toward him. They hold each other close and cry their hearts out. Caleb wraps his arms around both of them. All three sit for a moment, sharing the pain.

Maggie whimpers. "I want to kill him, Wesley. I want to be the one to do it."

Succumbing to her request, Wes gently grabs her by the face with both of his hands. "Okay, Maggie, we'll do it together." Softly he kisses her forehead.

Now at peace, she looks at her husband. "Thank you, Wesley."

CHAPTER 57

A S THE THREE ENTER the emergency room. Nicholas Rosewell, the physician's assistant who helped Vinnie, rolls his eyes when he sees Wes again. "I can't do any more favors."

Wes ignores the comment, fatigue on his face. He nods to Maggie and Caleb to go sit down. In an exhausted tone, he tells the PA, "She's two months pregnant. We were in a car accident earlier. She thinks she may have lost the baby."

The PA's demeanor relaxes. A genuine concern for Wes's situation is visible. "I'm sorry to hear that, Wes. What makes her think that?"

"She's been bleeding a lot."

The PA's eyebrows rise with concern. "She needs an ultrasound."

Wes dips his head in agreement. He waves Maggie over. "The doc wants to do an ultrasound, right now."

Wes tries to lead Maggie with a gentle arm around her shoulder, but she raises her hand to his chest. "I have to do this myself."

Wes's eyes soften, his brow furrows. "Are you sure?" he says, his words quivering.

"Yes."

Wes steps to the side. Maggie moves past him and follows the PA down a hallway.

Wes watches her as he feels pain growing in his eyes. He finally takes a seat next to Caleb. "You're not going with her?" Caleb asks.

"She didn't ... want me ... to."

Caleb shakes his head, leaning back in his seat.

Maggie is placed on an examination table and asked to lie down. The ultrasound tech, an older Filipino lady, squeezes clear jelly on Maggie's belly. Maggie flinches at the cold sensation on her bare stomach. The tech slides an apparatus around on Maggie's belly that looks like a video game controller. The monitor mounted on a rolling cart displays a grainy image of Maggie's womb. "We're looking for a heartbeat right now," the PA says.

Maggie stares at a medical poster on the wall. The poster is of a pregnant woman at full term with the inside of her anatomy exposed, revealing a baby ready to be born. Maggie's right hand shakes uncontrollably.

"Too cold?" the tech asks.

"No," Maggie says, solemn. She brings her hand next to her leg.

The ultrasound operator looks concerned after swiping Maggie's belly a few times. She shakes her head at the PA.

His eyes lower. Carefully, he addresses Maggie. "I'm sorry, but there's no heartbeat. That with the fact that you've been bleeding for a while, it's a safe assumption you've lost the child."

"I knew it inside the trunk," Maggie says to herself, not completely in the room.

"The car accident?" the PA asks, unsure.

"Yeah ... the accident."

"Bleeding may continue for another day or so. If it does, you'll need to come back."

Staring off into space, Maggie says, "Thank you."

The PA escorts Maggie back to the waiting room, where Wes and Caleb stand to meet her. Wes and the PA don't speak. He only offers Wes a small shake of his head. Wes looks down slowly. Caleb puts a hand on his best friend's shoulder.

Now standing with them passively, Maggie says, "Let's go home."

Together, the three leave the hospital.

CHAPTER 58

IT'S ANOTHER TEN MINUTES before the old work truck pulls up to a double-wide mobile home. In the front is Caleb's own truck, looking like it's been stolen and ransacked. Maggie eyes the injured vehicle with an angry look.

When Caleb climbs out, Maggie grabs him by the hand. "Thank you, Caleb." Gratefulness is in her face and voice.

Caleb's head swings left and right as he lets out a slight cough. He nods slowly, "Anytime, Maggie." He and Wes shake hands through the open window. "Keep your head on a swivel, brother. I don't think you're out of the woods yet."

"Yeah, me neither," Wes says.

"You've still got three full magazines. If anything goes sideways, call me. I'll be there in minutes. If not, call me tomorrow to let me know what the plan is."

"We should be good tonight. They're going to have to regroup, and I don't think anyone knows where we live," Wes says, sounding unsure.

Caleb shakes his head slowly. With his rifle slung over his shoulder, the young sniper heads inside.

Eventually, Wes and Maggie make it home themselves. "Sit here for a minute, sweetheart. I want to make sure no one is waiting for us."

Tactically, Wes goes through the back door, pistol raised, clearing each room in his house. *No one here; good. We're safe for now.*

Wes pulls the work truck to the back of the house. *In case someone drives by looking for us.*

Once inside, Wes says, "You should take a shower and relax, Maggie." She agrees. While in the shower, Wes makes a pot of coffee. Watching each drip of the dark liquid fall into the pot, Wes finds himself lost in thought.

What do I do next?

Should I call the police?

I killed someone and burned two bodies.

What's going to happen to Caleb too?

If we run, where to?

Where the fuck is Sean?

The droning sound of the shower stops, snapping Wes out of his meditative state. He brings two mugs of the fresh brew to the living room.

Maggie meets him on the couch. She's wearing light pink sweatpants and a white T-shirt. Her hair lies straight down, still wet. Her face is clean and a bit pink from the hot water. All the tear-streaked dirt has been washed away, leaving only her fatigue and a few light bruises she earned resisting her abduction.

She takes a sip of the coffee and balls up against Wes. Within a few minutes, he can feel her breathing deep, having fallen asleep. Carefully, he eases her down on the couch, putting a pillow under her head and covering her with a blanket.

Wes takes a long moment to look at her lying peacefully. *I love you so much, Maggie. I'm so lucky to have you back.* A single tear drops from his eye. *How's this going to affect you, baby? Your brother, your dad, our baby are gone. Taken.* His once dainty princess of a wife now wants blood for their lives. Wes can't blame her. He readied himself to destroy everything standing between them to save her life. *The things we do for those we love. Even killing.* He brushes a little hair from Maggie's face. *I hope she gets through this. I've seen people self-destruct over less.*

Not wanting to wait for something to happen, Wes decides he needs to act. Though it's almost midnight, he starts making calls to every location he knows the Professor has an association with. He eventually ends up calling the Love Patch, again. Another woman answers the phone. He asks for Valentina. It takes a long minute, but she picks up. Sounding half-asleep, Valentina begins to speak.

"Hey, Wes, did you find your wife?"

"Don't play sweet with me! Where's Sean?" Wes asks.

"I haven't seen him in several hours," Valentina says, absent her typical charm.

"Let me ask you something, *Val.* I understand all the women up there make an individual decision to spread their legs for money, but where do any of you draw the line?"

"What the hell are you talking about?"

"What I'm talking about is that a house full of women watched Sean punch my pregnant wife in the stomach and throw her in the trunk of a car. And none of you tried to help her."

There is silence on the phone now. Wes can almost hear emotional breathing from Valentina. Her tone softens. "I wasn't aware of that. Is she okay?" Genuine concern in her voice.

Wes ignores her question. "So, where's Sean?"

"The only thing I can tell you is, his flight instructor called up here before six p.m. to leave Sean a message."

"What was the message?"

"Just confirming their lesson tonight at the airstrip in town."

Wes is familiar with the Calvada Meadows Airport. It's a private airstrip for small aircraft. He has met Sean out there several times after one of his lessons. *I know where you're headed to, motherfucker.*

"What's the Professor's phone number?" Wes asks.

"Professor? I don't know who that is."

"The owner of the Love Patch," Wes says impatiently.

"I don't have the owner's number. But one girl here ..." She hesitates. "... keeps him company in Vegas occasionally. Let me check if she's working and I'll call you back."

Wes gives Valentina his phone number and they hang up.

Being utterly wasted and fatigued, Wes carefully slips himself underneath Maggie's feet, placing the pistol and phone on the coffee table next to him. Finally, getting his body in a relatively comfortable position, Wes leans his head back. Within minutes, he is sound asleep.

CHAPTER 59

Early the next morning, Wes is awakened by the sound of the neighbor's dog barking. It usually barks only when somebody is pulling up his driveway. As he processes the sound with his foggy brain, streaks of the early-morning sun jet through gaps in his home's front curtains. It only takes another few seconds for Wes's hypervigilance to reactivate from being turned off for the few hours he slept.

Quickly, Wes sits up and glances at Maggie, still curled up in the fetal position at the other end of the couch. With purpose, but still careful not to wake his wife, he slides off the couch and peers covertly through his window. An all-black Lincoln Continental is in his driveway. *Fuck me, it's the cops.* Another quick glance and Wes quickly figures out that, in fact, it's not the police.

Two large, muscular men wearing formfitting black Polos, slacks, and dark sunglasses exit the vehicle. *Who the hell is this?* One of the men opens the rear passenger door to the luxury sedan. An older man, maybe sixty, wearing what looks like golfing attire, steps out. *It's the Professor, shit.* Wes knows this, though he's never met the man before.

Nervousness invades Wes's body. Right now he regrets making those calls last night looking for this man. But he notices the three men's collective demeanor as they approach his home. *They seem relaxed. Not ready for a fight.* None of them have hard looks on their faces, and their strides are casual.

"Sweetheart, get up. We might have some trouble."

Groggy for only a moment, Maggie sits up quickly, concern on her face. "What's going on?" she asks, a little panic in her voice.

"I think it's Sean's boss."

A look of fear crosses her face. "Go in the bedroom and wait," Wes says.

It only takes a second for Maggie's face to change from fear to defiance. "I'm not going anywhere," she says, uncompromised in her tone.

A knock at their door interrupts the couple. Without hesitation, Maggie moves for the door.

Wes grabs his pistol. In a hushed tone he tells her, "Maggie, don't!" But she ignores him.

Angered by her actions, Wes prepares himself for another shoot-out. He posts himself in the blind spot of the front door's threshold. Before Maggie grabs the door handle, she gives her husband a *get ready!* look. *Fuck,* Wes thinks, nodding back at her. He raises his pistol. She opens the door, her face stoic.

An older, mature voice, absent of a threatening tone, says from outside the door, "You must be Maggie."

"I am."

"May I come in?" the voice asks.

Wes shakes his head no, hoping his gesture is seen by Maggie in her peripheral vision.

A long moment passes. Finally, she says, "Sure."

Damn it, Maggie. What are you doing?

Before anyone moves into the house, the voice says, "I'm confident your husband, Wes, is waiting on the other side of the door, ready to shoot me in the head as soon as I walk in."

Maggie's face tightens. "He is."

Why did you tell him that?

"I'd prefer he didn't," the voice says.

With Maggie having given up their tactical advantage, Wes steps out into the open.

On their porch, an older man stands in front of two larger goons. *Why is he standing in front of his security?*

He's an average-size individual. Relatively fit for a man in his sixties. Wearing a fitted, cotton golf shirt and tan slacks, his hair black with an adequate amount of salt-and-pepper mixed in. His olive-colored face is clean-shaven, showing off a strong chin. His eyes, more hazel than brown, are hard with deep lines. Creases on his forehead are also prominent. They don't require a scowl unlike many young men who paint on tough faces. By the way he's standing at their front door, an air of confidence, authority, and experience saturates the older gentleman.

"Are you the Professor?" Wes asks.

He doesn't answer Wes's question. Rather he says, "I'd like to speak with you and your wife."

"Why don't you push through and do what you're going to do?" Wes asks, his tone semihostile, caused by his nerves.

"Because this is your home, Wes, and we've all had a tough couple days."

Wes glances at Maggie. She looks back at him like she wants him to come inside. At this point, Wes is at a loss.

On one hand, he spent all day yesterday looking for this man with Maggie kidnapped in the back of a trunk. Plus, he burned a couple of the Professor's hired hands in a car.

On the other hand, if the Professor wanted them dead, why would he not kill them both right now? Instead, he's having a conversation at their doorstep.

Wes considers his options quickly. *I can either make our last stand here right now or hear what he has to say.* With Maggie obviously wanting to let him in, Wes steps to the side. The Professor graciously enters their home. His two men remain outside by the door. "They're not coming in?" Wes asks.

"Do they need to?" the Professor responds matter-of-factly. This time Wes doesn't answer. Rather, he puts himself in a position in their living room where he can cover the Professor and the doorway. He remains standing, keeping the pistol in his hand, but at his side.

Maggie points out a wing-back chair to the Professor. He takes his time sitting in it. All three look at each other for a long moment. To Wes, it feels like the president of the United States came to his home *so he can kill me himself.* The whole scene is surreal.

Wes breaks the silence. "Why are you here if not to kill us?"

Switching his gaze from Wes to Maggie, the Professor says, "I had your brother and his friend killed. But they stole from me.

Upon hearing confirmation to her fears, Maggie grows emotional.

Seeing her pain resurface, Wes says to the Professor, "You didn't have to kill her father."

"I did not endorse that. Lee and his wife can get a little ... heavy-handed. And from what I understand, Wes, you collected that debt yesterday at the dry lakebed." Wes chokes down any rebuttal and says nothing. The Professor continues. "Either way, I am sorry for what happened to your father, Maggie."

Maggie subdues her grief. Her face tightening back up.

"And what about Sean! That motherfucker kidnapped my wife and killed our unborn child," Wes says, emotions escaping his voice.

For the first time, the Professor's passive look changes to sympathy. "Family is the most important thing to me. I have a son myself. And a grandson. With that said, I gave Sean direct orders. And those orders never included taking your wife. He did that on his own."

"If you're not here to kill us, what are you here for?" Wes asks, now genuinely curious.

The Professor leans back in the wing-back chair, pulls out a cigar, and holds it up to Maggie. "Do you mind?" he asks.

"No," Maggie says politely.

The Professor looks at Wes, holding up a second cigar. "Would you like to have one with me while we discuss how to move forward?"

Before Wes answers, a scene from the movie *True Romance* written by Quentin Tarantino pops into his head. In the film, a pimp challenges Christian Slater's confidence after being offered to sit down at the table. It is the pimp's assessment that if Slater's character wasn't afraid, he would have sat down without "a care in the world." But instead, Slater shows his fear by posturing as if he weren't afraid. Heeding the fictional pimp's advice, Wes takes the cigar and asks the Professor, "Do you want some coffee?"

He gestures *yes*.

"Sweetheart, do you mind bringing me and our guest a couple of coffees?"

Showing no fear, Maggie asks the Professor, "Do you like your coffee with cream or straight black?"

"A little cream would be nice. Thank you."

Wes takes a seat next to the Professor. Still maintaining his coverage on him and the door. He puts the pistol on the coffee table with the barrel facing the Professor. A small smirk escapes from the older man's face.

While Maggie is in the kitchen, the phone rings. She answers it. Wes hears her say, "Hello …" and moments later, "Thank you." She comes back into the living room with two coffees and a flower vase. She sets everything down between Wes and the Professor and finds a seat next to her husband.

"The vase is for your ashes. We don't have regular ashtrays."

"Was that Valentina?" the Professor asks.

Maggie nods.

"What did she want?" Wes asks.

"She wanted to let us know he was coming to pay us a visit."

"Valentina's a sweet kid," the Professor says, handing Wes the cigar. He pulls out a cutter, snips off the end of his cigar, and hands the cutter to Wes. Wes does the same and notices a V-notch cut left in the end of the cigar. The Professor pulls out a shiny lighter from his shirt pocket. He flips the top and again Wes hears that familiar and distinctive *ping* sound. A soft flame shoots from the top.

Both men toast the ends of their cigars, taking a moment to get an even, hot ember started on their sticks.

"You know, I keep running into these fancy lighters," Wes says.

"How so?"

"Your man Lee had one. So did Sean."

Frustration contorts the Professor's face. "And that's our problem, Wes."

"How so?"

The Professor smirks. "Sean told me about you. He said you have balls of steel and are exceptionally smart. He also said you weren't afraid to get your hands dirty, but for some reason you would rather deal cards at the casino."

Wes doesn't respond. The Professor continues. "You and I have a problem, Wes. And that problem is Sean." Wes scoffs at the Professor's comment, but the Professor ignores it. "You don't get to live as long as I have in this business by taking the lives of innocents. On the other hand, you don't get far in this business by letting people run over your organization either."

"I had nothing to do with Russo. And you came after us," Wes says defensively.

The Professor shakes his head. "No, I did not. Lee and Amber were freelancers who did a lot of good work for me in the past. Unfortunately, as I said before, they went outside of their purview and, in my opinion, that's because of Sean."

Okay, now I'm curious, Wes thinks. "Besides taking my wife, what did he do?"

"You mentioned the lighter. I know for a fact that Russo kept his lighter in his safe because of its sentimental value. And in the same safe is where he kept the merchandise that was stolen."

"Okay."

"I gift these high-end lighters to those who work with me. A gesture of solidarity. But not everyone gets one."

The Professor stops for a moment and lets Wes and Maggie ponder this point.

"I never gave Sean a lighter," the Professor says.

Wes and Maggie look at each other, connecting the dots. Their eyes widen.

Maggie says, "Sean was in that safe too. So my brother didn't need to die."

"Not entirely true," the Professor corrects her. "Your brother and his friend in fact stole from me. But they didn't kill Russo—Sean did. And that's how he came into possession of this symbol of my affection and commitment." The Professor takes a drink of the coffee as he knocks off the long ash into the vase. He continues. "The problem with Sean is, his excessive ambition makes him erratic. And that's why I kept him on a tight leash."

Starting to understand the bigger picture, Wes asks, "So, you think he killed Russo ... for a promotion?"

The Professor bobs his head in agreement.

Admittedly, this is quite a bit for Wes to take in all at once. Maggie, on the other hand, looks like she's keeping up fine.

She asks, "So, what are you going to do now?"

"Well, Maggie, Sean is gone, and I figure Wes could help me find him."

Hearing this fills Wes's body with both excitement and dread. Excitement at the idea he might get to kill Sean. Dread because of any legal consequences that come with doing that. "And what if we decide to walk away?" Wes asks.

Calmly, the Professor explains, "I told you I had your brother-in-law killed. I also saw how you dealt with Lee and Amber. And I appreciate you pulling my product and cash out of their vehicle before ... *the accident*. What I haven't decided is, are you a friend or a threat? And seeing how you negotiated these recent challenges, I would have to deal with an enemy as dangerous as you ..." He pauses. "... swiftly."

This motherfucker just told me he'll kill us if I don't help him, Wes thinks.But he knows the truth inside his heart. He and his wife want Sean dead. And that's all Maggie can see at this moment.

"That sounds fair," Maggie says. Wes and the Professor cock their heads at her.

Feeling boxed in, Wes responds carefully, "I know where we can find him."

A pleased look appears on the Professor's face. He stands, takes one more drag of his cigar, and places the rest of it in the vase.

"From what I understand, sir, you have two openings you're looking to fill," Maggie says.

What the fuck did you say, Maggie! Not wanting to appear divided, Wes remains quiet.

A look of surprise transforms the Professor's face. And for a long moment, he eyeballs the young couple. Another moment passes and the Professor reaches into his pocket and pulls out the famous DuPont lighter. He looks it over and hands it not to Wes, but to Maggie. *What the fuck is this!* Wes thinks, feeling a bit emasculated. The Professor then reaches out to Wes and the two shake hands.

Now back on their porch, the Professor says to Wes as he points his head at one of the goons. "Gino here will pick you up tomorrow at nine a.m." Wes tips his head in acknowledgment.

The Professor and his security drive away.

Inside the house, Maggie is sitting on the couch upright, looking at the DuPont lighter. With regret and disappointment, Wes looks at his wife with sadness. *My precious, innocent, tender loving wife is gone.* "I hope you're ready to carry this burden for the rest of your life," he says.

Maggie ignites the lighter, looking at the flame. Not taking her gaze off the flickering light, she replies, "I didn't choose this, Wes—they forced it on me."

Wes recognizes her perspective. He and other soldiers used to have similar feelings when it came to shooting both men and boys toting AK-47 rifles and RPGs. And this only saddens him more.

CHAPTER 60

TWO DAYS LATER, IN a small Mexican casita in Sayulita, Mexico, thirty minutes south of Puerto Vallarta, the voice of a young woman with a thick, sultry Mexican accent calls out, "*Mi amor*, are you awake yet?"

Now I am, Sean thinks.

Before moving, Sean takes a moment to enjoy the feeling of the soft cotton sheet resting on his skin. The bedroom window is open, and a slight ocean breeze blows in. The distant sound and smell of the moving water relax him. It has been a long time since Sean has had any peace in his life. He doesn't rush the moment.

Eventually, he does sit up, swinging his feet onto the floor. The tranquility he felt from sleeping in a bed covered with the fragrance of a beautiful woman fades. It is overshadowed by the actions Sean took to get where he is this morning.

Every day since he left the States, thoughts of Wes and Caleb have popped into Sean's head. Residuals of guilt still fester in his stomach. Reflecting on what they've all become since Mogadishu is sickening to Sean. He considers Caleb first. *Go-*

ing from being the deadliest and most talented sniper I've ever worked with to a security manager. What a fuckin' waste. And Wes. What a limp-dick pussy he's become. I saved that kid's life, pulling that RPG out of him. And rather than working with me, he hands his balls over to Maggie, day in and day out.

Sean lies to himself so he can start his day without suck-starting his own barrel. *I'm embarrassed I fought shoulder to shoulder with these warriors turned bitches.*

Sean contemplates his tenure with the Professor's organization. "Arrogant piece of shit," he mumbles to himself. *It didn't matter what I did or what I brought to the table; it was never good enough.*

But the source of Sean's deepest contention is the Professor putting him under Russo. *That fat, greasy fuck.* Sean despised every time he found himself in the same room with Russo. Having to watch him parade around like the Prince of Sheba, sucking the Professor's dick. *It's like men aren't men anymore. Fuck 'em all.*

In the same room with Sean, an older wooden chest sits on the floor, secured with a padlock. The only key to the padlock is kept hidden. Even from Sean's beloved Leticia. She doesn't ask about the chest, and that's why he loves her so much.

Standing from the bed, Sean opens the chest. As he lifts the lid and gazes at his earnings, pride swells in his heart. Everything is there. As yesterday and the day before. Twenty-five thousand dollars in cash and the two kilos of high-grade cocaine. Sean still has Wes's Glock too. His mind continues to wander. *Oh, James. I bet you thought I didn't see you watching Russo's house. But I did. I appreciate you kicking in his door and getting the safe open. Leticia and I thank you for your sacrifice.* Sean snickers. *So do the fish.*

The cash shortage is a result of Sean's recent purchase of the two-bedroom casita he now lives in with Leticia. It's not a big place, but it's enough. It has a roof that doesn't leak, running hot water, and a flushing toilet. Plus, it sits on enough land to keep him from being right next to a neighbor. Even before deciding to buy this place, Sean thought about the chances of him being found. But the only two people who ever knew about this place and Leticia were Wes and Caleb. *Not anymore.* On several occasions, Sean had bragged to his former soldiers about having some big-booty Latina chick down in Mexico. And the casita he would rent while visiting her.

He tries convincing himself he's safe. *I shot Caleb myself and watched him sink to the bottom of the pool. I know he's dead. And Wes, not being much of a gunfighter, going against Lee and Amber, his chances of surviving are almost zero. I'll take those odds.*

Sean is even less concerned about the Professor. A few times when Russo was liquored up, he said the Professor was not in good standing with the cartel but he made another connection. That's why he became so giddy when he first showed Sean the coke. *So no, neither the Professor nor any associates would be showing their faces down here. I'm well insulated.*

Leticia calls to him again, "Sean, I made you a plate. Come and eat before it gets cold."

He calls back, "I'm up, thank you." *Damn, Sean, you did pretty good. You deserve this.*

As he strolls through his humble adobe home into the kitchen, the aroma of eggs, potatoes, chorizo, and fresh tortillas fills the house. Leticia, wearing only a white button-down shirt from Sean's closet, stands in front of the stove. She pulls a flour tortilla off the burner and slaps it on a plate with the potatoes and eggs. Enjoying her morning tasks, she brings the plate over to a small table in the kitchen. The plush green yard set against an ocean backdrop is visible through a window in the kitchen. Leticia sits across the table.

They both stare at each other for a moment. Sean basks in the quiet. "What are your plans today?" he asks.

"I wanted to work in the garden. I planned on picking some roses before dinner tonight."

Sean teases her. "That takes all day?"

Not quite getting his sarcasm, Leticia responds, "Nooo, *mi amor*. But I want to pick the right ones, especially if they're going to be on the table for a couple of days."

"Oh, I see," Sean says, smiling to himself.

Eventually, Leticia picks up on the joking tone and smirks at Sean. He smiles back, leaning across the table and kissing her. For a half moment, he considers Wes's life. *Maybe he had it right.* But quickly he puts the thought out of his mind.

The two sit for a few minutes before Leticia goes to the bedroom and changes. She comes back out still wearing Sean's shirt and a pair of her own formfitting jeans. Her hair is pulled back in a ponytail.

"Are you actually going to pick roses in a dress shirt?" Sean asks.

"Why not? I like the way it feels."

Sean shakes his head with a little smile, watching her sashay outside.

Eating his breakfast, he thumbs through a local newspaper with Spanish and English articles. He hears the sound of a clay pot outside being knocked over. "Did you drop something, *chula*?" he calls to Leticia. But she doesn't respond. Curious why she's not answering him, he goes outside.

On a gravel walkway leading from the front door around the side of the house where the rosebushes are, Sean looks for Leticia. At the edge of the rose garden, he notices a clump of fur or something furlike on the ground.

Getting to the clump of fur, Sean realizes he's looking at black hair bunched up on the ground. *What the fuck?* Nervousness grows in his heart. He rounds the row of bushes. He finds Leticia on the ground. His insides jump. *Motherfucker.* Looking closer, he sees the deep cut across her throat. Her head is unnaturally tilted to the side, caused by the damage to her neck. A chunk of her hair is missing from the side of her head too. Blood from her wounds pours into the soil while her open eyes stare at him. Her white shirt is ripped open, exposing her breast.

In shock, Sean stumbles backward and races back to the house. He bursts through the front door and rushes down the hallway toward his bedroom. He grabs the hidden key to the chest and tries to open the padlock. Fumbling with the key, he hears a familiar voice.

"Thought you could move up the ranks before your time, huh?"

Up to this point, Sean didn't have time to consider who killed Leticia. But now he knows.

He stops moving. He knows the moment he unlocks this chest, he will catch several rounds to his back. Sean turns around. Standing before him is the Professor, wearing an all-beige linen outfit. Outstretched in his hand, a black semi automatic pistol is pointed at Sean. Trying to be casual, Sean says, "I thought you were on the cartel's shit list."

"Not for a long time, Sean. They seem to appreciate access to American big rigs. Especially in Texas, New Mexico, and Arizona."

Sean smirks. *Of course you figured it out.* "So, what now?" Sean asks, not giving the Professor the satisfaction of observing fear.

The Professor shoots Sean in the stomach. Sean's ears ring from the gun blast before he feels the punch in his midsection. But it doesn't take long for the pain to catch up. Sean looks down and sees blood pouring out of his gut. A slow growl of pain exits his mouth. He falls back toward the wall. Gasping for air, he slides into a sitting position on the wooden chest. Grabbing his stomach, Sean yells. "You pussy fuck! All of this over that fat slob Russo?"

"Freddy was my cousin—my family."

A hysterical laugh from Sean fills the room. Neither of them had ever said anything about their family ties. *Sneaky rat fucks.* The Professor used Russo as a plant to hear who would speak ill of him and who remained loyal. Figuring he's probably going to die, Sean refuses to grovel.

Blood now running from his mouth, he says, "Well, then, sir. Fuck you and your dead, fat cousin! Let's get this shit over with!"

"Oh, not yet, Sean. You have more to atone for," the Professor says, turning toward the bedroom door.

What the fuck is he talking about? Sean thinks, squeezing the wound to his belly.

A man and woman enter the bedroom. Looking up from the pain, Sean feels his eyes grow wide and his heart heavy. With hardened faces, Wes and Maggie stand before him.

Sean recognizes, through Wes's reaction, that this is the first time Wes has seen him afraid and in shock.

Walking out of the bedroom, the Professor says to the couple, "We have to leave in fifteen minutes."

They both nod in acknowledgment.

Looking at Sean's condition, sorrow fills Wes's eyes. But the reaction is short-lived as Sean yaps his mouth.

"Wes, you slick motherfucker. How in the hell ... did you get Maggie back from those ... two rednecks and escape with your life?"

"I had a little help."

A little help? Sean shakes his head, trying to figure out who helped him. It only takes him a few seconds before he says grimly, "Caleb."

"Yea."

Through a painful chuckle, Sean says, "What the ... fuck, man! The way he fell ... in the pool..." He takes a deep breath, trying to suppress the pain. "I thought for sure I clipped ... him good. And then he ... he got all wrapped up in the pool cover." He grunts. "How did he ... get out?"

"He improvised, he adapted, he overcame," Wes says, repeating one of Sean's mantras he used to preach to his young war fighters.

Continuing to physically decline, Sean smiles, nodding in approval. "So, what's this? You brought Maggie to watch you kill me?"

"No, you worthless fucker. *I'm* here to kill you," Maggie says before Wes can respond.

Sean laughs and coughs hysterically. He tries to stand up but stops. Maggie has her Glock 19 aimed at him. "Sit the fuck down, Sean!"

Sean freezes in place and slides back onto the wooden chest.

Through the sound of gurgling blood, Sean says with a weak laugh, "I like this new Maggie, Wes. Not the whining bitch who kept you up all night on the phone telling you to come home."

Neither responds. Rather, they move into a better position to put Sean down. Coming closer to her ear, Wes says to Maggie, "You don't have to do this."

Sean mocks Wes by waving one of his arms in the air like he's signaling traffic. With an exaggerated squeaky voice, Sean mimics Wes. "No, Maggie, you don't have to do this."

"I am going to kill him," Maggie says with a steady voice, ignoring Sean's mockery.

Wes nods.

Like a lioness stalking her prey, Maggie approaches Sean. The two are nearly nose-to-nose. She stares into his fading eyes. With little strength, Sean takes hold of her shirt collar. Wes starts to move closer. "Don't," Maggie says. She wraps her hand tightly around Sean's. Sean begins to feel panic rush through his body.

What the fuck is wrong with her? Not being able to stand the pain any longer, Sean tries to push her to her limits. "Let me guess … when I punched you in the stomach, I killed—"

An explosion booms in the room. Sean screams. Maggie eases back and observes her work. Another hole in Sean's stomach leaking out blood.

Wes rushes Sean, putting the barrel of his pistol against Sean's head.

Through snarling, bloody teeth, Sean tells Wes, "Finish it."

Maggie waves the pistol off Sean. Giving Maggie a confused look, Wes steps back.

She leans in close to Sean again. Calmly, she says, "No, Sean, you don't deserve mercy."

Sean feels his expression weaken as fear overtakes him. This makes Maggie smile. She grabs him by his face with both hands and waits. As he fades for good, Maggie slowly inhales, taking Sean's final breath.

"What the fuck, Maggie?" Wes whispers to himself, mortified at what he observed.

Wiping her face, Maggie lets out an odd laugh of relief.

Wes shakes his head regretfully, grabbing the wooden chest off the floor.

EPILOGUE

Tʜᴇ ᴘᴀsᴛ ᴄᴏᴜᴘʟᴇ ᴏғ days have been long and tense for Maggie and Wes. Their small home looks the same but feels different after returning from Mexico. The cigar odor from their meeting with the Professor is still lingering a little. *The drapes and couch will need a good cleaning.* But that's not all Maggie is thinking about. Her life has been completely redefined. She contemplates her options. *What do I do now? Go back to catering? Start a new job? Leave Pahrump?* Trying to find balance in an unbalanced world feels futile to her.

During this entire ordeal, the young couple suffered an array of emotions. Of course, sadness and anger in various degrees. But Maggie gained peace too.

Staring at herself in a mirror, she examines every little detail about her face. Down to every skin pore. *Taking Sean's last breath as he died ... cleaned my soul. Okay, maybe not cleaned, but numbed the pain.* Her face softens. *Whoever said getting revenge doesn't bring you peace was wrong.* Having seen Sean bleed from his stomach and die slowly brought a level of satisfaction to

Maggie. *I can't say I've ever felt this way before.* Having the power to show or withhold mercy revealed something hidden in her.

I wonder if Daddy knew I had it in me with that poor dog on the road. The lesson was hard at the time. But that lesson paid dividends recently.

Maggie tries shoving away thoughts of what the future could've been with Wes and their first child. *I will always miss Daddy. And the child I never held. There will always be an empty spot for them in my heart. But I will fill that spot. No, I will feed the emptiness.*

Things have been different between Maggie and Wes since Mexico. *He has been looking at me differently. Like the way I looked at him when he first returned from deployment.* She thinks about their future. *I hope he embraces the change in me. Wes has killed people too, and I stood by him. I hope he does the same for me.* Maggie knows she will never be the same person. No matter how much Wes wants his simple housewife back.

Still staring in the mirror, Maggie has a more accurate understanding of how life and death coexist. She raises her chin and stands a little taller now, feeling a sense of pride in her emotional resiliency. She likes the woman in the mirror. Much more than her previous self. She is no longer scared or compelled to prove herself to anyone. *I have what it takes to push back and survive.* She is comfortable with violence. And what it takes to perform it. She is no longer self-serving. But instead, she is now becoming an agent of revenge. A tool for those unable to take it themselves. *With the Professor giving me this opportunity within his organization, I will capitalize on the position. Even if Wes disagrees. I will embrace the calling of the lioness.*

But Maggie doesn't consider the Professor her salvation. He is but an asset to help her on her new forged path. He made the mistake of giving Maggie his trust. Inviting the young couple into his circle so fast. *Could the Professor understand the strength a woman brings to a man? Maybe that's why he gave me his token of appreciation, and not Wes.*

Maggie feels a small grin emerge on her face. *Someday your gesture, whether or not genuine, will pay you back tenfold, Professor.* To Maggie, the couple who tortured and killed her father were the Professor's responsibility. And because they were, the Professor will pay this debt to Maggie in full. The same way Sean did.

If Maggie has learned anything over the past week, the long game is to be played only by those who can look past their nose. Unfortunately, as much as she loves Wes, deep inside, he still desires a long life built on peace. *I don't want peace. I want justice.*

Maggie runs both hands through her hair and forms a bun at the back of her head. Her path, now determined. *It may not be today, or tomorrow, or next year. But, Professor, you will pay your debt to me. And when your day comes, you will know your demise was delivered at my hand.*

AFTERWORD

Nevada Lowball was originally a movie script written by my good friend J. G. Blodgett. He invited me to partake in the first rounds of rewrites, which was an absolute blast. Eventually, a Lion's Gate producer optioned the script in 2012 for a whopping three months! You can imagine the excitement we both felt when we got the news. Unfortunately, as with many independent film projects, *Nevada Lowball* never got produced, and we shelved the script.

For the next twelve years, I produced several independent feature films while still enlisted in the US Army. Each film having moderate success. I eventually found myself exhausted by the process. No longer having the stomach for pretentious actors and outdated producers, I tried to take a break. But the creative itch remained. J. G. had already written two novels himself and suggested I consider doing the same. I examined the logistical aspects of writing and jumped in with *Nevada Lowball*.

The process was long, and I still have a lot to learn. By reading a ton of writing books, working with beta readers, and finding editors that also coach, I am ready to continue my writing journey. With that said, you can expect more stories in the near future.

I plan on writing three more books for the Nevada Lowball series that explore Maggie's new path as a vigilante and how that affects her relationship with Wes. Of course, there needs to be a final showdown between Maggie and the Professor. Also, being a fan of back stories, I'd like to write an anthology-prequel featuring our favorite antagonists and how they came to be.

ABOUT THE AUTHOR

As a youngster with average athletic abilities and looks, Antonio developed an ability to tell stories early in his life. That ability helped him secure the hand of his wife Deanna.

Married and broke with two young daughters, Antonio joined the United States Army. While serving, he advanced in rank and responsibility relatively fast. In 2009, Antonio was deployed to Afghanistan and served as a platoon sergeant for a maneuver element assigned to Combat Outpost Najil, earning him the Bronze Star.

After returning home, Antonio used his education benefits to earn a bachelor's degree in film studies from Nevada State University and a master's degree in business management and leadership from Western Governors University. While in school, he also produced several independent films.

At forty-eight years old, one month after retiring from twenty-three years of military service, he became a Las Vegas Police Officer.

www.ingramcontent.com/pod-product-compliance
Lightning Source LLC
Chambersburg PA
CBHW040857010826
48978CB00013BA/1054